The Lord of the Looking Glass and Other Stories

Also by Fiona McGavin

The Lord of the Looking Glass
and Other Stories

Fiona McGavin

IMMANION PRESS

Stafford England

The Lord of the Looking Glass and Other Stories
By Fiona McGavin
© 2019

Cover art and design by Danielle Lainton
Interior layout by Storm Constantine
Illustrations by Storm Constantine, pages 10, 30, 38, 56, 112 (with Danielle Lainton), 128, 142, 148, 230 and by Danielle Lainton, pages 12, 18, 40, 66, 106, 130, 166, 180, 196, 202
Editor: Storm Constantine

Set in Garamond

ISBN 978-1-907737-99-2

IP0150

An Immanion Press Edition
http://www.immanion-press.com
info@immanion-press.com

Contents

Publishing History of the Stories

All stories previously unpublished, except for:

'A Tale from the End of the World' – *Visionary Tongue*, 1996; *Visionary Tongue: A Selection of Stories & Poems from the Magazine*, ed. by Storm Constantine, NewCon Press, 2017

'Roses' – *Visionary Tongue*, late 1990s

'The Walking Man' (original version published as 'Twilight') – *Visionary Tongue*, late 1990s

'Magpie' – *Visionary Tongue*, early 2000s; *Visionary Tongue: A Selection of Stories & Poems from the Magazine*, ed. by Storm Constantine, NewCon Press, 2017

'Driving Home for Christmas' – *Darkest Midnight in December*, anthology, Immanion Press, 2017

Into the Looking Glass at the End of the World

An Introduction by Storm Constantine

Back when Louise Coquio and I were editing and publishing the magazine *Visionary Tongue*, sometimes stories would come to us that held an indefinable 'something'. One day we received a submission from a writer named Fiona McGavin. From reading only the first paragraph, Lou and I realised we had a wonderful story in our hands. This is what we read:

> *For a long time, the sea had been crossed only by screaming gulls, but one evening, as the sun began to set, a small boat with a white sail drifted between the rows of needle-sharp rocks and into the shadow of the towering cliffs. A man stood tall like a prophet in the prow of his vessel, his silvery blond hair billowing about him. He stared expectantly up at the crumbling settlement that perched above the sea. He smiled to himself as he drifted with the wind, but his smile was cold, and his eyes were as grim as the choppy waters. Then, once the village was passed, he spied the old crooked house and its spreading gardens, and he laughed aloud. This must be the place.*

This is the opening of 'A Tale from the End of the World'. From the first, we were drawn in by Fiona's style of writing, the sound of her 'voice'. There was a melancholy to this tale, as well as a pervading sense of menace, but also a sense of drowsy lushness that's almost narcotic.

Fiona's fascinated by stories of a post-apocalyptic world, and in 'A Tale from the End of the World' she began to realise her own vision of what this might be like. Gabrielle and Raphael Blood, a pair of weird twins, live in a huge, crumbling old house at the end of world – in both senses. They are at once wistful and innocent yet deadly. It would take a brave visitor to risk ascending the cliffs to reach them – or someone as dangerous as themselves.

'A Tale from the End of the World' was satisfying on several levels, and phenomenal for a writer just starting to send work out for publication. Lou and I, of course, snapped it up!

Fiona went on to write three more stories for *Visionary Tongue*: 'Twilight' 'Roses' and 'Magpie' – revised versions of which are included in this book.

Not long after I set up Immanion Press, I published Fiona's Gothicly-leaning fantasy trilogy, *A Dream and a Lie* – comprising the three volumes *A Dark God Laughing*, *Dreams of Drowning* and *The Fourth Cleansing*. We also published it in omnibus form some years later. Immanion Press will be releasing a revised edition of the trilogy in the near future.

It was only when I got back in touch with Fiona a couple of years ago, to ask if I could reprint her short stories in the *Visionary Tongue* anthology I was editing for Ian Whates' NewCon Press, that I enquired how many stories she'd written since we'd last spoken. Was it enough to fill a book, perchance? Happily, it was, and I told her I'd love to publish them in one volume. This book is the result.

Fiona writes across genres, sometimes mixing them up together, and the tales within this book present a wide range of stories. She's not a writer to stick to the obvious, however, and takes delight in playing with genre tropes – much in the same way that the late Tanith Lee used to do. Also, like Tanith, Fiona has a lyrical style to her writing – this was undoubtedly a large part of what made me fall in love with her writing to begin with. She has the gift of being able to write comedic as well as profoundly moving tales. Sometimes a story might contain both aspects, luring the reader from one emotion to another.

For this collection, Fiona and I decided the stories should be grouped into sections, because they cross so many genres. The book begins with 'Fairy Tales', the first of which, 'The Lord of the Looking Glass', provided the name for this collection. Among these tales are the charmingly strange 'The Post-Garden Centre Blues', which explores fairy abduction from a very different angle, and 'The Piper', Fiona's darker reinvention of the Pied Piper, a sinister tale set in a world resembling Europe in the time of Viking invasions.

'Fairy Tales' is followed by 'Ghosts, Vampires and Other Monsters'. I'm not usually a great fan of zombie stories, but found 'The Contraption' bittersweet and touching, without any hint of sentimentality – and certainly no brain-eating! Even when it's funny, it's poignant. Among other delights in this section, you'll also find the very unusual Frankenstein-inspired piece – 'Dr Franks and Mrs Stein'. 'Magpie' reveals a different kind of monster – a scavenger of the battlefield who foolishly robs a dying man she really shouldn't have dared to cross.

'Just Another Day at the Office' takes the reader into warped realities, where the crushingly mundane becomes something else entirely. It includes 'The Lottery Lady', a story that's more of a psychological thriller than horror or fantasy. 'The Last Days of the Jesus Star Mission' is science fiction, and the 'office' in this case is far from earth.

The final section, 'It's the End of the World...' includes a revised version of 'A Tale from the End of the World', the story that caught my attention over twenty years ago, as well as a beautifully bizarre sequel 'He May Grow Roots'. Also in this section are the stories set in another (or perhaps related?) post-apocalyptic world that Fiona is continually developing – and intends one day to write a full-length novel about. The collection ends with the intriguing 'The Census-Taker's Daughter', which leads us – and the protagonist of the story – out of this book and into a new world, which has yet to be written.

It's my great pleasure to publish a new book from this very talented writer. You'll find more about Fiona's inspirations in the afterword she's written for this book. Immerse yourself in her words and share her visions. You'll find yourself in some delightfully strange places.

Storm Constantine
February 2019

Fairy Tales

The Lord of the Looking Glass

I wake suddenly. It's the tapping at the glass again, sharp and insistent. For a moment, I don't remember what I must do and then I drift to the surface of the glass and slowly take form, like smoke, into the face she prefers to see. She's there on the other side of the glass with the room stretching out behind her and the gardens and the forest beyond. Inside the mirror there is nothing, only me, the Lord of the Looking Glass.

'Mirror, mirror,' she says. 'Am I the fairest of them all?'

I examine her through the glass, put my phantom fingers against it, as if I am reaching for her with longing. She is pretty with her silken corn-coloured hair and her clear blue eyes, her slim waist and full breasts. I reflect her own face back at her, but I let it change a little, arching her eyebrows and defining her cheekbones, making pretty into beautiful. It is a game I play with those who think they can command me. Sometimes, I show them something more beautiful than the reality and sometimes I show them crows' feet and double chins, yellowing eyes and greying hair.

'My lady,' I drawl, 'you are truly the fairest of them all.'

She laughs with delight, clapping her hands and for a moment I think maybe I could forgive her the spell that trapped me here behind the glass. She is just a child, a witchling. She is not the evil one in this story.

Who is the villain, then? Her father who gave her to a man twice her age to be his bride? Her husband for accepting her? The huntsmen who lust after her or the seven strange brothers hiding in the forest whispering unholy things about her behind her back, refusing to accept their new queen? Or is it her step-daughter, the other girl in this story, who lives so smug and secure in her father's love, never once doubting that she is loved by one and all? Or is it me, trapped and meddlesome behind the glass, a lost soul, a haunt of mirrors and calm forest pools?

I watch her move across the room, the swish of her skirts like music, the tinkle of the little bottles on her dressing table as she fusses with the reflection in the other mirror there, the innocent one where nothing lives. I want her to look at me, to talk to me, to need me for something more than the affirmation of her beauty. I am better than this.

The things I could tell her: tales of dragons and angels fallen down from heaven, stories of fairies and giants and magical kingdoms far beyond the mirror's glass; the magic tricks I could show her; the philosophies that would tell her how to live a worthwhile life; the jokes that would make her laugh until she ached, would let her touch, if only for a moment, the tiniest spark of happiness. I could be her friend, her confidante, as close as a lover, but instead I am her prisoner, condemned to answer that one question over and over again.

Mirror, mirror...

My anger is a cold thing. I drift like the thickest winter snow. I touch the glass, and frost patterns run across it like a tracery of flowers, born from spite. I have a hellebore heart, blossoming only when the air is coldest. I drift through my own thoughts and memories, remembering the sunlit forest pools and the beautiful women who came to admire themselves, the midnight rituals, the candles and apple peel. I remember roaring through carnival halls, distorting reflections, turning people upside down, twisting them into the most grotesque of monsters for their own delight. I remember shattering glass. I remember what it was to be free.

The mirror is small. It hangs on the wall opposite the window where I watch as the seasons pass, the daffodils giving way to the bluebells, the cherry blossom that drifts like snowflakes, the roses I cannot smell behind the glass. At night, when the garden is lit by torchlight and candle light, I see myself reflected in the window glass. I amuse myself by changing colour and shape. I flash through every colour, through azure and ochre and scarlet. I am triangles and hexagons and starbursts. I am sometimes the very fairest of them all. I want to weep, those nights alone behind the glass.

I watch my little witchling walk in the gardens, mostly alone with a book tucked under her arm, but sometimes laughing with one of the huntsmen and sometimes silently and dutifully by her husband's side. Sometimes, I see her with her step-daughter, the one they call Snow White for her flawless skin and the purity of her heart. It is easy, is it not, to be pure of heart when you have never been tested? And isn't purity of heart just another word for dull, for smug? I watch those two girls together and I can see that they will never be mother and daughter, will never be friends. A tension sparkles between them, and I press myself against the glass trying to taste it, trying to breathe it. The thought of it makes me tingle.

But mostly I sleep. I am fading away in my prison, dying for the lack of my mischief-making, my shaded pools and carnivals. Mostly, I am only awake when she comes and taps at the glass. I only know I exist when she asks me over and over who is the fairest of them all.

Tap… tap… tap…

I come awake slowly. I do not know how I know it, but I'm aware I have been asleep for a long time. Or perhaps not even asleep, for I have no dreams to prove I slept and was not simply gone, faded away. I think jealously of the huntsman and how perhaps she does not need me now that she has him to tell her she is beautiful. I cannot be cast aside like an outgrown toy. I will not have it.

I prepare myself. I am red-eyed and vengeful. I will not be forgettable any longer. I will not be nice. I come to the surface of the mirror in a blaze of blue flame. I form wings to clash and a voice to roar and howl threats and curses. I have horns and a tail, eyes of flame. All this I prepare for her.

She stares at me and then laughs. There is a tremor in the laugh, but it is laughter all the same. I do not care to be laughed at.

'Mirror,' she says mockingly, 'who is the fairest of them all?'

I arrange myself into the form she prefers, the delicate melting winter prince with his frosty hair and pale grey eyes. I do not answer, and she leans forward tapping her foot impatiently.

'Hmm,' I say doubtfully, 'certainly, you are beautiful beyond measure, but…'

Her eyes flicker to the window where Snow White is walking arm in arm with her father, their heads bent over a book as they walk, more like lovers than father and daughter. How hard it must be to break into that enchanted circle, how lonely to have to try. She stares at me, plays with a strand of golden hair. Suddenly, she looks very young, very frightened.

'But,' I proclaim cheerfully, 'you are without doubt the fairest of them all.'

She smiles but it is a watery smile, a shifting movement across her face rather than something that comes from within. She goes to her dressing table and her other mirror and fusses with pots of cream and rouge, wands of kohl. She calls her maids and they fuss with her dress and her hair before she dismisses them and reaches for the spell books on the shelf and sits in her painted glory, leafing through the pages, looking for spells to make her hair glossier and her lips plumper. And I could tell her how, such things I could tell her, if she would only ask me.

This becomes the pattern. I go to wherever I go when she has not summoned me. I come back when she taps on the glass. She asks her question and I answer her. I tell her time and again that she is the fairest, the most beautiful. And all the while Snow White walks in the garden with her father, and the huntsmen watch her, and the woodsmen watch her, and even the very flowers in the soil watch her, and the trees bend their branches down towards her.

No one watches the witch and me anymore.

Winter comes and passes, spring turns to summer. There are wild deer in the gardens, apples hang heavy in the branches. The sons of rich men come to visit Snow White and all are turned away. Snow White will not make the mistake of her step-mother and marry the first rich handsome man to come knocking. She will marry for love. Everyone who looks upon her knows this. It is only the second-best girls who settle for men they do not love.

I miss the whole season of autumn and wake to the tapping against the glass and find it is darkest December. I wake to cold and the endless rain against the window, the garden beyond full of dead leaves. There is music and laughter from somewhere beyond this room, but there are tears on my little witch's face. Her fingernails are bitten down to the quick and beneath the finery of her dress she is bone thin and gaunt. She and I are both dying, slowly fading into nothingness.

'Mirror, mirror,' she whispers, 'who is the fairest of them all?'

The truth is that I am the only one left who thinks of her. The truth is that I love her, this enchantress turned to nothing more than a silly, spiteful girl full of vanity and insecurity, turned into the wicked witch. I love her because I remember how her spell drew me, trapped me, how her voice was like music and her laughter sent me whirling and circling in the glass. I had been alone so long that when she stood on the other side of the glass waiting for me, it didn't feel like a prison at all. I love her because once I believed that she and I could create such wonderful mischief together. So, I ask you again, who is the evil one in this story? Who was it who took all the light and laughter from a young girl's life? I do not know the answer, but it is I who must set her free. There is no one else.

And I never lied to her until now. She was always the fairest of them all to me.

'My lady,' I say. 'It is true that you are fair beyond all measure, but Snow White is yet fairer.'

For a moment, her face crumples and her eyes fill with tears. She stands perfectly still, biting her lip. Thoughts whirl in her head, a turmoil of despair that changes slowly to anger.

'Snow White is a silly little princess who is only beautiful because she has seen nothing and done nothing and knows nothing of the world,' she snaps.

I can almost taste her rage, her fire.

'Yes,' I agree, 'but I cannot lie; she is fairer by far than you. If she was gone...'

For a moment, she doesn't move, then her face twists with rage and I can see what a strange and terrible pair we might have made. I can see that no one but me will ever love her again, that the road she has chosen leads into darkness.

She reaches forward, the sleeve of her dress brushing the glass, making me catch whatever it is I have that passes for breath. She tears the mirror from the wall and lifts it high above her head and hurls it with all her strength and a deranged scream at the wall.

It shatters. Smithereens rain down, lethal and sparkling, in the candlelight. Shards litter the carpet and the bedspread. I twist in my freedom, wrapping myself around her for a moment, breathing in her scent, her essence and the wickedness growing roots inside her and then I am gone, howling around the house, shattering the glass in every window and every mirror, and then out into the world and along roads of my own that lead to darkness, to freedom.

The Post-Garden Centre Blues

'I have become the kind of person who enjoys spending an afternoon at the garden centre,' Vicki proclaimed, as she set down two identical hanging baskets on the kitchen table in front of X. He looked at the baskets and then at Vicki and rose one perfectly arched eyebrow quizzically.

Vicki was not surprised to see him sitting there at the kitchen table flicking through *The Guardian* even although, when she had left for the garden centre, she had closed all the windows and locked the doors behind her.

'What's wrong with the garden centre?' X asked.

Vicki sat down opposite him. 'Nothing's wrong with it,' she said. 'It's just so dull and so middle-aged and middle-classed and ordinary. I just thought my afternoons might have been spent doing something more exciting – riding motorbikes or getting tattoos or something.'

X folded the newspaper and leaned back in his chair. He studied her with his jewel-bright eyes that made her think of emeralds and leaves and poison. She had the uncanny feeling, as she often did when he was there, that the neat black hair, jeans and shirt with the sleeves rolled up to his elbows, were just a façade and underneath there was something else. Something with floating hair threaded with leaves and shards of glass and bone, something that didn't walk but prowled and hunted young girls and stole their lives away.

'Did you enjoy the garden centre?' he asked.

Vicki nodded reluctantly. 'I did,' she admitted. 'I met my friends and we had coffee and cakes – you really can't beat a garden centre cake – we went round the shop and bought some bits and pieces and, of course, I bought these hanging baskets and my friends bought some hanging baskets. Everyone was buying hanging baskets. And when I was looking at all those hundreds of perfectly identical hanging baskets, I thought, is this it? Is this what my life has become? I'm someone who hangs out at the garden centre and has exactly the same hanging baskets as everyone else up and down the country. I'm boring. I live in a boring house in a boring town, I have a boring job and boring friends and a boring husband and two children who I love dearly but who are boring.'

X smiled. 'I don't think you're boring,' he said.

But Vicki carried on, caught up in her monologue. 'Do you remember the night we met? It was twenty years ago, and I was twenty. I'd left a party early with no money, and it was pitch black, and I was hitch-hiking when you stopped for me. Hitch-hiking! Do you know what? I tell my girls that under no circumstances must they ever hitch-hike because you don't know what kind of crazy person is out there.'

'Very wise,' X said, 'very sensible.'

'Sensible!' Vicki snorted. 'Everyone is so sensible nowadays. People don't hitch-hike anymore, do they? Do you remember? I was wearing the tiniest little dress that I'd made myself from a curtain I got in a charity shop. These days I couldn't even get one leg in that dress. I had red patent leather shoes with three-inch heels. Do you remember?'

X nodded. 'I do remember. I loved that dress and those shoes. It's why I stopped.'

'And now,' Vicki sighed, 'look at me.'

X looked at her expressionlessly. 'I think you look very nice,' he said, 'and before you say it, you are not fat.'

'I'm hardly skinny either. And you haven't changed a bit in twenty years. How is that?'

X smiled. 'I think you know why that is.'

Vicki thought she knew too, but she didn't dare say the words for fear that they would sound as insane in her mouth as they did in her head. But all the same, she remembered that night as if it was yesterday. He had taken her somewhere she had never been before, some night-club she had never heard of. She couldn't quite remember where it was. What she did remember was loud pounding music and beautiful young men and women with bright eyes and glossy hair, all dancing and dressed like the models in her copy of *Cosmopolitan*. She had danced with X, his arms wrapped around her and his eyes shining brighter than anyone else's in the place. She couldn't remember eating or drinking anything, but she must have taken something that didn't quite agree with her because she remembered seeing the colours blur together, the features of all the beautiful people turning into strange shapes and colours. She had had the impression that she wasn't in the night-club at all, but somewhere amongst tall trees strung with lights, raining blossom like snow. She had seen the stars through the branches and something huge and black had flapped across the moon. When she turned to X, she saw, for a moment, not him but something else. Something of midnight black wings, sharp teeth and fingernails that curved like claws. Then, all at once, it had shattered into a cacophony of images and sounds – trees, owls, butterfly wings and gossamer, the skirl of fiddles and a wild primal beat. And everyone whirling and twisting and laughing. She had stumbled, felt the crack as the heel of one of her patent leather shoes snapped and suddenly it was all gone, and everything was real and normal again. X had taken her home after that, and she must have passed out in his car, because when she opened her eyes, she was sprawled across her narrow bed in her student flat, her red shoes discarded on the floor and her dress coming apart at the seams and her heart full of loss and longing.

'Will you take me back there sometime?' she asked X.

He frowned. 'Sometime, maybe.'

She stood up to make coffee. She knew that he liked his coffee strong and black and that he claimed the coffee she made was the best he had ever tasted. She knew this to be a lie. Today she made it in the machine, but often she just made him instant and she didn't think he could tell the difference. He was all glamour and charm. She could have served him dirty dishwater and he would probably have grinned that wide grin, which lit his whole face, and told her it was the best thing he had ever tasted and she the most beautiful woman in the whole wide world. Flattery gets you everywhere.

'Did you pick up other girls and take them there?' she asked.

He sipped his coffee and sighed rapturously. 'All the time,' he said, 'but you were my favourite.'

She felt a flicker of pleasure, although she knew that he probably told all the girls that.

'Seriously,' he said, 'I've taken many pretty girls there – and some not so pretty – but you were they only one I let go again.'

She thought of that place: the branches decked with blossom and lights, the wild skirl of the violin, the whirling and laughing dancers. Butterfly wings and gossamer and magic. That's what it was. It was magical and a million miles away from her world of garden centres, school runs, spreadsheets and shopping centres. In her world, a special weekend was one where they took the kids to some overcrowded theme park. She wondered what it was like in

21

that other place when the music stopped. She imagined soft couches and cushions, soft-footed servants with silver platters of quails' eggs and sugared almonds, glasses of jewel-bright fizz and soft voices making conversations that never involved the price of petrol or the best route to take to Manchester. She imagined cloudless skies and the drowsy scent of rose gardens, the low drone of bees.

'I want to go back,' she said. 'Will you take me back, just once more?'

He put down his mug with its cheap print of yellow roses that she had once thought so pretty, so vintage and shabby-chic. He could make everything in her life tawdry.

'No,' he said.

Disappointment surged through her like an arrow to her heart. 'But you said I was your favourite.'

'You are,' he said. 'You don't understand. That place and those people – my people – none of them are happy. Do you think if we were happy, we would do the things we do? The baby stealing and changelings, the sneaking into your houses to clean and tidy.' He made a noise of utter disgust before continuing. 'Turning the milk sour and blighting the harvests, the stupid impossible tasks and endless spiteful trickery. And what I do – the seductions and the heartbreak. Do you think we would do any of those things if we were a happy people?'

Vicki frowned, remembering how reality had shattered into pieces, remembering the gleam of all those too bright eyes and how she had thought they were shining with happiness and excitement but now she wondered if, after all, they had been shining with desperation.

'Those other girls,' she said slowly, 'the other ones you took and didn't let go? What happened to them?'

He drained his coffee and reached across the table to take her empty mug. She watched him walk to the sink and rinse them under the tap. He could make something as ordinary as washing the dishes look like a work of art.

'They died,' he said, 'but I think you know this. They wasted away, and they died. Our food started to taste like dust to them, their feet ached from dancing every night. Their dreams filled up with monsters. They missed their jobs and their families and their friends, and they missed things like petrol stations and motorways and offices and garden centres.' He laughed. 'They wasted away, and I drank up their sadness and loss and grew stronger and more beautiful. It's what I do, Vicki, it's a terrible life, but it's what I do because I can't do anything else. The music plays, the dance goes on and we can't do anything else but dance. But you can – you can do anything, go anywhere. You can earn money and spend money, you can make friends, you can eat new foods and go to new places. You can have children and bring them up and you can fall in love. Real love, not some silly courtly idea of what love is. You can grow up, grow old and leave this world different in whatever small way from the way it was before you were there. You matter. We don't.'

Vicki frowned. 'What made me different from those other girls?' she asked. 'Why did you let me go?'

'I don't know,' he said. 'It was a whim. I wanted to know someone, to live a life through someone else's. And I liked your red shoes and your dress that was quite obviously made from a curtain.'

Vicki smiled faintly. 'And have you?' she asked. 'Have you lived your life through mine?'

She remembered that he had been there in the background somewhere during every pivotal moment of her life – her graduation, in the church on her wedding day, delivering bouquets of red roses after the birth of each of her children, at her father's funeral, at the back of the school hall during nativity plays and countless school assemblies, in the pub where she had celebrated each and every one of her promotions, drifting through supermarkets listlessly pushing an empty trolley, grinning at her from the mirror in John Lewis or M&S, flying up the motorway behind her in a fabulous car. He was always there somewhere.

'No,' he said. 'I haven't lived my life through yours. You have, and your husband, your children, your friends and colleagues and neighbours. But not me. I have watched, but I have only lived my own life. Here's the thing: I have eternity, but you have the chance to be truly alive. Ask yourself, which you would rather have? I know what I would choose.'

He sat back down at the table and for a moment she saw his other self, his fairy self: a thing of purple wings and ebony hair threaded with leaves and petals and shards of bone. Bones, she knew, from every beautiful girl whose soul he had stolen. She should be afraid of him, but she never had been. Instead, she had loved him, or the idea of him, without ever understanding. He had told her his name once and it was long and unpronounceable – a thing of hisses and whispers and clicks – so she called him X and knew he liked it. He had told her what he was and of his many other names: Reynardine, the Glancomer, the Elf-Knight, the fairy seducer. He had seduced her, no doubt about it, but just as surely as he had seduced her, she had seduced him with her life so completely devoid of glamour that it was something magical itself.

'I will take you back there,' he said, 'when you are old and at the very end of your life. When your limbs don't work, and your eyes don't see, and your ears don't hear, when your mind is just fog. I'll take you back and we'll dance beneath trees hung with blossom and stars. We will dance across the sky, you and I, and you will blaze like a star, like a comet, until your light goes out and mine shines on its cold and empty light. We will do that, you and I.'

Vicki sat still and silent for a long time after that. She looked round her kitchen at the children's drawings stuck to the fridge, the washing machine waiting to be emptied, her husband's muddy boots sitting on a sheet of newspaper. All those ordinary things that when put together made a life, and a life that was worth living.

'I'd like that,' she said at last. 'I'd like that very much.'

He nodded and smiled. 'Then it's a deal.'

Vicki nodded and smiled back. 'In the meantime,' she said, 'would you like to come to the garden centre with me next time I go? It's dull and it's boring but the cakes are good, and the rows and rows of identical hanging baskets are worth seeing. It's beyond dull, but I think you'll like it.'

He grinned at her, all teeth and smile and poison green eyes. 'I would like that,' he said. 'I would like that more than anything.'

The Piper

This is the story of our sorrow.

We saw lights far out to sea one night, so the next day we went to see the Spider-King in his cave. We took offerings: flowers and cakes and pieces of gold and silver; a yellow bird in a cage and a wooden doll. We left them all outside the cave and waited, but the Spider-King did not come.

That evening, we saw more lights out at sea and this time they were closer, moving fast up the coast towards the larger settlements. We dowsed our own lights and kept curfew and the raiders passed us by, but we knew it was only a matter of time.

The next day, we went back to the caves and found that the yellow bird and its cage were gone, and the cakes and flowers had been torn apart into crumbs and petals. We left jars of scented oil and rounds of salty cheese, strings of wooden beads and seashells. Some of the braver members of our party ventured a few steps into the darkness and called out to the Spider-King, telling him that raiders were coming from across the sea and we needed his ripping, tearing arms and legs and the plagues of rats and locusts he could summon from the place between worlds where he lurked.

But still he did not come.

We laid traps and caught birds and small animals – gulls with angry beaks, fat pigeons and baskets of tiny mice. We left them all at the entrance to the cave and waited. We told the Spider-King of our troubles, but he did not come.

Word reached us from further up the coast of burning and looting and tall ugly men with shaggy beards and a bloodlust in their eyes. They were righteous with the fury of a god that was not ours, and they bore weapons of steel and iron and the iron hurt our eyes and made our heads spin. Our people were murdered and taken as slaves, forced into marriages, forced to worship a cruel new god. We called them Rat Men for they were greedy and numerous, and their eyes were sharp and cruel.

Bad things happened, and strange things of ill omen happened. The sky rained blood, and the earth shook and rattled great boulders down the mountainside and over the cliffs to the shore. Packs of wild dogs roamed the moorland, scavenging and looking for easy prey. A child was missing from her cradle and some said it was the dogs that took her, and others that the Spider-King had stretched out his long arms and snatched her up.

But worse than all of this was the news that the raiders were moving down the coastline, attacking villages and settlements from both the sea and the land, slaughtering farmers and fishermen and sending captives far away over the sea in their long boats. The smell of smoke carried down the coastline.

We went down to the caves. We lit torches and stepped into the empty blackness and it seemed that nothing lived there except for bats and pale moths.

'Please,' we whispered into the darkness, 'please be real. Please help us.'

And in the deep black where the tunnels crawled into the mountainside, something stirred.

A man stumbled into the village bloodied and raving with one arm almost severed from his shoulder and before he crumpled and died, he told us the Rat Men were coming, they were three days away by foot, maybe two by sea, and they were heading south to where the larger towns and cities were. Everything in the way, they were decimating. Their carts were piled high with bones and booty.

People ask why we didn't flee, but where would we have gone? Our homes, our families, our livestock and crops were all here. Our eight-armed god slumbered uncaring in the caves and we could not leave him. There was nowhere to go where the raiders wouldn't find us.

When the man died, we took his body to the caves and laid it before the entrance for the Spider-King.

We made a bargain. 'Take this man now,' we said, 'and we will bring you more when the Rat Men are all gone.'

We waited. Night fell, and the bats left the cave in a black cloud, but still he did not come.

The next day, a stranger came. He wore a long, ragged coat and had hair the colour of ashes, grey eyes and a wide smile. We asked him about the raiders and he made a dismissive gesture with his arm and sat down on the ground to unpack all the treasures in his pack. He had brought such wonderful things: coloured bottles full of scent, jars of spices, buttons and beads and spools and skeins of silken thread of every colour in the world. For a moment, we looked at those wonderful things and forgot our troubles, but then the smell of smoke came with the wind and all joy was stolen from the moment, and we knew we couldn't linger looking at gewgaws from a peddler's pack. We started to wander away – back to our fortifications, back to our spell-making and prayers and sharpening knives and stowing away our few treasures. Back to finding hiding holes and hoping against hope that the raiders would pass us by.

And then we heard music, soft and sweet at first, but then rising into something faster and louder, the notes weaving in and out of one another. It was like nothing we had ever heard before. The sound was like bird song in the early morning, like waves on the shore and rain against windows, it had in it hints of fire crackling and grasshoppers singing, a high note like a woman's voice and a lower note that made us think of distant thunderstorms and the noise of boulders rolling down the mountainside. It was hypnotic – a lure – it drew us away from our futile preparations and back to the square where the peddler was waiting with his fantastical wares, only now there was a reed pipe at his lips and his fingers were moving over it, drawing out that irresistible sound.

When the whole village was gathered before him, he laid his pipe on the ground and smiled his wide smile.

'Do not be afraid,' he said. 'When the raiders come tomorrow, stop up your ears and stay in your houses. I am here. All will be well.'

And then we understood. Some of us even saw for a brief moment, not this dusty moth-like stranger but a black many-legged thing with faceted eyes that burned like rubies and a sharp beaklike mouth. We saw, and we were grateful.

The next day, we did as we were bidden. We hid in our houses, peeping out from between the shutters with our ears full of cotton and beeswax. We watched the silent world and waited.

They came with the noonday sun, faces painted blue and green and whorled with patterns and pictures, mouths agape with fury we could not hear. They carried torches, swords and flails, and we had never seen such rage, such unthinking hatred and violence. We cowered in our homes and fingered the long threads of spider-silk we had bought the day before.

'Please,' we whispered, as they set flame to our fishing boats. 'Please.'

Those of us who dared to watch, saw the piper step out of the shadows and into the road before them and for a moment, he was nothing more than a grey man wearing a tattered coat with a sack of treasures slung over his shoulders. We saw the Rat Men laugh at the sight of him, saw their mockery die when he raised his pipe to his lips and began to play.

How we longed to hear that music again, but how glad we were that we had stoppered up our ears. We watched as the piper turned and began to walk through the village and out towards the caves. We saw how the Rat Men followed him, their faces slack and rapturous, their weapons falling from their hands unnoticed.

A few of us dared to follow at a safe distance, and we saw the piper lead the raiders along the narrow path where our crops grew on either side and our livestock grazed unharmed. We saw him lead them to the mouth of the cave and how they all followed him inside without pausing to look at the remains of our offerings left there: the bones and petals and shining things.

They all followed, unthinking, deep into the darkness where our monster-god lives.

And that should be the end of our story, the end of our sorrow, but in truth it is only the beginning

We had made a bargain, you see. We gave the Spider-King a man's body and we promised him more, but we did not keep our side of the bargain. We thought – I don't know what we thought – perhaps we thought it was enough that he had taken a whole army of Rat Men, perhaps we thought it was enough that we continued to leave birds and small animals and other things that were valuable to us. We were not ungrateful. In truth, our failing was perhaps that we were too kindly, too squeamish.

Our little village prospered, became a town. We had things we had not had before: a baker's shop, a tavern, a farrier. Our harvests were good, and the sea was generous. Children laughed and played in the streets. New strangers came from over the sea, but they were kinder. They brought with them a distant god in the sky.

And then, one festival day, when the sky was a clean cloudless blue and our children wore white for the dancing, the piper came back. Most of us ignored him for he was a shabby, dusty thing, a moth surrounded by the bright flapping of butterflies. A few of us followed him to the marketplace, eager to get our hands on some of his spider-silk thread. But this time he did not lay out his wares, he simply lifted his pipe to his lips and began to play.

And we heard no sound. It was like the day the Rat Men came, when our ears were full of beeswax and cotton. We heard none of that fantastic music. But the children did. They dropped what they were doing and began dancing: jigging and carousing and laughing as they followed him through the town.

When we realised what was happening, we tried to stop it. Parents grabbed children, but the children had grown savage in their need to dance, to follow the piper. They kicked and bit and had gained an unnatural strength. Some of us ran ahead and tried to plead with the piper, but his eyes were black now, unfeeling, completely alien. We tried to tear the pipe from his hands, but it was impossible. He had too many arms, too many legs, a sticky substance like gossamer protected him from our knives and clubs.

All the children of the town followed him out into the countryside in a long happy procession, all the way to the caves and into the darkness inside. And then the earth shook and boulders bigger than houses fell from the mountainside and over the black mouth of the cave, sealing it shut forever.

The Frog Prince

I'm a frog prince. You know how it goes – wicked witch, beautiful princess, very fortunate frog, a kiss and all that malarkey. I'm here to tell you that that's not really the way it is at all. So, maybe once there was a witch and maybe once someone did get kissed by a beautiful princess, but it's different now.

First of all, I'm not actually a frog. I'm not exactly a man either but I would definitely say I am more man than frog. I have two arms, two legs, one head. I walk upright with no leaps or waddles. My skin is pale and under certain light it does have a mottled greenish appearance. I wouldn't say I'm ugly like a frog is, but let's just say my appearance is an acquired taste, and let's just say that the ladies – princesses, if I may – find that taste much easier to acquire when they find out just how much money me and my brothers have.

I'm the youngest of three brothers. We are all frog princes. My oldest brother married young and now he lives in a penthouse on the Thames with his model wife and two of her glamourous friends. He drives an Aston Martin and works in a glass office in the city and every year that passes he looks less like a frog prince and more like a fat self-satisfied toad. His wife tells people that she didn't marry him for his looks or his money, but for his *personality*. The middle brother rebelled and took off one night, leaving behind his wealth and his beautiful fiancée and we think he's teaching yoga on a retreat somewhere in India. He was always very bendy.

My father was a frog prince once, and I suppose now you could call him the Frog King, but he doesn't like that. He prefers to be called The Right Honourable Sir Sidney Wetmarsh. My mother is one of the Goldington sisters. They all married into money, but she has done best of all. They have a mansion in the Cotswolds with a lake, a maze and tennis courts in the grounds, and a flat in Belgravia, and another home in the middle of nowhere on a Scottish moor. We want for nothing.

So, you're going to think me just the worst kind of goggle-eyed, ungrateful little freak when I tell you this story about something that happened to me two years back, when I was twenty years old and my parents took me to my first ever Butterfly Ball.

The whole point of the Butterfly Ball is to find a mate. Everyone knows that. The parents watch their children like hawks, nudging them towards suitable matches, nudging them away from the less suitable. It wouldn't do, for example, for a Cinderella to end up with a Beanstalk Boy or a Sleeping Beauty to shack up with a dwarf. That's just not how it works.

My parents took me in the Rolls, but once we got there, I saw my friend Jack at the drinks table pouring something into the punch bowl and looking shifty. Jack is a seventh son of a seventh son and, frankly, knowing that whatever adversity happens, he will always come out on top, has made him somewhat reckless and smug. He was also given the name Jack and he's not above telling the princesses that he's a Beanstalk Boy or a Giant Killer.

I helped myself to some of the punch anyway, and Jack and I watched all the comings and goings. As always there were a lot of Cinderellas at the ball. They breed like rabbits and there are never enough Prince Charmings to go round. Some of them had gone full out for the ball gown and glass slipper look, but the fashion was more for rags that revealed a lot of leg and cleavage. Of course, each Cinderella was trailing at least two ugly sisters behind her. I'd feel sorry for them, except that at boarding school I met more than my fair share of ugly sisters and those girls are mean. It was an ugly sister who first nicknamed me Kermit and that name has stuck so everyone calls me Kermit now.

Jack told me that he was going to have a shot at one of the Sleeping Beauties camped out near the cages where they would release the butterflies at the end of the night. The Sleeping Beauties are a feisty lot and anything but sleepy. Of course, they're all promised to a particular kind of rosebush-hacking prince, so there couldn't be anything serious with Jack, but he was game for anything. His parents and family had already arranged a beautiful princess for him. By the time he graduates with his law degree, his six older brothers will have tried and failed to gain her hand and there will just be some impossible task to complete before they can marry. I watched him crossing the room to the Sleeping Beauties and then looked round the room for someone else to talk to. There were a lot of non-specific princesses and I knew that my future wife was one of them but when I looked at them, I didn't feel anything.

I didn't want any of them, and I knew they didn't want me. They wanted my money and my name and the house in the country and the flat in the city my father would buy for us when we married, but they didn't want me.

And why would they want little bandy-legged me when there were all those handsome princes and Giant Killers and Dragon Slayers and Huntsmen and Beanstalk Boys? Even the Beasts that lurked at the back of the hall in a vast shaggy group reeking of real ale had more to offer than I did.

But still, it was my life. It was what I'd got and even though it's not what I would have chosen, I was OK with it. Or rather I was OK with it until I saw her.

No one wanted to talk to me, so I wandered off through the maze of backrooms, trying to avoid gaggles of Fairy Godmothers all ripe for meddling, and the heaving forms of Cinderellas and Prince Charmings hard at it under piles of everyone else's coats. So tawdry. I opened a door hoping to find the kitchen and a snack a bit more substantial than the trays of canapes the mice boys and girls were handing round, and instead I found myself in some sort of cloakroom and it was full of hissing angry geese. There was a girl there standing in front of a mirror on the far wall frowning at her reflection.

'Oh,' I said. 'Sorry. I thought this was the kitchen.'

The girl turned round and right away I could see that she was beautiful in that quaint understated way that goose girls have. She was wearing a grey dress and a snowy white apron, and her hair was loose down her back with a few artful pieces of straw arranged in it. It's not impossible for a goose girl to hook up with a non-specific prince or hero but it is unlikely. I wondered if she was Jack's type.

'Nope,' she said, 'this is just a room for avoiding other people.'

'Right,' I said, and I started backing away. 'Sorry to have disturbed you.'

She smiled at me and the smile went right through me. 'What are you?'

'Frog prince,' I said. 'And you're a goose girl. I can't be around geese. They eat frogs.'

'Mine don't,' she said. 'They get corn and breadcrumbs. Cake when they're lucky. Do you want to dance with me?'

I didn't reply immediately. Not because I was being rude, but because I was trying to work out how dancing with one girl and ten geese would work, especially when I was scared of geese. But she thought I was being rude.

'Right,' she said, 'of course not. How silly of me to think that a frog prince should lower himself to dancing with a goose girl.' She turned back to the mirror. 'Mirror, mirror on the wall, am I a princess or a peasant?'

The mirror remained silent.

'Um,' I said, 'I think that's just an ordinary mirror.'

'Are you still there?' she said. 'I know it's an ordinary mirror. I met this wicked step-mother who had a magic mirror that told her she was beautiful until one day it didn't, and she went ape-shit and murdered her Snow White and all the dwarves. Killed them stone dead without all the nonsense with the Huntsman and the poisoned apple. She was such a lovely person until she went psycho. The mirror is still around somewhere, looking for a replacement for her. That might be fun to get hold of, don't you think?'

I shook my head, edging away from one of the geese. 'Those mirrors are not toys,' I said. 'They can be dangerous. They tell lies.'

'Well, this whole world that we live in is a lie, isn't it?' she said. 'It's a lie that a Cinderella has to marry a Prince Charming and a Beauty has to marry a Beast. It's a lie that no one knows Rumpelstiltskin's name – everyone in the entire world knows what his name is. It's a lie that ducks and geese don't know a cygnet from their own little ones and it's a lie that a frog prince can't have one dance with a goose girl.'

'I could have one dance with you,' I conceded, 'but I don't know how it will work with those geese everywhere. I don't like geese or ducks or swans. I like foxes. My favourite story is Chicken-Licken.' I was aware that I was babbling, and I was babbling because she was beautiful, and I was not good at talking to girls.

'The geese will wait in the courtyard,' she told me.

'OK,' I said dubiously.

We walked along the corridor with half the geese waddling self-importantly in front of us and the other half waddling behind taking the rear guard.

'What's your name?' I asked.

'Sally,' she said, and I nodded. All goose girls are called sensible names like Sally, Joan or Greta. 'What's yours?'

'Augustus,' I said and sighed. 'People call me Kermit.'

She hid a smile. 'Well, I won't,' she said. 'I'll call you Augustus or August or Auggie or Gus or whatever you want me to call you.'

'Gus,' I said. Jack called me Gus, but to my family I was always Augustus and to everyone else I was Kermit. I liked Gus.

'Sally and Gus.' She laughed and took my arm. I almost pulled away from her but then I decided to go with it.

We found a door that led out into a courtyard that was all strung up with fairy lights, roses dropping pink and scarlet petals on the ground. A Sleeping Beauty was having a shouting match with a Rose Red at one end of it, and at the other some Beasts were sitting at one of the little filigree tables arm wrestling and cheering one another on. Two ugly sisters were gossiping into their mobile phones beside the fountain. This was supposed to be a peaceful place but people like us can never be at peace for long. There was a door that led back into the ballroom and I headed towards it.

'Wait,' Sally said, and she led me to a wooden bench. She bent down to the same level as the geese and started whispering to them and making little honking noises. I had to look away to stop myself from laughing, but when she was finished the geese all settled quietly on the grass beside the bench.

'There,' Sally said, 'now you're safe. Not that my geese would have harmed you. Let's go dance.'

'I should tell you,' I said, 'that I can't dance. I know all the steps. I can perform the steps to perfection but it's not dancing. It's just walking in an odd, jaunty sort of way. Frogs don't dance.'

Sally laughed and pulled me close to her and the next thing I knew, we were in a hold and my hands were on her hips and she was grinning at me and her smile was wide and happy and beautiful, and I knew, I just knew, that I was falling in love with her.

At first no one noticed us. They were all caught up in their own fairy-tale romances as they paired off while the night drew to an end, but then I was aware of a silence falling over the ballroom, and it was a silence weighted with outrage and disapproval. I caught sight of my parents, and my father's eyes were bulging and my mother looked like she wanted to cry. All the non-specific princesses were horrified as they watched their chance at my inheritance disappearing. Gradually, the other couples on the dance floor thinned until there was only me and Sally. And I was dancing. The steps were in the wrong order, but we were moving and whirling to the music, locked together and laughing. Frogs don't dance, but I dance when I'm with her.

We married two weeks later. Sally's family came, but mine were absent. A week before the wedding, my oldest brother tried to talk me out of it. He pointed out how happy he is with his wife and her two model best friends, all living together in some weird bigamist arrangement that for some reason is perfectly acceptable in a way that a frog prince and a goose girl marrying is not. And he is happy, but he's different from me. My other brother sent a garbled email about destiny and chakras, and a few weeks later a singing bowl arrived in the post from India with a note to say that its vibrations will bring us fertility.

My parents struck me out of their wills. No inheritance for me. No house in the country, no flat in the city, no Aston Martin or Rolls Royce, no castle in Scotland. My father shouted, and my mother cried. They called in a gaggle of fairy step-mothers to try and talk me out of it. The non-specific princess they had been considering for me cried too and then called me a cad and a cheater, despite the fact that I'd never met her before and never promised her anything. Her father and my father came to blows over the whole affair. It was quite a scandal.

Jack came to the wedding with his six brothers. He approved whole-heartedly, although he admitted he would never dare stray from his path as I have done. He admitted that he's scared of whatever ordeal he will have to get through before he can live happily ever after.

It turns out, we don't need my inheritance. Sally's family are farmers – free-range geese that roam over fields in the Shropshire hills. They've got plenty of land and money of their own. I can't say I enjoy being among the geese, but I'm keen to pull my weight and help out. When Christmas draws nearer, I feel a certain smug satisfaction when I look at them. Sally herself is always surrounded by her own personal gaggle of geese, but I've got used to that. I can even talk to them a little in that hissing, whispering, honking language Sally taught me.

'So, what happens to these geese at Christmas time?' I asked Sally one morning when we were lazing in bed with breakfast and the papers and ten fat geese.

'Nothing,' Sally said.

'What makes these ones different from those outside?' I asked.

36

Sally smiled. 'These are the ones that lay the golden eggs, of course.'

Of course. So, what else can I say except that no one calls me Kermit anymore? I'm Gus now. And Sally and me, we're very busy living happily ever after.

Ghosts, Vampires & Other Monsters

The Contraption

The dead man moved into the shed at the bottom of the Mitchells' garden at the end of October. He wore a black fleece jacket and desert boots, and his hair was neatly trimmed. There was something quite respectable about him. Even the supermarket trolley that he wheeled up the alleyway and into the garden through the back gate seemed to hold nothing more than a few carrier bags and a duvet with a rather tasteful blue and white cover.

Annie Mitchell watched him from the window of her office as he broke the lock on the shed door with a quick efficiency and went inside, leaving his shopping trolley on the garden path. She watched as he methodically removed the contents of the shed – the lawn mower and deckchairs and half used pots of paint – and placed them neatly on the lawn. He was very careful not to step in the flowerbeds or the vegetable patch and when he looked up and saw Annie standing at the window watching, he looked away quickly, as if he was embarrassed.

Annie watched him as he began to transfer the contents of his shopping trolley into the shed and then went downstairs and called Mike.

'There's a dead man moving into the shed,' she said.

'How does he look?' Mike asked.

'Healthy. He looks healthy.'

'Good,' Mike said. 'Don't go near him. It's Hallowe'en on Thursday. He'll be gone then.'

All afternoon, Annie tried to concentrate on her work. She was writing a thesis on twenty-first century zombie literature and the irony of having a dead man at the bottom of the garden had not escaped her. The trouble was that in the literature, the zombies were always brain dead and violent. All the dead people Annie had seen had been somewhat apologetic and slightly confused. Of course, she'd seen the terrible things on the news – whole countries razed to the ground by plagues of angry dead men and women, and sometimes there were incidents locally. Just recently a pack of dead dogs had started terrorising the car park at the local supermarket, and there was a terribly sad tale of a dead child wandering the streets, crying and shivering all through January until finally an old lady took pity on the thing and opened the door of her nice warm bungalow to it and had her throat torn out as a reward.

The dead were unpredictable, that was the trouble. All the townspeople had taken their training, and the Neighbourhood Watch had just got the only government-authorised Contraption in the county, but you still had to be careful.

At about three o'clock, Annie saw the dead man come out of the shed and begin to walk up the garden path towards the house. He was carrying a tin mug and his face was peaceful. He barely looked dead. It was only his deathly pallor, and the fact that moving into someone else's shed was not normal, that gave him away. Annie ducked down, but at the same time the dead man looked up and she was almost certain he'd seen her. A moment later there was a knock at the door.

Annie got the crossbow and pepper spray and still hesitated to open the door. The man didn't look dangerous, but you couldn't be too careful. She opened the door on the chain.

'Yes?'

The man smiled blankly at her. When he was alive, he had been a handsome man. He still was. He had blue eyes and black hair and he looked as if he had gone running or cycling often when he was alive. There wasn't a mark on him. Whatever it was that had killed him, it looked as if it had been a peaceful death. He was the most inoffensive dead person she had ever seen.

He held the tin mug out to her.

'Did you let the rabbits out again?' he asked.

'What?'

'One single to Atterbury Common, please,' he said.

Annie had read that the dead could still think but their thoughts got confused with old memories and conversations. Sometimes, what came out of their mouths was the memory of an old conversation and not connected to what was really going on their heads.

'Makka Pakka,' the dead man said.

'Would you like a cup of tea?' Annie asked. She supposed that she could do that.

'It's already past your bedtime.'

He held the tin mug out again and smiled showing perfect white teeth. Annie took it.

'Wait there. I'll just pop the kettle on,' she said.

She closed the door again and locked it. She was almost certain that he was safe, but she was also aware that she was prejudiced. Just because he was attractive, and didn't smell or have bits hanging off him, did not mean he was safe. That was the first thing they had learned in their training. It had been illustrated with a basket of dead kittens that had purred and played adorably until the instructor released a live mouse into their midst. Though, Annie had argued, that that was just what cats were like.

She made him tea in the white tin mug and poured herself a coffee from the machine. She realised that she should have offered him a choice of tea or coffee, and asked if he took milk or sugar, but she was afraid that might just confuse him further.

She opened the door on the chain again and passed the mug back out.

'My favourite word is quagmire,' the dead man said, 'what's yours?'

'Bamboozle,' Annie said. 'I hope you're comfortable in the shed. You can stay for as long as you want, as long as you don't cause any trouble, but I should tell you that Mr Stephenson from the Neighbourhood Watch will be using the Contraption on Hallowe'en.'

The dead man smiled. 'We're all going to Disney Land,' he said, 'isn't that exciting?'

'Yes,' Annie said, 'but the Contraption – do you understand? Nod or shake your head or stamp your feet if you do.'

The man blinked several times and his body twitched alarmingly. Annie took that as meaning that he understood.

'Well, maybe here isn't the safest place for you to be,' Annie said.

'We've got maybe six months left,' the man said.

'Oh, you poor thing.' Annie thought she understood then. The man had died from cancer or some other terminal illness. At some point a doctor must have told him he had six months left to live.

'You mustn't interrupt when the grown-ups are talking,' the dead man said.

Annie nodded. 'Well, if you need anything let me know.'

'Can you make sure the report's complete by lunchtime? I'll need it for my meeting.'

'In case you don't know, Hallowe'en is the day after tomorrow. That's two nights. Two sleeps. Maybe you should go out into the countryside, out of range.'

The man's face contorted. He seemed to be trying very hard to think of something or to tell her something. 'I never loved anyone until I met you,' he said.

Annie smiled. 'That's nice. I'm pleased you had someone. I'm sure she, or he, misses you very much.'

'Igglepiggle,' the dead man said sadly.

She couldn't concentrate on her thesis after that, and after a while she gave up and went down to the kitchen. She made some ginger biscuits and started chopping vegetables for dinner. The dead man was sitting on the lawn outside the shed in a deckchair. He didn't seem to be doing anything except sitting. He was still holding his white mug but there was something else in his hands.

Annie frowned and then took two ginger biscuits and put them on a paper plate. She picked up the crossbow and tucked the pepper spray into the waistband of her jeans and then went outside and walked down the garden towards him.

'I thought you might be peckish,' she said.

The man looked at her. 'I beat my best time by ten seconds,' he said.

'I made these biscuits,' she said. 'They might still be a bit warm.'

'Katie's making steak pie tonight. Did you feed the rabbits? She's too little to be all alone. It's only forty pounds a month for two of us. The haahoos never do anything much, do they?' He was getting agitated, his hands twitching, sloshing tea onto his black jeans. Annie saw that the thing he was holding in his other hand was a photograph.

'Would you like to show me?' she asked.

'Quagmire,' the man said.

'Bamboozle,' Annie smiled. 'Can I have a look?'

Very gently, one hand on her pepper spray, she took the photograph from him. He twitched and muttered something about family cars and mileage, but he let her take it. It was a photograph of a woman and a little girl. The woman had a mass of curly black hair and a wide smile. She looked like the kind of person Annie would have liked to have been friends with. The child looked to be about two years old with the same curly hair. There was a tube running into her nose.

The man made a pointing motion, not pointing at the photograph but vaguely at the sky. 'What Katie did,' he said.

'This is Katie?' Annie said. 'Is she your partner? Your wife?'

'I could eat five chocolate oranges in one sitting,' the man said, 'I really could.'

'Me too,' Annie said. 'Is this your daughter? Is she sick?'

'I wasn't even drunk,' the man said. 'Blooming cats digging up the flowerbeds again.'

'They're beautiful,' Annie said and then, against everything they'd been told in the training, she reached out and touched the man's pale cold hand. 'What's your little girl called?'

'Upsy Daisy,' the man said and made a noise that was halfway between frustrated laughter and a sob.

Annie told Mike about the dead man over dinner.

'I think he died and there's something unresolved between him and his family. That's why he hasn't passed over.'

'You shouldn't get attached and go looking for explanations,' Mike said. 'You know that sometimes people don't pass over the way they're supposed to. It doesn't mean anything. It just happens sometimes. Don't get attached to him, because Mr Stephenson is going to use the Contraption soon.'

'I know,' Annie said. She didn't tell Mike that she had warned the dead man about the Contraption. She knew he wouldn't understand. When their neighbours' dog had been put to sleep and then come back, Mike had shot it with the crossbow. It was the right thing to do, Annie knew that, but all the same...

'Mr Stephenson is unveiling the Contraption tonight,' Mike said. 'Do you want to go? I think there will be some nibbles and maybe even wine.'

'You know me,' Annie said, 'I'm never one to turn down free nibbles and wine.'

Mr Stephenson lived in the biggest house at the end of their road. There were three flagpoles in his front garden. One flew the Union Jack, one the Neighbourhood Watch flag and the third was one that Mrs Stephenson had stitched. It showed a crude cartoon zombie with a red cross through it. In his back garden there were floodlights and outdoor heaters.

'I'd like to see their electricity bills,' Mike whispered.

Mr Stephenson was a big man who wore camouflage trousers and tight tee-shirts. He usually wore a tool belt that was hung with his knives, pepper spray, and his government-authorised pistols and crossbow bolts. Annie and Mike often laughed to each other about how proud he was of his position as head of the Neighbourhood Watch.

The Contraption was in the back garden underneath a tarpaulin. Mrs Stephenson was small and busy and reminded Annie of a meerkat. She was bustling about with trays of crisps and peanuts. Mike helped himself to a beer and Annie poured herself a glass of white wine from a bottle that was chilling in a metal bucket. Mr Stephenson was holding forth to a group of neighbourhood men about an epidemic of dead people in London that was spreading northwards. Apparently, some of the dead were getting on buses and trains and moving about the country, and they weren't always being recognised as dead people. Even worse, people were helping them move about, humouring them and treating them as if they were harmless. Plainly, this would not do.

'Look at what happened in Berlin,' Mr Stephenson said. 'They've only just got the city back under control. Two hundred dead – ripped to pieces. We can't be too careful. We can't get soft and sentimental about this. I'm as sorry as anyone else, when someone dies, but the dead should stay dead. They shouldn't be coming back. We've got to keep this under control.'

Mr Stephenson unveiled the Contraption at 8.30 pm. Atterbury Common was the first town in the area to get a Contraption so Mr Stephenson told everyone what an honour it was that their Neighbourhood Watch had been chosen to have it. He explained that the Contraption was lightweight and had wheels so that it could be moved around. He asked for volunteers to help move it into his truck to take round the other towns and villages in the weeks following Hallowe'en. Mike raised his hand and Annie suppressed a frown.

Mr Stephenson and one of the other neighbours pulled back the tarpaulin, and Mr Stephenson explained some of its key features. It had an extra loud noise-maker that would attract any dead people and animals in the town and also within a ten-mile radius around it. For health and safety, it needed two people to operate it, but Mrs Stephenson had just passed her exams, so she'd be able to help with it. The doors at the front that opened to the Other Place, were not as wide as on some models, but they were mirrored so the bright light was magnified.

'Compact, mobile and above all humane,' Mr Stephenson said proudly. 'Rest assured, neighbours, we are in good hands with this baby.'

Mike told everyone about the dead man in the shed, although Annie had asked him not to. He couldn't understand why she wouldn't want them to know. After all, it was nothing to be ashamed of and these people were their neighbours. They had children and pets. They had a right to know.

'It's nothing to be alarmed about,' Mike said. 'He's peaceful. We're keeping an eye on him.'

'Who is he?' someone asked. 'Is he local? Should we know him?'

Annie remembered the dead man talking about buying a single ticket to Atterbury Common. 'I don't think he's local,' she said, 'I think he got the bus here.'

Just before bed, she took the torch and walked down the garden to the shed. The door was open, and the dead man was lying on his back on his duvet, staring up at the ceiling. The white mug was on the floor beside him and there was pink teddy-bear and a blue toy rabbit propped against the wall next to him. The photograph was still in his hands.

Annie cleared her throat politely, but the dead man didn't move.

'Bamboozle,' she said.

There was a silence and then the man spoke. 'Quagmire,' he said.

'Good night,' Annie said, 'sleep tight.'

'I'm sorry,' the dead man said, 'he's not at his desk at the moment. Can I help you at all?'

The next morning after Mike had gone to work, Annie put together a pack for the dead man. She filled a thermos with tea and packed cheese and pickle sandwiches and a packet of chocolate digestives. For a moment, she hesitated and then she opened the treat cupboard and took out a chocolate orange someone had given Mike for his birthday. She put it in the pack with the other things and then added two apples and a bottle of water. She made some coffee in the machine and poured out two mugs and then took the pack and coffee and went outside.

The dead man was back in the deck chair. He looked at her and his face twitched as if he was trying to smile.

'Quagmire,' he said cheerfully.

'Bamboozle,' Annie said. She gave him his coffee and put down the backpack and sat down on the lawn beside him. It was only when she was sitting down that she realised she'd left her pepper spray and crossbow inside.

'Booze and pills,' the dead man said, 'that'll do the trick. Nothing gets any cheaper these days, does it?'

'Listen,' Annie said, 'you have to go away from here. We've got a Contraption and we're going to use it tomorrow. If you leave today, you can be far enough away that it won't affect you when they sound the noise-maker. You need to be more than ten miles away.'

'How can you be scared of the Pontipines when they're so tiny?'

Annie frowned. 'Do you understand? It's not safe for you here.'

'We just don't have the money to go to America for treatment we don't even know will work.'

'I'm sorry about that,' Annie said, 'I really am, but you have to know that it's not safe here. You have to go.'

'We binged out on a boxset last night.'

'Mike and I do that too,' Annie said. 'Listen, I'll drive you out of town. We'll finish our coffee and then I'll take you.'

The man's face twisted and contorted. 'Makka Pakka,' he said. 'Tombliboo Ee. Qwerty keyboard. Kale chips. Dammit.'

Annie touched his hand again. 'It's OK,' she said, 'it's OK.'

The man's fingers twitched as if he wanted to take her hand but couldn't. 'The bus gets in tomorrow at noon,' he said.

'Yes,' Annie said. 'I'm sure it does.'

They sat in silence drinking their coffee and watching the clouds cross the sky. Annie decided that she would take him out on the moor road and drop him off in the big layby where the viewpoint was. She'd suggest he follow the footpath and not speak to anyone. She was pretty sure that he wouldn't meet anyone, but if he did, they wouldn't be able to tell that he was dead, as long as he didn't speak.

'Popo-Bear and Hoppity-Blue-Rabbit will keep you safe in the darkness,' he said. 'We should catch up soon, have a few beers, what do you think?'

'That sounds like fun,' Annie said. 'What's your name anyway? I don't think I told you mine. I'm Annie. What's your name?'

He frowned. 'Mr... Mr... We're going to be late if you don't get a move on. Is there really a Contraption here?'

Annie felt a surge of relief. He understood, he recognised the danger. 'Yes,' she said, 'and tomorrow they're going to use it.'

He smiled. 'That's good. It's cheaper to get it in Aldi, but that's a ten-mile round trip, so it all evens out. She was blazing drunk, you know, she made such a fool of herself. I said I'd give it ten minutes. The bus gets in at noon tomorrow, don't forget. What's the Wi-Fi password? Do you really think all those drugs are doing her any good? Oh, my name is Igglepiggle...'

Annie smiled as he rambled on. She finished her coffee and then stood up. She took the mugs back to the house and picked up her car keys. She paused for a moment in front of the cabinet where the crossbows were and then shook her head slightly and went back out jingling the car keys.

'OK,' she said, 'let's get going. Take the backpack. It's got some bits and pieces in it for you. Do you want to take anything else? We can't fit your trolley in the car, but we could take the cuddly toys and some other things if you want.'

He looked slightly puzzled, but he followed her to the car without taking anything except the backpack.

'She's too little to go alone into the dark,' he said as Annie reversed the car out of the driveway, hoping that none of her neighbours would notice her passenger.

He became agitated when they reached the edge of town, grabbing the steering wheel suddenly and nearly sending them into the path of an articulated lorry leaving one the industrial estates that sprawled into the countryside. He started shouting and she had to pull into a bus stop.

'The Contraption,' he shouted. 'It's here. Don't you see? Idiot.'

Annie shouted back. 'Yes, I see. That's what I'm trying to save you from. You're the idiot.'

'Cantaloupe melon,' the dead man shouted and despite everything Annie burst out laughing.

Her laughter seemed to calm him down. 'Katie?' he said.

Annie shook her head. 'No. It's me. Annie.'

'Do you want me to get you anything while I'm out? The pink

ones are my favourite.'

Annie tried to explain again. 'I have to take you out of town because it's not safe for you. Tomorrow, Mr Stephenson will start the Contraption and it will open the doors to the Other Place and you'll have to go. You won't be able to resist.'

'All little girls go to heaven,' he said. 'The wheels on the bus go round and round. The agapanthuses are beautiful this year. Mummies and Daddies go to heaven too.'

Annie looked away, biting her lip and blinking back sudden tears.

'We just don't all get to go at the same time.'

Annie watched the traffic in silence. The dead man fell into a silence too.

'The Contraption,' Annie said at last, 'you came here deliberately because we have a Contraption?'

'There's a moose loose aboot the hoose.'

'Are Katie and your little girl arriving tomorrow? On the bus?'

'It takes two hours on the bus. I said that I'd pop in on my way home, just to say hello.'

'OK.' Annie turned the key in the ignition and turned the car round. 'Would you like me to meet them? At noon?'

'I've always wanted to go to Barcelona.'

'Me too,' Annie said sadly.

'Pills and booze,' the dead man said when they pulled back into the driveway, 'that'll do the trick.'

Hallowe'en was a perfect crisp autumn day. Annie set the pumpkin lantern Mike had carved the night before on the window ledge and poured fun size chocolate bars into a bowl with monkey nuts and some satsumas that she knew the children wouldn't want. She made coffee for the dead man and took it to his shed.

'Bamboozle,' she said.

The dead man managed a smile. 'Quagmire,' he said.

Annie packed the pink bear and blue rabbit into the backpack. 'You should take this when you go. You might need it.'

'I'll always go first so that you don't have to go alone,' the dead man said. 'Penguins are pretty speedy when they're swimming, you know.'

'Listen,' she said, 'this is the plan. I'll pick up Katie from the bus station at noon and take her straight to the Stephensons' where the

Contraption is. I think they're going to start it at about one o'clock, so that should be plenty of time. When you hear it, I don't think you'll be able to resist but just in case, when you hear the noise-maker, go down the driveway and turn left and it's the big house at the end of the road with the flags in the garden. Do you understand? Show me that you understand.'

The dead man was silent, and she could see him trying desperately to form the right words. 'Pets Win Prizes,' he said at last. 'I'm really sorry, but if you're late again this week I'm going to have to inform human resources.'

Annie squeezed his hand. 'I'll go and get them, then.'

The bus station was busy and crowded, and Annie wondered if she'd made a mistake coming here. She was worried that she wouldn't spot Katie in the crowds or that she wouldn't recognise her. The bus station was busy with people from the other towns and villages close by, and it looked as if most of them were on a day trip to see the Contraption in action. They were carrying picnic baskets and blankets, hurrying towards the shuttle buses that Mr Stephenson and the Neighbourhood Watch had organised for just that purpose. Annie stood on her tiptoes cursing that she didn't even know where Katie was coming from, so she couldn't wait at the correct bus stance. But finally, she spotted a woman with untidy curly hair, a child clutched close to her chest, heading towards the shuttle buses.

'Katie,' Annie shouted. 'Katie.'

The woman didn't hear her so Annie had to push through the crowds and grab the shoulder of her jacket just as she was about to step onto the bus.

The woman turned to look at her, her expression flustered and annoyed. In that moment, Annie could see how right she was for the dead man. Her slightly quirky way of dressing, the flash of irritation in her eyes that could so easily turn to anger was the perfect foil for his neatness and calm. The child stared at them through huge eyes. She was painfully thin and pale. A tube ran into one of her nostrils, the other end of it hidden in the large corduroy bag Katie was carrying. Annie bit her lip, unsure if the child was dead already.

'Katie,' she said. 'There's a dead man in my shed. I think he's your husband. Your partner? His favourite word is quagmire. He has a pink teddy bear with him.'

Katie stared at her. 'Is he OK?'

'Yes,' Annie said. 'Well, no not really. He's dead, you know.'

'I know,' Katie said.

'There isn't much time,' Annie said. 'They're switching the Contraption on at one o'clock. We can take my car. It'll be quicker.'

Katie hesitated for a moment and then nodded. 'Thank you.'

Katie laid the child on the back seat of the car and sat beside her. As they drove through the town towards the suburbs, she told Annie that the dead man had been an advertising executive when he was alive. She said that the little girl was called Maisie. She was their only child.

'He said her name was Upsy Daisy,' Annie said.

Katie laughed sadly. 'They used to watch that programme together. He'd get home from working late, just in time for bedtime, and they'd watch together. Then when she got sick, we told her that it would be just like going there. That Upsy Daisy and Igglepiggle and all the others would be waiting for her. We said don't be afraid, but we were all afraid.'

Annie didn't know what to say. 'I'm sorry,' she said, 'I'm so sorry.'

'There's nothing for you to be sorry about,' Katie said. 'I'm going to be in so much trouble, you know. I took her from the children's hospice. I stole her away from all the machines that were keeping her alive and put her on a bus and brought her here. The police are probably looking for me, and social services. But it wasn't life, you know. Where she was, it was just a hinterland between life and death. It was just prolonging her pain and her suffering.' Her voice broke and she fell silent.

Annie concentrated on the traffic. She didn't know what to say and she felt helpless and immature. She could live to be a hundred, she thought, and she'd never be mature enough to handle this.

They were part of a long stream of cars and buses heading towards the Stephensons' house. Katie was suddenly afraid that they wouldn't make it on time, that they'd be stuck in a traffic jam when Mr Stephenson turned on the Contraption.

'Is she still…?' Annie asked delicately.

'Yes, Katie said. 'Yes, she is, but not for long.'

'And afterwards, will you be all right? What will you do?'

'I don't know,' Katie said, 'I haven't thought about that. I'll be all right, I guess.'

The child whimpered, and Katie made her voice sound light and cheerful again. 'It's OK, sweetie,' she said, 'we'll see Daddy soon. Daddy's going to take you to the Other Place. You'll be safe with Daddy.'

The Stephensons had wheeled the Contraption into the street and there were crowds milling around it, sitting on garden walls, and spreading out their picnic blankets on the front lawns of the neighbours' gardens. There was a hotdog van and an ice-cream van, a man selling balloons and someone else selling tee-shirts with pictures of the Contraption on the front. The flags in the Stephensons' garden danced merrily in a warm autumn breeze. Members of the Neighbourhood Watch walked amongst the crowd, giving out leaflets and free pens and notebooks stamped with the Neighbourhood Watch logo. Annie spotted Mike talking to a group of young men, campaigning to get them to join, and hoped that he would not notice her.

At exactly one o'clock Mrs Stephenson began cranking the levers and pressing the coloured buttons on the Contraption in a complicated sequence. Mr Stephenson made a show of holding up the big key that would unlock the doors to the other place. He said a few words, but Katie couldn't hear them above the crowds. There was something about it being his great pleasure, and something about zombies and something else about cleansing the streets before the children went trick or treating, and then he fitted the key into the lock, pressed a few buttons on the machine, and the doors slowly began to slide open. At first there was nothing to see. The doors just opened into a grey metal box, but as Mr and Mrs Stephenson darted round the Contraption, pressing buttons and cranking levers like bees dancing on a hive, the space inside the doors began to expand, spreading wider than should have been possible. It appeared to tear a hole in the air and through the hole, a clear golden light began to shine.

'The bright light,' someone close to Annie said. 'It's working.'

Katie stroked Maisie's hair. 'That doesn't look too bad, does it, darling?' she said. 'A beautiful light and on the other side, there's the Night Garden. Daddy will come soon.'

A strange noise began to come from the Contraption. It was a low, soft humming interspersed with sounds like waves on a pebbled shore, like someone crushing cotton wool, like wind through trees. The animals came first. The pack of dead dogs from the supermarket car park in a happy, barking mob were first. The crowds parted for them as they raced headlong into the light and were gone. Birds tumbled from the sky into the light, a fox bounded in, some roadkill rabbits and hedgehogs followed, and an old badger shambled in after them. The woman from a few doors down, gave an anguished cry when a fat black cat with a red collar bounded into the light after it.

Then the dead people began to arrive. The first was an old man with a Zimmer frame and tartan slippers. The crowds cheered and clapped as he made his way through them, drawn by the strange noises and the light. After that, they came thick and fast, unable to resist. Mostly they were elderly and confused. Everyone got a round of applause before they went in and Annie felt a surge of warmth towards her neighbours.

'Where is he?' Katie asked. She stood on her tiptoes and searched through the crowds.

He was close to the back of the crowd. It seemed that in death, like in life, he was kind and patient. He'd got stuck behind a group of slow-moving dead people with shattered limbs and horrific injuries and was too polite to push past them.

Annie jumped up and down waving frantically. 'Bamboozle,' she shouted. 'Bamboozle.'

'Quagmire,' the dead man shouted back.

Katie ran to him, Maisie still clutched to her chest. She threw her arms round him and held him. The dead man was speaking but Annie couldn't tell what he was saying. People tried to prise Katie away from him.

'You've got to let him go,' someone said kindly.

The dead man was carrying the backpack Annie had made up for him on his back and Annie could see the smiling faces of the pink bear and the blue rabbit poking out of it. Maisie's face broke into a weak smile and she tried to point to them. The procession of the dead moved around them, and Katie, Maisie and the dead man stood in the midst of it, holding one another. The dead man was twitching, his face contorting as he fought to resist the call from the Contraption.

Annie moved towards them and put her hand on Katie's back. 'Let them go,' she said.

'I love you,' Katie sobbed, 'I love you both.'

'Somebody answer the phone,' the dead man said. 'We're going to be late if we don't get a move on.'

'I can't,' Katie said. 'Don't leave me, please don't leave me. I love you.'

'It's cold out,' the dead man said, 'take my scarf. Drive carefully.'

Then he took Maisie from her arms and let Katie go. He held the child close to his chest and walked towards the light. Just before he stepped into it, he looked back and his eyes met Annie's and she knew he was trying to say thank you.

'Quagmire,' he said.

'Bamboozle,' Annie whispered.

And then, the child wrapped tight in his arms, he turned round and walked backwards into the light, his eyes fixed on Katie's so that she was the last thing they saw before the light swallowed them up and the doors of the Contraption swung shut with a satisfying metal clang.

Grey

Their eyes meet, the yellow of the bird's meeting the brown of the boy's, unblinking, until the boy looks away. The bird turns its gaze to the water and its beak stabs downwards like a knife, misses its prey and comes up again. It eyes the boy as if amused by its own failure and then stretches its great wings and a takes off, sweeping low over the fishing pool and across the reed bed to the second smaller pool, where the water is shallower and the fishing easier. Calum presses the shutter on the camera and shoots, catching the bird in flight. He's pretty sure it's a good shot though he won't know until he loads it onto the PC. He watches a moment longer as the heron sweeps the perimeter of the pool and chooses its spot, settling into a perfect stillness at the edge of the water to watch and wait, as if it has always been there, will always be there.

'Bloody things,' Dad says as Marie spoons soggy vegetables onto his plate. 'Fishing stocks down for the third year running.'

Calum and Marie make noncommittal noises. Calum's thinking of his art project. He's called it 'Game' and it's supposed to represent both the wildlife on the estate and the people who come to hunt and shoot it. Miss Sealey says it has potential, but he needs to work on the narrative as well as the photographs.

'We'll get it sorted tonight,' Dad says. 'You and me, Cal.'

Calum groans. There was a time when he might have argued, claimed homework or appointments with friends, but he's wise enough now to know whatever he says will be overruled. He's just biding his time until he's sixteen and can get out of here for good. In the meantime, he can't do anything to upset Dad.

'Aren't they protected?' Marie asks.

Dad shakes his head. 'We're talking about a grey heron not a bloody golden eagle,' he says. 'This old thing's been hanging around for years, breeding more of the little bastards. He needs taking out.'

Dad doesn't care if birds are protected. Calum and Marie both know he's poisoned eagles and ospreys, shot a wild cat once for going too near his precious pheasants. They've grown up surrounded by death and for the most part it doesn't bother them.

They understand the need to cull deer. They know that what Dad calls Rich City Boys bring money and jobs into the area. They know that where there's beauty, there's savagery.

The evening smells of gorse and chimney smoke. They leave Marie to wash up and walk down towards the fishing pools, with Buddy prancing at their heels, barely able to contain his excitement. In the distance, there's the sound of fiddle music and an occasional burst of laughter. There's a party going on at the Lodge and Calum knows that this is what has spurred Dad into action. If a Rich City Boy has paid thousands to experience some hunting, shooting and fishing, he doesn't expect to go home empty-handed. It's up to Dad to make sure the fish are biting and there's a big, kick-ass stag ready for the taking.

It's still hot and clouds of midges are hanging low over the water. Swallows dart after them. There's something ecstatic about their flight, their daring, as they swoop lower and lower over the water. Calum would have liked to have had his camera. Capturing the swallows in flight would be a challenge that even Miss Sealey would be impressed by.

'There,' Dad says, and he points to the far side of the pool.

The heron is in the same position among the reeds, standing still in the shallows, watching and waiting. The evening light has washed the green from the reeds and the bird is scarcely visible. It looks up and sees them and although it's too far away to see, Calum pictures its beady yellow eye unblinking, uncaring. They are not intelligent, Calum knows this, birds don't think, birds don't learn, birds don't feel. Dad has drummed this into him from before he could think for himself, but still Calum imagines the bird looking at him, recognising him and believing itself safe. He turns away, not wanting to witness this and for a moment he thinks of waving his arms, of shouting or racing towards the bird in a frenzy, anything to scare it away before Dad's ready.

'Here,' Dad says suddenly, and he thrusts the shotgun towards Calum. 'Have a go. You need to get some practice in.'

Calum shakes his head. 'I'll miss.'

Dad's in a good mood. On evenings like this, he's easy to be with, like a dad ought to be. He wants to teach his son and he wants his son to do well.

They crouch low among the reeds and Calum lifts the gun

reluctantly. There was a time before when he'd liked the feel of a gun in his hand, when he'd relished the moment when he caught whatever he was aiming at in the sights and slowly, so very slowly, squeezed the trigger. He'd shot his first pheasant before he was ten and his first deer – a doe – on his thirteenth birthday. They'd celebrated that night with venison and chocolate cake, and Calum had been allowed to drink a whole can of lager. Until recently, he'd kept the skull in his bedroom. But that was before Mum left and before Marie became a vegetarian and before Miss Sealey, who Dad says is a southerner and hasn't a clue.

'Steady,' Dad says, 'take your time. Doesn't look like the cocky old bastard's going anywhere.'

Calum finds the bird in the sights. Magnified, he can see that it is watching them, its head cocked slightly to one side, its yellow eye unblinking before it turns back to watching the water. Calum knows birds don't think, but he also knows that the bird thinks it knows him, thinks it can trust him, thinks it's safe.

'Got him in your sights?' Dad says. 'Good. Keep it steady.'

There's a moment when things could be different. There's always that terrible moment of one decision or another, of 'what if'. Calum sees himself leaping to his feet, waving his arms, roaring a warning, sees the bird unfurling its great wings and taking off, never to be seen again. He sees all that and at the same time he sees this precious moment with Dad passing into shouting and rage and affirmations of how useless and pointless his offspring are. There's a moment and it passes. He squeezes the trigger.

The noise is first: the roar of the gun breaking the evening calm; the dog, unable to contain itself any longer, barking with pure joy; a flock of mallards taking off in panic from the reeds. Then he sees, and for a moment he thinks he missed. The heron stands still and then, horribly, begins to flap, one-winged, in a desperate panic. The dog takes off round the pool still barking.

'Good lad,' Dad says. 'Could have been cleaner but Buddy will finish it.'

Calum looks at the gun in his hands and slowly passes it back to Dad. He doesn't speak, even when Buddy drags the remains of the bird back to them, struggling valiantly through the long grass with the weight of the thing that must be several times more than the pheasants he's used to retrieving. In death, the bird looks smaller, its feathers bedraggled and bloodied, it's beak less like a blade. Only its yellow eye is still bright as it stares sightlessly at nothing.

'What'll we do with it?' Calum asks.

'Leave it for Buddy and the foxes to dispose of,' Dad says, 'leave it as a warning to the others. You did well tonight, Cal. We'll make a gamekeeper of you yet.'

And even though the last thing Calum wants is to be is a gamekeeper like Dad, he can't help smiling with pride.

Calum wakes that night, and there's fear and disbelief, but more than that, there's pain in his wing. Terrible burning pain where the wing joins the body. Calum sits upright in bed and tries to stretch his broken wing, tries to lift off from the bed, and finds that he can't. He fumbles for the light and switches it on and remembers that he has arms, not wings.

Dad's out all day taking the Rich City Boys deep into the moor and he'll probably stay on at the Lodge with them, drinking and eating until late, and Marie's at her Saturday job so Calum's alone in the house all day. He's behind with his art project and his other homework, but Dad's left him a list of jobs to do and they come before any school work. Calum's known for a long time that he only goes to school because the law says he has to. He'll be leaving next year when he's sixteen.

He's in the yard with the heavy-duty gloves pulled up past his elbows, cleaning out the ferrets – a task that Marie begged him to do the night before because the ferrets are nasty and smelly and vicious, and she will owe him big time if he does it for her just this once. He's reaching in to grab one of the little monsters when, inexplicably, he's terrified of it. He remembers its black eyes and sharp teeth and remembers what it was like to have those teeth tear pinions from flesh before he twisted his long neck and stab, stab, stabbed it until it ran away, and he took to the sky away from the place by the water where it and the others like it lived, where he'd never go again.

He shakes his head to shake the memory out and stares at the ferrets. Dad's always said he's a witless daydreamer with too much imagination. But it lingers, more than a daydream: the feeling of air under his wings; the way the fishing pools and the loch look from above; the shape of a boy amongst the reeds with a camera round his neck.

There are feathers in the yard. They're grey and bloody and Calum tells himself that they could be easily be from a pigeon or a seagull. He stoops and picks one up and knows it's too big to belong to anything but the heron. The dog or one of the many feral cats that haunt this place must have brought it up.

This is mine, Calum thinks, *this is part of me.*

When the chores are done, he works on his project. He downloads the photographs of the heron and zooms in on the images, pleased that they are sharp and in focus. The bird stares out at him from the computer screen and Calum remembers how he had admired its stillness, its patience as it waited amongst the reeds for the fish. The other birds that came were noisy and quarrelsome, snapping at one another, chasing and flapping, quacking and honking. The heron was always still, and there was something alien and almost supernatural about its calm. The photographs are among the best he has ever taken, but he feels sick and ashamed when he looks at them. He knows that Miss Sealey will be full of praise when he shows them to her. She might even print one of them out and put it in a frame for the school art exhibition in the summer, and she will almost certainly suggest that he writes something to go with the photograph, or search through her books of poetry to find a few lines of verse to match the photo. He'd always liked that kind of thing and had taken to going to the art room at lunchtime instead of hanging around in the cloakrooms with the other boys. Miss Sealey was always pleased to see him, the two of them at the computer screen, playing with Photoshop or bent over her photography books and poetry books.

He can't show Miss Sealey these photographs. His stomach churns at the thought of her admiration of the shot, her praise that he doesn't deserve. She will almost certainly say something about how magnificent the bird is, and he will do nothing but smile and nod, his mouth full of the taste of pond water and blood.

He presses the delete key and the photograph is gone. There's no point anyway. It doesn't matter how many A's he gets in art, he's never going to be a photographer or an artist. He'll be a gamekeeper like Dad and Granddad and that will be that. Dad has poisoned his future as surely as he poisons the buzzards and peregrines.

Dad's drunk when he comes in. His mood swings between good humour and bad temper. He's pleased because they had a good day's shooting and fishing but angry because Marie hasn't returned from her job to make dinner, and when Calum offers to cook something he shouts and insists it's Marie's job now that Mum has gone. Calum slips away to the bathroom and texts a warning message to Marie and, as he turns to unlock the door, he catches sight of his reflection in the mirror and sees for a moment another face superimposed over his own: a long grey face with a beady yellow eye and a beak designed for stabbing. He reaches for the glass and it ripples beneath his fingers like water. When he draws his hand back, his own face stares back at him from the glass, wide-eyed and afraid.

'All right?' Dad says when he gets back to the living room. Dad is flicking through the channels on the television looking for football and settling instead for a Saturday night talent show. There's a glass of whisky on the table beside him. He hasn't showered since coming in and he smells of blood and butchery. The Rich City Boys are happy to shoot and kill, but they are not so happy to do what needs to come next if this is to be more than just pointless killing. There's a lot of talk amongst them of knowing where your meat comes from, of respecting the animal, humane management of the landscape. *A complex issue*, Miss Sealey says. *Cruelty to animals*, Marie says. *Load of old bollocks*, Dad says, *but who cares as long as they continue to pay my wage.*

They watch the television in silence, Dad laughing along with the audience. Inexplicably, he loves this kind of thing and the more deluded and less talented the contestants the better. Calum watches with half an eye and with the other, watches the night fall outside and wonders where his sister is, and he can feel in his feathers that it will rain tomorrow and that his chances of catching a fish will be higher in the loch than the pools.

The beep of his phone jolts him out of something that is part daydream and part memory. It's Marie texting back to say she's not coming home tonight. She'll stay at her friend's and go straight to work tomorrow. She promises she'll be home in time to cook the Sunday dinner, but if she's not, maybe Calum could start it off. There are instructions in Mum's recipe book. Calum sighs and glances at Dad and decides not to tell him Marie's not coming home just yet.

'Dad,' he says instead, 'do you believe in ghosts?'

Dad tears his eyes away from the television. 'They say there's a white lady up at the Lodge,' he says. 'I've never seen her, but Davy MacLeod swears he saw her. Mind you, it was Hogmanay he saw her. And there's some say that Maggie Hamilton's girl that had the car crash on Christmas Eve comes back every year and crashes her car over and over again.'

Calum frowns. 'Do you think the animals we kill come back?'

Dad sits up a bit straighter. ''Course not. Why?'

Calum shrugs his shoulders. 'It was just a thought.'

'Dead's dead,' Dad says. 'Dead's the end. There's some cultures believe the spirit of dead animals passes into the hunter that killed them. Load of old bollocks. The animals know its tooth and claw out there, survival of the biggest and the strongest. It's the way of the world and always has been, no matter what your animal rights people and vegans and other crazies say.'

Calum nods and they both turn back to the television. Dad laughs happily when one of the judges tells a contestant exactly how talentless and foolish she is. Calum looks at the screen and sees heather moors and mountains, the silver sparkle of water below him and the clouds above.

He wakes shaking in the middle of the night, convinced that the bed is full of feathers and blood and fish bones, and finds himself tangled in the sheets. There's a tapping at the window, as if something with a beak is outside trying to get in, but when he opens the curtain there's only rain beating against the glass and the perfect pitch blackness beyond.

He reaches for the bedside light and clicks it on and stretches out to pick up the long grey feather from his desk. He holds it in both hand and pushes away the feeling that it is part of him.

'I'm sorry,' he whispers. 'I'm sorry I shot you. I'm sorry I couldn't stop Dad and that I didn't try to.'

The feather lies inert in his hands and the rain, or something else, taps on the window. He thinks of his sister safe in the village, probably drinking wine with one of her friends and gossiping and dreaming about universities and cities. His sister will get away from here one day, but he knows he never will. He belongs here, amongst the fishing pools and reed beds, like his father and his grandfather and the thousands of generations of grey herons and men before him. There is a comfort in that, and a terrible terror.

He doesn't go to school the next day or the next. He tells Dad some story about in-service days and knows Dad doesn't care. He spends the days wandering round the fishing pools and across the moor to the loch, where a scrub of bog myrtle, heather and silver birches fringe the water. He wades out until the water is up to his knees, bitingly cold, and stands perfectly still watching the water with one beady eye and the sky and the shoreline for predators with the other. When he sees fish gliding beneath the water, he swoops down with his sharp sharp beak to stab at the water, but he always misses.

At night he dreams of flying.

Marie doesn't come home. Dad curses and threatens to go and find her and drag her home, but his heart isn't in it. He misses having someone to cook dinner and clean up after him, but Calum can do those things, and Marie is just a girl. A silly girl, Dad says, who will come running home again soon enough.

The fourth day that Calum misses school, Marie does come home, and Miss Sealey is with her. Calum is in his room and he is not sure if he is boy or bird. He's talking to the bird in the mirror, saying over and over again, 'Leave me alone. Leave me alone. Leave me alone,' when he hears the car pull up outside.

He hears voices, just talking at first, and he catches his own name and then there's shouting, mostly Dad, but Marie is shouting too and Miss Sealey's voice has taken the tone it sometimes does in class when someone is messing around. When he looks out of the window, he can see Marie shouting at Dad and Dad, red-faced and hungover and furious, shouting back, thrusting his face into Marie's, calling her a whore and a slapper and a snob. Miss Sealey is stepping forward, holding up her hands in a conciliatory way and slowly unbelievably, Dad's hand forms a fist and he punches Miss Sealey sending her reeling backwards against her little red car.

Calum doesn't think. He finds himself half running, half flying down the stairs, pausing in the kitchen to snatch up the carving knife from the drawer, and then out into the yard. He feels rain on feathers, sees an eagle gliding too far away to be a danger, hears shouting and the dog barking hysterically and panic wells in his chest. For a moment he longs to open his great wings and fly away from here, forever and ever, but then everyone is looking at him and Dad is coming towards him roaring something unintelligible, all teeth and smell and noise, and then his long beak is stab, stab, stabbing, and there's screaming and shouting, and blood and Dad falls and twitches and is still.

There's a long moment of silence, and then Marie sobs and Miss Sealey's voice asks someone to send an ambulance and the police quick. He looks down and sees not wings and feathers, but his hand, bloodied and clutching the long red blade and Dad on the ground, the dog running circles round him, and his eyes staring sightlessly at the sky where the huge grey shape of a heron is fading into nothingness.

Roses

This is a haunted house.

The ghosts walk the long corridors and gardens and drift like smoke through the rooms I still use.

I used to hear them at night, screaming from their resting places and calling out to be released from the eternity of their punishment. Behind the bricked-up windows and doorways, I heard them scratching at the walls and often at night I dreamt there was someone in my bed with me. I felt long limbs entangled with mine and smelled some strange scent of orange blossom and ginger. When I reached up to push my hair away from my face, I found it wasn't my hair at all but that of some other creature I could not see or feel once fully awake, but whose presence was very real. Sometimes I felt the scratch of fingernails sharpened like claws and woke screaming, convinced that the bed was full of blood. But always, I awoke to an empty room, the curtains billowing at the open window and the garden below full of shadows.

I am not afraid of the dark or of the shadows and I wish only to see their faces. I imagine that they are beautiful beyond description, the women with long flowing hair, either ebony black or the palest yellow, and the men standing tall with chiselled faces and all of them with eyes that shine like jewels. They are both old and young, not like anyone who lives in the world now.

But they are gone: bricked up in their rooms centuries ago to die of their blood thirst, for all that their ghostly screams still echo round this house.

I was never afraid here, not even in the very beginning. At the very most I have felt a little unsettled, perhaps uneasy. In those first few moments after I arrived, I stood alone in the hallway with my bags at my feet and felt the house shift around me. I felt peaceful. I felt as if finally, after all my years of wandering and never settling, that I had come home. There were dust sheets and cobwebs, windows grimy and cracked hung with moth-eaten cobwebs. There were rats and pigeons rustling in the attic and something else, a scratching sound, like something sharp being drawn slowly down a brick wall.

My feet echoed through the rooms and I breathed in the dust and marvelled that it had all been left to crumble and fall apart for decades.

In the rooms at the back of the house, I found glass-fronted cases still full of books. There was an old piano, wardrobes full of antique clothes and satin slippers. On the walls hung rows and rows of portraits of young and beautiful people, smiling and laughing with their eyes full of mischief and passions. I walked past bricked-up doorways and was certain that I heard sobbing and whispering from within.

I chose my own bedroom for the unruly climbing roses outside the window. They flowered with a bloom of such a dark red it was almost black, and the scent filled my room night and day. It was intoxicating and no matter how much I cut back the long stems, the scent still stretched into my window, refusing to be shut out.

In short, I was not afraid of my new home and whatever I might be sharing it with. I was merely fascinated.

I had been warned about the house beforehand. Not by the estate agents in their expensive London office who only wanted a quick sale, but by the nearest neighbour who still reluctantly held a key and some sadly-neglected caretaking duties. The man did not come with me to the property when I called to collect the spare key, just told me that the previous owners had left in a hurry. The official story, he explained, was something to do with bad debts but the unofficial story was that they had become afraid of the dark and the shadows. The noises gave them nightmares they could not forget even when they were far away.

'I never seen nothing myself,' the man told me, 'but you hear things. They say there's monsters there, bricked up behind the walls. The people before you were going to open up those rooms, but they never did in the end. Ran out of money. Or something.'

The caretaker was the friendliest of the villagers and that was not saying much. The others eyed me suspiciously. They did not like strangers and they especially did not like strangers who lived in that house. They watched me as I passed, and I felt their eyes follow me whenever I ventured into the village. I could not help but feel that they had secrets: dark secrets, old secrets, shameful secrets.

My reasons for moving there were simple and dull. I had divorced recently, and the children went to live with my wife.

Although I had had the best of intentions, I saw less and less of them and it seemed that they were happy enough with this arrangement. I had a very well-paid job that took me all round the world, but it felt like an empty, shallow existence, as if I were an actor playing the lead role in a rather dull play. I earned enough money to retire very early and I did so with the vague idea of travelling some more – though truly I felt I had been everywhere I wanted to go – or starting some small homespun business, or finally writing the novel I had been considering writing all my adult life. But instead the house consumed me.

On the first night I began to read the books the first occupants had written themselves, their black spidery writing covering page after page of brittle yellow paper. I read of the parties they had thrown, the lawns full of wealthy glamourous people, the friends who came to stay and never left and village people who they lured up to the house and who were never seen again. And of the quieter moments: lying in bed until noon, reading and writing and daydreaming in the sunlight. Theirs was an easy, carefree life, who could not help but be envious?

And so, I stayed, fell into their trap and my novel remained unwritten, my ideas of starting a business forgotten. My old life, my ex-wife and children and my job, might never have existed.

I have lived here for a long time now, but I do not think of it as being my house. I am a guest, a passer-through who stretches hopelessly for something that is just out of reach. The changes that I have made to the house are clumsy and ugly against their ageless, elegant decorations. They have always been here, and they will always be here. I am simply passing through, a traveller, a tourist, a guest, in their home.

On summer nights, the scent of the roses they planted drifts in pollen-laden wafts through my bedroom window and I feel closest to them. I hear them calling out to one another, the pad of their feet along the corridors, deliberately finding the floorboards that creak. I glimpse their shadows ahead of me in the corridors and, in the garden, shapes move among the roses, the birds cease their singing and even the wind stands still, and I know that something is there. The scent of the great frothy roses is narcotic, a drug to lull the unwary to linger longer. I find myself singing strange old-fashioned songs I never knew before, listening with anticipation for a footstep on the stairs, a knock on the door that never comes.

Of course, I decided to unseal the bricked-up rooms, to silence forever the screaming and the scratching on the walls. With this accomplished, I felt that the house could become a happy home once again. A haunted house still, but a haunted house where the ghosts were happy ghosts.

It was a long tedious task for I could find no one in the village to help me and, besides, I felt a strange reluctance to let anyone into the house. The work was back-breaking, and I was ill-suited to it, but I could not bear the thought of workmen being there with their small talk and radios and flasks of tea. I worked by myself and each time I broke through the walls, I found the rooms within empty, ice cold and dark. There were no bones and no blood, only the scratches on the walls to give away the truth.

When the final room was unsealed, the house seemed to breathe more easily. There was no more screaming or crying in the night. But now I hear them moving around me even in the daytime. I catch tantalising glimpses of pale clothes and dark hair, I hear voices calling out my name. My dreams are no longer my own and when I awaken in the morning, I find my few possessions have been packed away into boxes. Their books sit on the shelves where mine once sat, their clothes hang in my wardrobe. When I look in the mirror my reflection is not always there. Instead, I might see a young man, dark-haired and pale-skinned, laughing out of the glass at me, or a woman wearing a white dress stained with red. But then the apparitions fade and my own very ordinary face gazes back at me and I feel disappointed. I know I am being packed up, cleared away. All traces of my existence here are being eradicated and I do not care.

The scent of roses is everywhere, and they have never bloomed as they do this year: blood red, pale pink and the purest cleanest white. I drink in the scent and pollen and become intoxicated and dizzy. Things shift out of focus; reality fades and I can almost see their faces.

I am close to becoming one of them. I am a ghost just waiting to die.

Wintertide's Eve

I remember the cold. The way it crept into my basement and froze the water in the pipes. Icicles hung like daggers and snow fell soft over the city night after night, and I could find no pleasure in any of it anymore. It had all blurred into one – autumn, spring, summer, winter – and I was just passing my days waiting hopelessly for oblivion. There is such a thing as living too long, there really is, and with every day of my long life that I squandered, I had come to understand this even more. I truly believed that I was the last of my kind and this made me sad and hopeless beyond all measure. So, you may find it strange that it is a story of love and hope that I have to tell.

But it is, for I fell in love in this cold winter city at the end of world where they burn witches on Wintertide's Eve and the city rings with their screams.

The city was grey and brown. Even the snow soon turned to grey slush and the air had taken on a yellowish tint, so thick was it with foul-smelling smoke from the factories and refineries. I had been hiding in the murk for centuries, deadening my yearning for companionship with red wine so sweet and thick it clung to the sides of the glass. I had been alone for so long, I had forgotten how to behave with other people, and I had become afraid of the shadows that stretched across the narrow, twisting alleyways and fell monstrously across the wide city square. I had almost forgotten that there was a world beyond this bleak northern city and I had lost all will to see it. Most days I lay in bed in my basement, and it was so cold that ice patterns bloomed on the window panes and began to stretch across the window ledge and down the walls and over my rumpled sheets. In short, I had become quite depressed and melancholy.

But on Wintertide's Eve, I ventured out of doors, not to watch the frenetic insanity of the witch burnings, but to attend a ball at Josiah Crawford's tall house on Cathedral Hill. I took some care over my appearance. I wore my best black and silver dress, painted some colour into my face, braided silver thread into my hair. I have always been able to keep up appearances.

It was difficult to leave the house. The crowds gathering in the square chanting for the death of the witches were not far from my destination. I stood for several long moments in my hallway, reaching for the door handle and then snatching my hand back again and again until I found the strength to turn the handle and step outside into the frozen air.

I walked quickly to Josiah's house. When I am out of doors, I think too much about the soot in the air and how it finds its way into my lungs. Last time I was out of doors, I became so sure my lungs were filling up with smoke that I tried to carry on without breathing. It was Josiah, my host for this evening's revelries, who took me home in his carriage, blue-faced and choking.

But I am a fashionable guest for there are still a few who remember my past glories, and my appearances are scarce enough to be something of a novelty. When I put my mind to it, I can look good on anyone's arm and from time to time I say something outrageous enough to buy me a fleeting popularity.

It was in the alleyway that runs behind Josiah's house that I saw him for the first time. I was going in the back way, through the kitchens and the servants' quarters, because a shyness had taken hold of me. I would have turned and gone home if it had not meant passing back through the crowds gathering for the burnings. I do not enjoy death, despite what you might have heard of me.

The alleyway was dark. Tall houses lined one side and on the other was a high wall of smoke-blackened bricks. It was so long since I had tasted anything but sickly red wine, that I barely registered the scent of blood in the air. I recognised it, but in an abstract way that was completely devoid of desire.

I carried on walking with the scent of blood in my nostrils until I came upon them – two figures struggling in the darkness. I watched them, the air around me full of the coppery scent of blood and my heart clamoured in my chest. My thoughts were in turmoil, until one figure crumpled and fell and the other straightened up. I stood back, watching as he neatened his clothes, wiped his mouth on the back of his hand and reached for his hat where it lay in the alleyway. Only then did he sense my presence, spinning round in the darkness to search for me. Too late, for I could easily have destroyed him by now had I wished to. His scent filled the air, fresh and clean like summertime.

It was like a knife twisting in my heart, that feeling of recognition. They say there's no such thing as love at first sight, but in that alleyway with a concerto of witches screaming in the background, I fell so much in love that I still hear his footsteps, though he walks on the other side of the world.

He looked at me and I saw the same recognition in his eyes. A wide grin spread across his face as he tipped his hat at me and offered me his arm. He was young, so young that standing next to him, I felt as if I was drinking his youth, that it was rejuvenating me. We walked in together, our arms linked although we had not yet spoken. I could smell blood and alcohol on his breath and he felt so strong, so alive. I was drab and paltry in comparison.

'Ah, you two,' Josiah cried when he saw us together. 'I had hoped to introduce you, but I see you have found one another.'

My companion smiled and leaned forward to embrace Josiah and thank him for the invitation.

'Everyone is here,' Josiah said, 'and you can see the burnings from the balcony.'

We watched Josiah disappear into the crowds, gaudy in his fashionable red and gold silks.

'Shall we dance?' he asked, and I nodded and let him lead me onto the dance floor, where other couples spun and whirled in the flickering candlelight. We leaned close to one another, our fingers entwined, and I was pleased that he was taller than me, that I could rest my head against his chest and listen to his heart beat in perfect time with mine.

'Vampire,' he whispered.

I did not deny it. With him it stopped being a shameful thing. This polluted, northern city on the edge of the Wilderness breeds monsters in its dark twisting alleyways and shadowed tenements, and we were only one kind of monster.

As we danced, he told me a little about himself. He lived with some friends in a large sparsely-furnished house near the cathedral. His family were still alive, but they did not understand him, and his friends had begun to look at him oddly. He had begun to crave their blood. He told me his name was Henry Steeple, though I do not believe this to be his real name. When he spoke of his friends and family, he sounded detached and disinterested, all his attention fixed on me.

Later, Josiah told us that the young priest who had signed the death warrants for the witches was at the party. He pointed out a young man dressed in midnight blue and green with hair of such a dark red it was almost black, as if it had been washed in blood. I thought he looked like a demon, although he was also rather beautiful – blue-eyed and pale-skinned and little more than a petulant child. As I said, this city breeds many kinds of monster.

'I'll have his blood before the night is out,' Henry said, 'and next year, you and I will save the witches from the pyre.'

Later that night, Henry and I followed the young priest home and pounced on him outside his tall white house. But his blood tasted bitter, like poison, and we left him twitching and half-finished in the gutter and ran home to my basement to laugh over our wickedness like naughty children.

After that, Henry stayed with me. He refused to live in the basement and threw open the windows in the upper rooms to let out the mustiness and to let in the city smell of smoke and chemicals. While I lay on the bed, too afraid to go out, he walked through the city and brought back young girls for me to drink from.

'Come with me,' he begged but I thought of the witches burning in the city square and was afraid. I could not say exactly what I was afraid of. It made no sense, even to me, but it felt as if going outside was a risk and surely now that we had one another, we did not need anything else. But he continued to go out alone, and I crept back downstairs to my narrow bed in the basement and lay there waiting for his first footfall on the step, imagining that they had caught him and put a stake through his heart and left him screaming for me to help him. And I did not know if I would. That was the worst of it. I did not know if I would ever leave the house again, even to save him.

I began to wonder at his need to go out, for it seemed a foolish thing, a thing he would come to regret as he grew older. It seemed insane to go out and risk discovery and disapproval, to walk, talk and laugh with other people and then drink them dry. I began to think of bricking over the doorway and all the windows, so that neither of us could go outside. I imagined the long days and nights we would spend together, our bodies taut with desire, our limbs entangled. But when I spoke of it, he laughed and shook his head. He said he needed to go out. He said he would die without blood and sunlight.

'You will dry up and wither away,' he taunted me.

He was young and still reckless and impetuous. There was still magic in the world for him, new things to see and learn, new stories to tell, new books to read and lands still unseen. But I am old. I have seen those things and done those things and I know that they soon lose their lustre. Better to give up hope and joy now than to lose it slowly over the centuries. It is kinder that way.

So, I ordered the bricks and the mortar, and I was pleased when he lay lazily on the bed and watched as I set to work bricking over the first of the windows.

'You are mad,' he said and stood up. I watched him select a hat and scarf and knot it jauntily round his neck.

'You're going out,' I said flatly.

'Yes,' he said, 'just a few drinks with friends. Come with me.'

I thought of the immorality of having friends whose blood you later drank and shook my head. He sighed and then embraced me, pulling me tight against him and holding me for a moment too long.

'I love you,' I said and kissed him, biting his bottom lip and tasting his blood.

'I know,' he said. 'I have to go. They're waiting for me.'

I watched him go and I suppose I knew, for I ran to the door and called his name, watching as he turned round in the street, the oil lamps making the tears on his face glitter.

'You will come back,' I said, 'won't you?'

'Yes,' he said. 'I'll come back.'

I finished the windows and began bricking up the doorway. I left a space only large enough for him to come back through, but he didn't come. I waited all that night and the next and the next. I am still waiting now in my almost bricked-up house. I wait even though ten Wintertide's Eves have passed and neither of us has rescued any witches.

But I know he will come back when he is older and wiser, and this city and its monsters begin to creep into his dreams. He will realise that only I can truly understand him, only I can wash his nightmares clean. We will close up the door and live together in perfect blackness, our bodies touching, our hair, our limbs, our very heartstrings tangling into one. Ice and cobwebs will cover us over and that is how we will live happily ever after. I hear his heart beating on the other side of the world, and it still beats in perfect time with mine. That's how I know he'll come back.

Dr Franks and Mrs Stein

It was the last day of July when Mrs Stein moved into the house next door. I watched from my living room as she came up the pathway with a man behind her, who I could just tell was from the university – you live round here long enough, and you learn how to spot them. She didn't have much, just a couple of bags that she carried in, while he followed behind with a cardboard box, and two pet carriers that they took out of the back seat of his flashy car. I tried to see what was in them, but I couldn't from half way behind the curtain. The house was let fully furnished so I suppose she didn't need much.

She walked with a limp and her head down, poker-straight red hair hiding her face. She was wearing a very unflattering coat with the hem of a floral skirt hanging down under it. But even then, I thought I'd seen her somewhere before, though I couldn't place her.

I heard them moving around through the walls. They're paper thin. I could hear every word that the last couple who lived next door said to one another, and if I'd had anyone much to talk to, and they hadn't been so busy shouting at each other, I've no doubt they'd have heard every word from me. I could hear the shuffling, uneven sound of her footsteps on the floorboards and the mumbling sound of their voices. Then he was gone. I watched him walking down the garden path to the kerb where his big Mercedes was parked in next door's disabled spot. He was handsome enough – tall with a slightly rakish look about him, silver grey hair just slightly too long. But arrogant. I could tell that just from the way he walked. He had a look about him that told me the world had never been unkind to him. It turns out, I was wrong about that, but I'll get to that in due course.

I was curious. I'm always curious. My nephew Tom who stays with me from time to time says it's my only fault. I heard the couple next door talking through the walls once and they referred to me as 'a nosy old cow', but I don't think I'm nosy. I'm just interested in people. I like people. I like to people watch, and I like to know what's going on. I think it's neighbourly.

I gave it half an hour and then went through to the kitchen and had a look through my cupboards to see what I had. Nothing very exciting to be honest. I'm not one for luxuries, but at the back behind the Nescafe and PG Tips there was a tin of Earl Grey tea leaves that someone gave me at Christmas time and that I'd never opened because I didn't have a tea strainer. I had a box of salted caramel cookies in the cupboard unopened too. I'd been saving them for next time Tom visited, but they'd do.

I went next door and knocked on the door. Through the frosted glass, I could see the shape of her moving closer and closer. She was slow, and she had an odd way of walking as if one leg was shorter than the other, which it may well have been for all I knew.

She opened the door and looked at me, half smiling, half curious, and she had such a pretty face. Pale skin and high cheekbones and a scattering of freckles across the bridge of her nose. Her eyes were green and her hair long and straight and a wonderful shade of red that I could tell was natural. The rest of her didn't match. There was the unflattering floral dress for one thing that hung slightly squint to just below her knees and the big black boots she wore with no socks. I guessed they must have been orthopaedic boots to help with her limp. She was plump round the middle, but her legs were skinny and the sleeves of her grey cardigan that she'd pulled down over her wrists couldn't quite disguise that she seemed to have one hand much bigger than the other. But I liked her. She was smiling, and she looked kind and that was good enough for me.

'I'm Kathy,' I said, 'I'm your new neighbour. Welcome to the neighbourhood.'

I held out the tea and biscuits to her and she took them and examined them and made a little exclaiming noise.

'Thank you,' she said. 'I'm Julia. Julia Stein.'

I smiled, and we looked at each other with that awkwardness of strangers who are not friends but who want to be, neither of us wanting to be pushy and overstep the mark.

'Would you like to come in?' she asked, just as I was opening my mouth to invite her to mine for a cuppa. 'We can have some of this lovely tea.'

I followed her inside. It was a long time since I'd been in that house. Four or five different sets of tenants had lived next door to me over the years and not one of them had invited me in. She led me to the kitchen where there was a breakfast bar and two high stools. I perched awkwardly on one of them while she busied herself with making the tea.

'Lucky the kettle came with the house,' she said, 'and there's a teapot somewhere.' She searched through a cardboard box and found a fat, stripy teapot and two spotty mugs. 'Have you lived here long, Kathy?'

'Almost thirty years,' I said.

'Wow. You must have seen a lot of changes.'

'You could say that,' I agreed and then my eye fell on one of the pet carriers sitting on the kitchen floor. It was open, and I could see that it was empty now. I listened for that all too familiar pad of little feet upstairs but there was silence. My heart twisted with a sudden longing. Even after all these weeks, I still missed my Smudge.

'You have a cat?' I asked hopefully.

'One of each,' she said.

I looked at her and she laughed. 'That's what Victor and I used to say. A dog and a cat – one of each.'

'Victor?'

'My… friend. Victor Franks. You might have seen him. He helped me to move in.'

There were so many questions, I didn't know where to start. I wanted to know about her and her *friend*, I wanted to know about the cat. I wanted to see the cat, to feel the softness of its fur and have the warm weight of it in my lap. The only thing I wasn't interested in was the dog.

'Do you have a husband?' she asked me.

I shook my head. 'Not anymore. He passed away five years ago. Cancer.'

'I'm sorry,' she said, and it sounded like she really was sorry.

'My nephew stays with me sometimes. He's a sales rep so I'm not alone much. And until recently I had my Smudge.' She looked at me quizzically. 'My cat. He was put to sleep about six weeks ago. I still miss him.'

She nodded, and her expression was so kind, so caring, that I could feel tears welling in my eyes. She reached across the breakfast bar and took my hand.

'It's stupid,' I said. 'When my husband died, I barely shed a tear and I loved him to pieces, but I only have to think of Smudge and I'm a mess.'

She nodded. 'It's a different kind of grief, though,' she said. She limp-shuffled over to the kettle and I was struck again by how oddly-shaped she was. The best word to describe her was lumpen. Her body was lumpen, but her face was not. She didn't spill anything, but her movements were awkward and clumsy. I wondered if I should offer to help her or if she might find that offensive.

'I always think that when you lose a person, the grief goes down deep inside you like a stone sinking into your heart forever,' she said, 'but when you lose a pet, it's agony at first but it's closer to the surface. It goes away quicker.'

I nodded. 'Have you lost someone?'

She didn't reply at first. She poured the tea out into the spotty mugs and carried them over one at a time, very carefully, like a small child would, using both hands. 'Sometimes it feels like I've lost everyone,' she said.

I could have hugged her then. I wish I had, but we were practically strangers and it wasn't the done thing, was it? Instead she steered the conversation elsewhere. She asked me about Tom and about the neighbourhood and I asked her if she had any family – she didn't, there was just Victor – and if she worked and she said that she couldn't, not anymore. I got the sense then that something had happened, an accident I supposed, that had changed her.

Just before I left, I asked her about her cat. 'I'd love to meet him. Or her. Just for a little stroke.'

'Oh,' she said, 'she's shy. They both are. We rescued them, you see. They've been mistreated but they're safe now. Just shy and scared of people.'

'Maybe another time, then,' I said.

She nodded. 'Maybe.'

When I left it was almost dinner time and I'd promised Tom I'd make him my lasagne that he loves to eat even though it's a fiddle to make. I was late starting because I'd spent much longer with Julia than I expected, but I was happy. I'd had a good afternoon and I was pleased that Julia seemed as if she would be a good neighbour.

I got on Google that evening after dinner. It surprises people, but I'm good with technology. Tom got me a little tablet that I sit with every evening. Sometimes playing games, sometimes watching films and TV, sometimes just browsing the internet. I call it wandering because there's so much there that you can go from link to link to link and forget what it was you were looking for in the first place. I typed in 'Julia Stein, Cambridge' and nothing came up. There were plenty Julias and plenty Steins and even plenty Julia Steins but none of them were her. I scrolled through the list of Facebook accounts studying the pictures of each Julia Stein and she wasn't there. So, I tried again and typed in 'Victor Franks, Cambridge' and this time I asked Google to give me images, not text, and there he was, at the top of the list.

Dr Victor Franks, Doctor of Medical Physics, whatever that was. I scrolled down through photographs of him in his office and in his lab, what looked like a passport photo, a picture of him in his running gear standing between two much younger men with the caption: 'Vic is raising money for The British Heart Foundation, visit his Just Giving page to donate.' I scrolled on a bit further down and then I found her.

It was a photograph taken at some happy formal occasion. His silver hair was swept back from his brow and his bow-tie was loose, the top button of his shirt undone. He had his arm carelessly round her shoulder and she was grinning and glowing as if she was the happiest person in the world, all that red hair tumbling round her shoulders and her eyes glittering and green and laughing. It was her, only I saw a moment later that it wasn't her. The woman in the photograph was tall and slender and there was an elegance to the way she was standing. My heart went out to Julia, it really did, for it was plain that they were sisters and poor Julia was the ugly one.

The caption underneath said that they were Dr Victor Franks and his wife, Dr Karen Stein. It was easy after that. I just typed in Karen Stein and there were links to her academic papers, links to her Facebook page and Twitter account but the first thing that came up was her obituary. I read it and almost wept, it was so sad. She was only twenty-six with a long and brilliant career ahead of her. She and Victor had only recently married and were talking of having children. She had died in a car accident on the way to the vet. No other vehicle was involved, and it was thought that one of the pets must have distracted her. They all died, Karen Stein, her cat and her dog.

I had Julia over for a cuppa a few days later. Nothing fancy, just mugs and digestive biscuits at the kitchen table. She loved those biscuits, though. I could see it in the way she leaned back slightly to savour every mouthful. I pushed the packet towards her.

'Go on,' I said, 'they're just digestives. One more won't do any harm.'

She frowned and then took one. 'I shouldn't,' she said. 'Victor doesn't like me to get fat.'

'What business is it of his?' I asked. 'He's not your keeper, is he? He's your friend. If he was any sort of friend, he wouldn't begrudge you a couple of digestives.'

She was still frowning, as if something was puzzling her. 'He used to buy me chocolates,' she said slowly. 'Expensive chocolates in little round boxes with gold writing on them, tied up with ribbons. Champagne truffles, sea-salted caramels, pralines, and my favourites were raspberry creams coated with thick dark chocolate. How I loved those. We'd have one each day after dinner and that was just enough.'

I was puzzled now for she was talking as if they were husband and wife, as if they had lived together. But he was her brother-in-law, not her husband.

'Did you live together, then?' I asked. 'You and your sister, before the accident?'

'My sister?' she said, and her brow creased with confusion. 'I'm sorry, I don't, I can't, I don't always remember things very well. My sister?'

I nodded. 'Karen. Victor's wife. She died, and I am very sorry for your loss.'

Poor soul, I thought, she really wasn't quite the full ticket, but she was sweet and lovely. I felt bad for bringing it up.

'My sister?' she said again and then nodded, her face clearing. 'Of course. My poor dead sister. So sad.'

'It's good of Victor to carry on looking after you. A lot of men wouldn't.'

She smiled uneasily. 'Yes, Victor is very good to me.'

'But you mustn't think he's all you have.' I reached across the table and squeezed her hand. 'If you ever need anything, you can always come to me.'

She nodded, and her eyes filled up with tears. 'Thank you, Kathy,' she said, 'that's very kind.' She wiped her eyes with her hand and when she lifted her arm, I caught a whiff of something unpleasant, something off that was gone in a moment and replaced by the smell of her perfume, which was always just a bit too much. I pushed the box of tissues towards her. 'Don't cry.'

'I'm sorry,' she said, 'it's just that no one's ever kind to me anymore.'

'Oh, tosh. I am and I'm sure Victor is too, in his own way.'

She smiled. 'In his own way,' she repeated.

I made us some more tea and we chatted about some other things – the new shop opening a few doors down, a TV talent show, an exhibition at the Fitzwilliam that we both agreed we'd like to go to – and the time passed quickly, the way it does between friends.

She left about four thirty saying that she had to walk the dog, but the funny thing is, I never saw her walk that dog. Not that day, nor any other.

I saw the cat in the garden that evening, though. I love cats. Tom says if I had the choice, I'd take them all in and become a Crazy Cat Lady, but even I could see that this was an exceptionally ugly cat. It had a weird way of walking, and I don't mean this to sound cruel, but it walked like Julia. That same shuffling gait as if its legs were all of different lengths. Which they were, as it happens. Even from the upstairs window, I could see that its front legs were shorter than its back legs. I watched it for a few minutes doing what cats do – grooming and scratching against the back fence, rubbing up against the rusting patio furniture – and a great empty hole opened up inside me when I thought of my Smudge. I nearly cried, but then I saw Julia come out into the garden with the food bowl and the cat ran towards her, and I swear I never saw a cat wag its tail the way that that one did.

Victor came to see me the next morning. I knew it was him before he knocked because I'd heard his car drawing up and peeped out between the curtains and saw him walking up the garden path. I thought he was going to thank me for being kind to Julia, but I was wrong about that.

'Kathy,' he said, 'I don't know if you know who I am?'

'You're Julia's friend.'

'Yes,' he said, 'and you are not. Nor will you ever be.'

He was such a handsome man, even as he was saying such ugly words. I remembered how happy he had looked in the photographs on the internet and I saw the sadness lurking behind the anger. Some people don't know how to show weakness or sorrow, so they wrap it up in anger and hurtful words. I forgave him.

'Julia's not quite right,' he said. 'Of course, you know this. She has problems remembering things. She forms attachments to things and people that are not good for her. She doesn't need you putting ideas in her head.'

'Putting ideas in her head? We had tea and biscuits, that's all. I was being neighbourly.'

'People take advantage of her and she can't tell the good from the bad. I'm asking – no, I'm telling you to keep away from her in the future.'

He didn't give me a chance to respond. He was off down the garden path towards his fancy car with his arrogant little swagger.

'Dr Franks,' I called after him, 'I was very sorry to hear about your wife.'

He didn't have the grace to respond. I watched him get in the car and pull out of the parking space and when I was sure he was gone, I went next door and rang the doorbell. The dog started barking inside, that high pitched yappy noise that small dogs make. She didn't answer, and I pictured her inside, confused and upset and not knowing if she should open the door. I thought she might even be frightened because she and Victor had had some sort of argument before he came round to warn me off.

I bent down and pushed open the letterbox. I was intending to tell her that it was all fine and I wouldn't bother her, but she could come to me whenever she wanted, but instead I found myself stumbling backwards gagging at the stench that came through the letterbox. There was a cloying scent of too much air freshener but beneath that, something rotten, like meat left out in the sun. So, I didn't say anything, just left and went home feeling very odd and disturbed.

I was starting to get funny ideas about them. Crazy ideas. I won't write them down because you'll think I'm just a loony old lady, but they were there, taking shape in my mind all the same.

I did as I was told and kept away. I thought she would come and see me when she was ready, but she never did. Victor came and went, pausing sometimes on the garden path as if he knew I was watching. He took in boxes and bags of things and once a bouquet of pink and white flowers, but he never took her out with him. I never saw the dog, although I heard it barking through the walls, and it was driving Tom insane whenever he stayed with me.

'Bloody pointless, yappy, little dogs,' he said. 'Why can't people have sensible dogs? Labradors, collies, spaniels? I go to sleep and it's barking, I get woken up countless times in the night by it barking, and it's still barking in the morning. I've a mind to go round and complain.'

'Don't,' I said. 'She's got enough on her plate. Her sister died and she's, you know, a bit different. Special, if you get my drift.'

He nodded. 'Well, you know best.'

I saw the cat out in the back garden a few times. One sunny morning, I saw it sprawled out, luxuriating in a sunny spot and I smiled because sunbathing was what my Smudge loved to do, right up to the end. But the weird thing was that the front half of the cat was sleek with black velvety fur, but the back half was brown, and the fur was more wiry, as if the back half and the front half didn't quite belong together.

A few days later the yapping got the better of Tom and although I begged him not to, he put on his shoes and went marching next door. To complain, I thought, but he came back a few minutes later and went straight to the telephone table and pulled out the Yellow Pages.

'What are you doing?' I asked.

'Calling social services.'

'What? Why?'

'I went next door to offer to walk the bloody dog and see if that might shut it up. Something's not right over there.'

'What do you mean?' I asked although I was really looking for confirmation that I wasn't going mad.

'She opened the door and I could see inside, and the house is immaculate – floorboards gleaming, not a speck of dirt – but she was a mess and she stank. There was enough air freshener that I could taste it in the back of my throat, but she stank like rotten meat, like something dead. She looked sick. She was grey, and she was thin but bloated looking at the same time. One of her eyes was all jellied and she could barely walk. She said it was kind of me to offer but the Dog-Cat and the Cat-Dog were completely fine.'

'Did you see the dog?' I asked.

He nodded. 'Stupid little thing about the size of a cat. It was walking funny. I'll need to call the RSPCA too.'

I put my hand on his. 'Don't. I'll call her friend, Dr Franks, and let him know she's letting herself go a bit.'

'A bit?' he said and then nodded. 'All right. Just promise me you'll call someone else if he's not interested.'

It wasn't easy getting in touch with Victor. There was an email address on the internet, but it didn't seem right to send an email. I wanted to speak to him. I found a phone number on the internet that took me through to a secretary at the university who, it turned out, wasn't his secretary anymore, but she gave me another number and that person passed me on to someone else and so on until eventually, I got through to him.

'Dr Franks,' I said, 'it's Kathy. I don't know if you remember me. I live next door to your *wife*.'

I said 'wife' very deliberately and he was silent for a long moment, but he didn't deny it. I told him that Tom was threatening to call social services and the RSPCA, and I told him about the very bad smell that no amount of cleaning, bathing, air freshener or perfume could mask. I told him I was worried about the Cat-Dog and the Dog-Cat and he didn't laugh or protest or call them by any other names.

'Dr Franks,' I said at the end, 'your wife is a wonderful, sweet person but I am afraid that she is very, very unwell.'

'I know,' he said, and I heard the utter sorrow in his voice. 'Thank you for letting me know. I shall have to – well, I shall have to do something.'

'Don't hurt her,' I said. 'Please don't let her suffer.'

He was silent for so long I thought he might have hung up, then he spoke again. 'I'm afraid it's rather too late for that.'

I put the phone down and I didn't know what to do with myself. I just knew I couldn't be in the house when he came round for her. So, I put on my nice trousers and a pretty top and I took myself off to the Fitzwilliam to see that exhibition we had talked about. And then I had lunch and walked round the shops and along the riverbank and sat with a takeaway coffee on a bench and watched the tourists and students going to and fro. After that, I called up Tom and arranged to meet him in a restaurant for dinner and I got quite tipsy and when I got home it was late and Julia, Victor and the Dog-Cat and the Cat-Dog were all gone from next door and the To Let sign was up again.

I saw Victor some months later quite by coincidence at an exhibition Tom took me to. He was standing perfectly still in front of a case of old medical equipment and I recognised that silvery hair at once.

He recognised me too. 'Kathy,' he said politely. Some of the swagger and arrogance had gone. He looked smaller, older, somehow.

I asked after Julia's health and he looked away. 'I'm afraid she passed away shortly after she moved out,' he said.

'Oh,' I said. 'I'm sorry.' And I was. She had been so kind and warm. We could have been good friends. 'How did she—?'

He looked away. 'She just… she just didn't make it,' he said which struck me as an odd thing to say because he could have said it was cancer or a heart attack or some kind of accident. It was his way, I suppose, of acknowledging that he knew that I knew that something very wrong had been going on.

'I'm glad to have met her,' I said, 'I didn't know her for very long, but she was special to me.'

He nodded. 'She was very special to me too. I loved her so much.'

I wondered if I should say something, if I should squeeze his hand or hug him, but I didn't say anything, just stood beside him for a few moments, until he turned and started to walk away and then I suddenly thought of something.

'Dr Franks,' I said, 'what about the Cat-Dog and the Dog-Cat? Did they make it?'

He smiled briefly. 'They did,' he said. 'Funny how things turn out, isn't it?'

'Well,' I said, 'I know you're a busy man and I know that pets need time, and those particular pets have their own difficulties and special needs, but I have time and I'm an animal lover and— oh, never mind.'

Well, a couple of days later, there was a knock on the door and when I answered it, there was no one there except for two pet carriers on the doorstep and a yapping was coming from one and a purring from the other.

I took them in, of course, and we couldn't be happier even if

Fiona McGavin

the Dog-Cat is yappy and drives Tom to distraction, and the Cat-Dog smells a bit off despite all its rigorous grooming. And they are both ugly and put together all wrong, but they fill an empty space, so much so that when the new people moved in next door, I scarcely noticed.

Bridge 52

I go straight from work most afternoons, parking the car by the *One Stop* shop and setting off through the housing estate, inappropriately dressed in my work clothes and walking boots. I take the footpath down onto the old railway line and start walking west towards Bridge 52.

I walk with the sun in my eyes and the sky turning to blood and rubies. The unending roar of the motorway grows louder and louder as I walk towards the bridge. The people in the cars and lorries above have no idea that they are even passing over Bridge 52. They fly past northwards and southwards to wherever they are going, and they don't feel the place where the air suddenly turns chill, where the murk under the bridge deadens the blaze of sunlight for a few moments as you pass underneath. It's not as if the place is an accident black spot or anything like that.

Bridge 52 is a brutalist monstrosity. Parallel lines of concrete pillars support the motorway as it roars past above. Graffiti adorns its walls and the ground is littered and treacherous with wet leaves and broken glass. It smells of damp and the poison fumes from the traffic. It is not a place to linger. The dog walkers, joggers and cyclists quicken their pace when they pass into the gloom, the dogs pulling on their leashes. Linger too long and the shadows between the pillars start to shift; you get the impression that the graffiti people are moving, whispering and laughing amongst themselves when you turn your back on them. When you pass under the bridge, you hear footsteps behind you and nine times out of ten, when you turn round, it's a dog walker or a jogger. But not always. Not every time.

I've recently bought an expensive camera and I set up the tripod under the bridge and point the video camera towards the row of pillars opposite and switch it on. There's a yellow-haired graffiti doll painted on the wall with white button eyes that follow me as I walk around in the gloom taking pictures with my mobile phone. I'm considering setting up camera traps like wildlife photographers use, so that I can see what's happening under here even when I'm not around. I know I'm obsessed, but it doesn't matter. What I'm doing is more important.

I try to capture the blackness under the bridge and the scarlet and orange of the sky on the other side, try to capture the silhouettes of the leafless branches against the sunset. If anyone asked me what I was doing, I would tell them that it's for a photography project, something to do with post-industrial landscapes. I wouldn't tell them that what I'm really trying to do is photograph a ghost.

I didn't used to believe in ghosts as a rule. I was living a very ordinary life, working in an office during the day, the weekends taken up with family and friends and a new boyfriend, Jack, who I hadn't quite made my mind up about. I was getting older and my increasingly sedentary lifestyle meant that I was getting a little overweight. It was hard to fit in exercise, so I'd started cycling in an attempt to get fit quick. I'd get up early in the morning and fly along the old railway line with the sun rising behind me. I was not a confident cyclist, so the early morning loneliness of the old railway suited me. I'd see foxes and deer sometimes and that always made it feel worth the effort. I started taking photographs, logging the sunrises and the changing seasons. Some mornings, I'd use the video recorder on my phone to record my ride. Once I managed to capture a fox running across the path in front of me, but mostly it was just cats, rabbits and a few early morning joggers. Often, I didn't see another living thing.

I didn't really think much about Bridge 52. I didn't even know that the bridge had a number. It was just the motorway bridge to me back then. I didn't much like riding under it but that was more because I worried about the broken glass on the ground puncturing my tyres. Sometimes, I'd feel a sense of unease, but on a bicycle, you're under the bridge and out the other side in seconds.

It started one morning in October. I'd set up my phone to record, and I was cycling west with the sunrise behind me trying to break through a sky full of storm clouds. It had rained all night and the path was littered with wet leaves. I came off the bike under the bridge. I was going too fast and the ground was wet and slippery. There was a moment when I tried desperately to gain control and then it was over. I hit ground, the force of the fall jarring my body, the bike on top of me, wheels still spinning. I lay there for a moment and then wriggled free from the weight of the bike. I was bruised but unhurt, and the thing I was most relieved about was that there was no one there to witness what had happened. I stared down at the bike with a sudden hatred. I was covered in mud, and the leg of my glasses was twisted askew, the screen of my phone was cracked. I stood in the gloom under the bridge, with the traffic passing above oblivious and the graffiti people watching me, and I wanted to cry.

A hand touched my shoulder and I whirled round. There was a man standing there. He wore a cloth cap and a dark coat. There were mud-spattered boots on his feet and he was smoking a cigarette. Its end glowed amber in the gloom.

'Are you all right, my dear?' he asked.

I stared at him. I hadn't seen him ahead of me on the path. He must have been in the shadows around the pillars. I tried to laugh.

'Just wounded pride,' I said. 'I'm OK.'

I bent down and picked up the bike.

The man nodded and took a drag on his cigarette. 'Be careful, then,' he said. 'Maybe walk for a bit before getting back on the bike.'

He had an Irish accent. His voice was so kind, and I was so shaken by the fall that I felt tears well in my eyes again.

'Don't cry,' he said, 'there's no need to cry.' He reached out and touched my hand. It was an odd thing for a stranger to do, but I didn't mind. His touch was light and cool, his hands big and strong.

I smiled. 'Thanks,' I said. 'Well, I'm going to go home. Thank you again.'

I wheeled the bike out into the sunshine and started walking back home. I turned round once to wave to the man, to reassure him that I really was OK, but he'd already gone.

By the time I got home, I was feeling better. I'd already formulated the incident into a funny story I could tell Jack to make him laugh. I was annoyed about my broken glasses and phone, but I was unhurt. I met Jack for lunch and we went into town. I got my phone fixed and made an appointment for an eye test that was overdue anyway. We went out with friends in the evening, so it wasn't until the next morning that I remembered I'd had the video running on my phone when I fell off the bike. I was curious about what the camera had captured of my fall. I thought it might be something else funny to add to the story of my mishap. Although it hadn't been a particularly bad fall, it seemed to have shaken me, left a lasting impression. I wanted to turn it into a joke.

I played it back and at first it was what I expected: just the path stretching out straight in front, lined with trees, a rabbit that ran out in front of me and a cat disappearing into the undergrowth. No foxes or deer this time. The fall happened fast on the camera, a chaos of fast-moving trees, sky and ground and then just the ground and the sound of the wheels spinning in the background.

And then nothing. Just the ground and the sound of the traffic passing over the bridge above. My feet in their grey trainers came briefly into shot and then there was my voice telling someone I'm all right, trying not to cry. This was where the man should have been talking back, but there was no sound of his voice. The scene changed as I picked up the bike, showing the grey pillars that supported the bridge, the graffiti on the walls. There was no man. Where he should have been standing in front of me and the bike, there was nothing.

I played it back again twice and there was nothing. There was me and the bridge and there was nothing else. The third time I played it back, I noticed something in the background, just a quick movement, a splash of colour that was gone in a moment. I played it back again and for a moment I thought I saw a group of figures in the background, almost lost in the gloom. I couldn't see what they are doing, but the splash of colour I saw looked like a spray of blood.

No one believed me. My friends and family told me about faults in the filming – my phone had been broken after all – or that perhaps I'd hit my head when I fell and imagined the Irish man. Jack suggested I visit A&E to get checked over, just in case. But I knew I hadn't hit my head – all my bruises were down my right leg. That's where I'd taken the impact of the fall. I watched the video footage over and over again, but he wasn't there and no matter how hard I tried, I couldn't find that group of dark figures again, couldn't see that arc of red spurting through the air.

I went back the next weekend. I went on foot, setting off from the car park at the *One Stop Shop* in the nearest housing estate. It was a bleak dank morning, the type of day I'd normally spend indoors with a fat novel or a boxset. More leaves had fallen, and the path was dappled with their colours; the branches above were stark against the grey sky. I was reassured by the sound of birds and squirrels in the branches above me, but as the sound of the motorway increased, I felt my heartbeat picking up. When I saw the grey-black opening of the bridge before me, I felt an almost overwhelming urge to turn back.

There was no one else around. No dog walkers or joggers. The traffic moved relentlessly above, but beneath the bridge the air felt stale and stagnant. Even the graffiti was washed out and faded that morning. There were broken bottles on the ground and a litter of crisp packets and chocolate wrappers, so I knew that people must come here, linger here drinking, but there was no sign of anyone now.

An emergency vehicle flew past on the motorway and in the howl of sirens, I thought I heard another sound: a man's voice shouting in agony and terror.

I didn't wait any longer. I turned and almost ran back the way I'd come.

I did some research at the library. There was a book of local ghost stories and it told a story about a labourer who'd been murdered, and his body walled up in the pillars of the bridge when they were constructing the motorway in the 1950s. It was from this book that I learned that the bridge was numbered Bridge 52, but it didn't tell me much else. It didn't give a name for the labourer or tell me what happened or why. There was a website for the book's author, a J D Bennett, and on it there was an email address. I contemplated a quick polite email asking for more information, but then threw caution to the wind and typed the whole story into an email and sent it off: how I'd fallen off my bike, the kind stranger who didn't appear in the video on my phone, the dark figures and the spray of blood, the voice crying in pain.

I did a bit more research into bridges and read about rainbow bridges and crybaby bridges, trolls and children walled up in the supports of London Bridge to appease some spiteful river deity. And not just children and not just in London. It seemed that this had been a common practice once, that bridges represented something mystical, passing as they did from one side of a river to another, forming a natural border, a natural defence, between lands and territories.

But this was a motorway bridge passing over a disused railway line. It was nothing like that, was it?

It scared me, but for some reason I couldn't keep away. I found myself walking to the bridge almost every day. I took photographs of it, some just straight through from one end to the other, others at strange angles capturing the row of pillars, the litter and graffiti and the curve of its roof. At home, I enlarged the photographs, played with the filters, hoping to find something in the shadows but there was never anything there.

I took audio recordings on my phone, but they were nothing more than the noise of the traffic and the sound of the wind rustling the last of the leaves.

The only thing I couldn't capture was how it made me feel. It drew me and terrified me in equal measures. There were times when I stood under the bridge and I could feel someone standing behind me, but as soon as I turned round, whatever it was had gone.

One day, I brought flowers. I felt self-conscious about it, but I felt I had to do something to show that I cared, so I bought a small bunch of carnations from the *One Stop Shop* where I parked the car and laid them against one of the pillars.

I looked round to check that there were no dog walkers who would think I'd lost my mind and then spoke. 'These are for you,' I said. 'I'm sorry for what happened to you.'

I turned to go and there was a noise behind me, like a sigh. I whirled round and he was there, standing between the pillars, in his workman's clothes and muddy, steel-toe boots. There was a fragility to him this time, a transparency. He was fading away before my eyes. I snatched the phone out of my pocket and managed to take a couple of quick snaps before he was gone completely.

When I checked the photos at home, he wasn't in them, but the graffiti doll on the wall behind him dripped blood from its eyes.

Jack was worried about me. He thought I was becoming obsessed and he was right. I was worried about myself, so when he suggested a weekend break in the countryside, I was really happy. We spent a long weekend lazing in our room or in front of the hotel's impressive open fire, and we left our phones and tablets in the bedside drawers as much as possible. We took a long walk through the countryside from one quaint sandstone village to the next and ate a massive lunch in the pub. I started Christmas shopping, and I think it was at this point that I realised this was the man with whom I wanted to spend the rest of my life.

But every night, I dreamed of the bridge. I was always on my bike, flying along the old railway, faster and faster and unable to stop. When I reached the bridge, there was a group of black-clad people lurking between the pillars, their faces hidden behind grotesque masks, before the ground disappeared from beneath my wheels and I was falling and falling to wake with a jolt in the big double bed in our luxury hotel room with Jack sleeping peacefully beside me.

A couple of weeks after we came back, I received an email from J D Bennett, the author of the book of local ghost stories. *Things are not always what they seem,* J D Bennett wrote, *I would like to meet you to discuss this.*

I almost deleted it. I'd had a lovely weekend doing normal things and I wanted to get back to that ordinariness. I didn't want to be wasting my time trekking along the old railway line in all weathers to what was really a very ordinary, very ugly bridge. I didn't want to be using up my thoughts and energy thinking about it. I wanted to be thinking about work and friends and starting a life together with Jack, maybe moving in together soon, getting a dog, going away on holiday again. All those lovely things were ahead of me and yet I couldn't quite bring myself to delete the photographs and video footage and sometimes, when I was alone, I found myself swiping through the photographs, pausing on one or another to enlarge it, searching for dark figures in the shadows and blood on the walls.

I picked up my phone to delete J D Bennett's email and instead found myself opening the photographs one more time. I swiped through them until I found the first video footage of the morning when I'd fallen off the bike, and I watched it again from start to finish – nothing. I watched it again and again, almost as if something was compelling me to do so. I must have watched it at least ten times before I saw something half hidden behind the pillars that hadn't been there before.

I hit pause and stared. It was him. It was the man, the Irish labourer. He was on his knees and behind him there was a crowd of dark-clad people, each of them wearing a mask. Some were no more than scarfs wrapped round to hide features, others were cheap Hallowe'en masks with garish colours and bright nylon hair, others were more elaborate, painted and carved into beaks and horns. Each figure held a knife in their gloved hands.

I stared, my heart racing. I wondered if there was any way of capturing this image as a still, but I couldn't work out how to do it. It didn't matter anyway because I was pretty sure that if I tried, there would be nothing to see except the concrete pillars and graffiti. And sure enough, as soon as I pressed the play button again, the labourer and the other figures were all gone.

I emailed J D Bennett back and told him, or her, that I would very much like to meet to discuss Bridge 52.

We arranged to meet on a Saturday afternoon in the shopping centre. J D Bennett had emailed back almost immediately and said it was important to meet somewhere bland and modern and noisy to discuss what we had to discuss. *The positive energy of many, many families going about their business will counteract any negativity*, he, or she, said in an email. It sounded like hokum to me, but I was living in a world of hokum by now and I felt comforted by it.

Of course, I didn't tell Jack or any of my friends who I was meeting. I made an excuse about Christmas shopping and went to meet J D Bennett.

It was the worst possible time to be at the food court and normally I'd have done anything to avoid the place. There were queues at every counter, and every table seemed to be occupied; people milled around with their trays searching for somewhere to sit. It was noisy and bright and crowded, and I knew without tasting it that the coffee I'd bought was going to be little more than dishwater. I realised too late the folly of arranging to meet a complete stranger here. I should have at least found out if J D Bennett was a man or a woman. I milled around with the crowds looking for anyone I thought might be him or her until someone tapped my shoulder and spoke my name.

J D Bennett turned out to be a woman. She was tiny, stick thin, but a mass of energy. All scarves, necklaces and bangles with a mass of black frizzy hair and skirts down to her ankles that almost hid her rainbow-patterned boots.

She didn't tell me her first name but said that people called her J D. She had already found a table near the escalators and laid claim to it by spreading out her shopping bags and coats, along with a detritus of empty coffee cups and food wrappers.

'So,' she said as soon as we sat down, 'tell me what you think is going on.'

'I think a man – an Irish labourer – was murdered, and his remains walled up in one of the pillars that supports the bridge,' I said. 'I think it might have been some sort of sacrifice. People used to make sacrifices in the old days to protect bridges. And I think he's still haunting the bridge where he was murdered.'

J D nodded. Her movements were fast and bird-like, her eyes very bright and shrewd.

'That's what I thought too at first,' she said. 'When I was writing my book that's exactly what I thought, too, but then I realised it didn't add up. You have to look at it in a different way.'

'What do you mean?'

'The bridge was built in 1958. Within living memory, but no matter how hard I looked and no matter how many people I spoke to, no one knew the man's name, no one could remember a police investigation taking place. All they knew was that there was something under that bridge. It was 1958 – someone should have known something. So that's when I started to look at it differently.'

'How?'

'Well, for starters I discounted any notion that what is haunting Bridge 52 is a kindly Irish labourer.'

'But I saw him,' I said, 'I had some video footage. He was in it. You can't see him now, but I saw it. I know I did. He spoke to me. I saw him being murdered. There was blood.'

J D shook her head. '*Something* spoke to you.'

Despite the noise and the bright lights and the crowds, I shivered.

'You shouldn't go back there,' J D said. 'It's got a hold on you and you need to break its grip. You must do everything you can to forget about it.'

'But if it's not the Irishman, what is it?'

'That's the question,' J D said. 'I don't know if there's a name for it. You know, in folklore and mythology there's a tradition of things pretending to be things that they're not. Sirens, for example, and kelpies, starving children that turn into ravenous monsters as soon as some silly fool invites them over the threshold.'

'But that's ridiculous,' I said.

J D raised one eyebrow. 'Is it any more ridiculous than believing a murdered labourer has come back from the dead to haunt the place?'

I frowned. 'But there are explanations for ghosts, aren't there? Scientific explanations. Something to do with a build-up of energy?'

J D sipped her coffee. 'You can believe that. You can believe what you want, but just don't go there anymore. Stop visiting, stop taking photographs, stop looking at the photographs. In fact, you should delete them from your phone right now. Don't do anything to make it think you care. That's how it gets a hold on people. It makes them care and then it destroys them.'

'Why? What does it want? And why is it there? It's not very nice under the bridge.'

J D smiled. 'So many questions. I don't know the answers. I can only guess. Why there? I suppose because bridges are mysterious places, thresholds. This particular bridge is ugly and modern, but it passes over an old railway line. It's possible that the thing – whatever it is – isn't haunting the bridge at all. It's haunting the railway line or something older that was there before there was a railway. But I don't think any of that matters. The bridge has given it a focus, a set of new possibilities. As for what it wants, I don't really know. I believe that it wants what it doesn't have – warmth, family, life – and it tries to take them from those it latches on to, those it can make care.'

'But why me? People drive up and down the motorway every day – why not one of them? Or one of the dog walkers or joggers or other cyclists? Or the kids who go there to drink and graffiti the walls? What did I do to deserve it?'

'I think because you stopped,' J D said. 'You fell off your bike and even though you weren't hurt, you were shocked and vulnerable. We fall all the time when we're children and it doesn't really bother us. But as adults we hardly ever fall down. When we do, it's a shock even if we're not hurt. We feel stupid, vulnerable, embarrassed. It shakes us up, if only for a moment. I believe that all those feelings drew it out and it gave you what you wanted in that moment – a kind word – to draw you into its web. It wants you. It wants what you've got, and I believe it will take everything from you if it can. You mustn't go there again.' She reached across the table and grabbed my hand. 'Promise me you won't go back there.'

I frowned. 'All right. I'm wasting too much of my time going there anyway.'

'And promise me you won't look at the photographs again, that you'll go home and delete them all without looking at them.'

I nodded. 'OK.'

'And you'll stop thinking about it. If you catch yourself thinking about it, you'll distract yourself with something else.'

'I'll try,' I said.

J D shook her head. 'That's not good enough. You need to put all thoughts of it from your mind. You mustn't let it in. It's got a grip. I just pray it's not too late.'

It was easy to distract myself that afternoon. I went shopping in the Saturday crowds. I bought some new clothes for work and a couple of books to keep my mind occupied. In the supermarket, I bought a bottle of wine and the ingredients to make Jack and I a nice meal that evening.

I drove home and put some music on and started chopping vegetables for the dinner. We hadn't made any plans to go out that evening, but now I wondered if the pub or the cinema might provide enough of a distraction to stop me thinking about the bridge and whatever was under it. I left the dinner simmering on the hob and called Jack to see if he wanted to go out.

'Hey,' he said. 'Guess where I am?'

'Where?'

'Under that creepy bridge you're so obsessed with.'

'What?'

'Thought I'd try and get some photos for you. And guess who I met?'

'Jack,' I said, 'get away from there. Come home. Now.'

He laughed. 'I met your Irish friend. We got talking about the bridge and I said you'd fallen off your bike and he said he'd been there. He said—'

'Jack!' I shouted. 'Get away from there. Come home. It's not safe.'

'OK. OK, I will.' His voice sounded puzzled. 'Are you OK?'

'Yes,' I said, 'just come home.'

'OK. I'm on my way. See you soon.'

'Love you,' I said.

Five o'clock came, then five thirty, six o'clock, six thirty and seven. He should have been home within half an hour. I swallowed down panic. I tried to eat the dinner I'd cooked. I texted some of his friends to find out if he was with them. I didn't know how long to leave it. I didn't know what you were supposed to do when someone went missing. I emailed J D Bennett, but she didn't reply. It was too late, she had warned me, and just as she had feared, it *was* too late.

At seven thirty, I took a torch and drove to the *One Stop Shop* and parked and walked along the old railway line. It should have been pitch black but there was a glow of lights up ahead. As I drew nearer, I could see the lights going past on the motorway above and the flash of torches and high vis jackets below. I saw that there was police tape and crowds of people. I could feel a scream building up in my chest, building and building, though it didn't come out just then. I walked a little closer and saw people in white jumpsuits bent over something on the ground, and I didn't need to see anymore to know what it was, who it was. My legs wanted to give way but somehow I managed to walk a little further on.

'Are you all right, my dear?' a voice spoke behind me, an Irish accent.

And then I was screaming, and the world was spinning around me as the traffic passed above on the motorway, unknowing, uncaring.

So that's why I come here despite everything J D Bennett said about not going there and not thinking about it. I go because I want to see a ghost. Because if there's a monster under the bridge that means monsters are real and if monsters are real, then there's a good chance ghosts are real too.

I take photographs and videos. I study them obsessively, but I never see him. Even if I did, how would I know it was him and not a new manifestation of the other thing under the bridge? I find that I don't care. I just want to see his face one last time.

Magpie

Winter had taken all the colour from the world. The trees stood stark and black against a grey sky and the ground was hard and barren. A bleak wind blew from the north and I could smell the battlefield on it – a stench of death that had once made me retch, but now filled me with excitement. My father looked back at me and smiled, and I grinned back. I wasn't afraid of the battlefield, and the circling crows above it made my heart race with anticipation.

The battles came more and more often, and my father and I followed just behind the marching ranks with their bright uniforms and glittering swords and armour, just behind the bands of servants, cooks and whores. We gave our allegiance to no side and we were as drab as sparrows. Turnip-faced yokels, someone had called us once, and failed to notice that my father's pockets jangled with coins, or that I wore pure gold round my neck and in my ears. They didn't see us, or care for us. They followed tall kings with bright eyes and golden crowns, their heads full of glory and honour. We couldn't afford glory and weren't sure what honour was. We knew that they rode through our villages and that their battles ravaged our lands and our crops. They took our livestock to feed their ranks, and our women to feed other appetites, but they didn't see us.

But we saw them, and we saw the mess they left behind in the fields where we'd once grown our crops. Some people said that the battlefield was no place for a girl, but my father laughed and threw his arm round my shoulder and said that I was as brave as any of his sons. I was his magpie – able to spot the things that glittered and shone from far away. My corner of the room I shared with my sisters was decorated with belt buckles, glass beads and brass buttons. Things that shone in the bleak, grey world we lived in.

I followed my father into the carnage, carefully lifting my skirts above the mud and he laughed at my fastidiousness. I picked my way through the tangle of broken limbs and armour and closed my ears to the sounds of dying men and screaming horses. A hand snatched at my skirts and I glanced down, but it had no rings. I walked on.

It was instinct that took me towards the oak tree that stood tortured in the aftermath of the battle. In the summertime, when it was dressed in greenery, it might have been as proud as the king of trees, but now it made me think of witches.

A king had fallen here. I knew that from the tattered remains of his banners that had caught in the tree's branches and waved helplessly at the crows. The king and his guard were long gone, but they had left behind them a mess of twisted armour and dead horses. I picked through the rubble looking for anything of any value and at first, I didn't even notice the voice that called to me.

'Help me.'

It was such a soft voice, I wondered if I was imagining it at first. Battlefields can do that to you: make you imagine ghosts and voices when there are none.

'Help,' it came again, and I turned, searching the carnage. Of course, there are always pleas for help amidst the screams and groans. Some men mistake me for a nurse and dare to believe I'm their last hope. But this voice was different, so lost and so alone.

'Help me.'

I found him half crushed beneath some other man's horse. He was not a rich man, for he had no armour, just a leather coat spattered with gore. Pale hair and an angel's face, blue eyes clouded with pain. *He might live*, I thought, and then dismissed the thought.

'Help,' he whispered.

I shook my head. He ought to have been dead already, half crushed like that. I crouched down in the mud beside him and fingered the collar of his leather coat and decided that it would do for one of my brothers if we could get the blood out of it. His other clothes were ruined with blood and dirt.

'My wife,' he said, 'please tell her.'

I ignored him. He cried out when I took his coat and clutched at my arm.

'Please,' he whispered, 'tell my wife.' He gave me the name of a village not far from here and I did consider it, I swear I did.

I shook my head again and his eyes closed. I busied myself going through his pockets. There were a few coins, a few crumbling cubes of sugar he must have taken for his horse. That made me sad. There was a lot of blood and that made me feel better. It wasn't likely that anyone could have helped him anyway, even if they'd been inclined to.

My father says sometimes it's kinder to kill them, but I've never done that. They ride into battle, they get paid for it, they know how they'll die and that it will be horrible. It's not my problem.

There was a ring on his fourth finger. Just a thin band of silver, not worth anything really. It wasn't even gold as wedding bands ought to be. But I liked it. I liked that it was worth nothing, but it meant everything to him and his wife. I took it and his eyes flickered open again.

His voice was almost gone when he spoke. 'Please,' he said, 'give that back to my wife. It's not worth anything to you.'

'It's mine now,' I said.

'Thief,' he whispered, and his voice was bitter at the end. It trailed away, but I thought I could just make out his last words. 'She'll find you.'

I shrugged my shoulders and I thought again of riding to his village and finding his wife. Maybe I wouldn't give her his ring, but I could at least tell her that he'd died thinking of her. Perhaps it would make widowhood easier for her. But what was the point? When he didn't come home, she'd know anyway, and what use was the ring to her, in any case? She probably had one of her own, and I didn't, and that was that.

I stood up to go and, just then, he died. I felt him go and when I turned round, I saw his spirit fading into the blackening sky and it was all the colours of summertime. I could hear him laughing, although I might have imagined that amongst the noise the crows made as they all took to the sky at once.

My father and I left the battlefield, our cart bursting with booty. We had broken armour and helmets, swords, knives, cannon shot, clothes, jewellery and even religious books and prayer beads. I wore the dead man's ring on the fourth finger of my left hand where I'd slipped it on without thinking. I twisted it round and round, but when I tried to take it off, it wouldn't slide back over my knuckle.

I tried again later with soap and water, but it still wouldn't budge, and I was annoyed now. I'd thought it a pretty, shining thing, but now I could see that it wasn't even real silver, and it was tarnished. No amount of polish could make it shine. It was a piece of cheap rubbish, I could see that now.

I couldn't sleep that night. My room was full of shadows I couldn't explain and the crows in the trees outside kept me awake all night. I could hear the rustle of their wings and the cackling, cawing sound they made. The ring was a dead weight on my finger.

And every time my eyes began to close, I was awoken by someone laughing. I thought it was him and he was laughing as his spirit melted into a pewter sky and beyond him, someone else was coming for me. I could hear the swish of her skirts, the sound of her heels on the iron-hard ground. His wife, I thought, and woke with a jerk, trembling, and seeing not a pretty, pink-cheeked country girl but a crow woman with cruel eyes and the taste of blood in her mouth.

I was on edge for days after that. I kept feeling that there was someone behind me whenever I was alone. I'd whirl around expecting to find someone – something – there, but there was never anything although the air felt different. Wrong, somehow, as if something had turned askew in the world. Things shifted behind my reflection in the mirror and the ring on my finger was turning black as it dug into my flesh.

But I wouldn't let it beat me. A man had died on a battlefield, so what? He'd asked me to help when he was beyond help. He'd asked me to tell his wife but what good would that have done? I'd taken his ring, but it was no use to him. I didn't make the war, it wasn't my fault.

I decided that I would wear his leather coat myself. It was a good fit – the leather was soft with wear and the lining was a little shabby, but I didn't mind that. It kept the rain and the cold out and it showed him and his wife that I wasn't afraid. It smelled of him – of leaves and herbs and a little of blood and sweat, for all that I'd scrubbed the stains away. I tried not to, but I couldn't help wondering who else had cleaned his coat and washed his clothes, who now watched the road for the young men returning from battle and twisted the ring on her own finger and waited and longed and ached for him to return.

And sometimes, when I wore his coat, I could smell a woman's perfume as well, something musky and dark. I thought of long fingers caressing his pale skin, ruby lips and black hair the colour of crow's wings. I tugged at the ring on my finger, but I couldn't get it off.

Ten days after my father and I went to the battlefield, I put on his coat and walked down to the river and found her there. It seemed that she grew out of the earth like the willows. She was a winter thing, a thing of northern winds and battlefields, of ice and endless sleet and sorrow. She wore a black dress and her lips were as red as berries. They were the only colour left in the world.

Wordlessly, she held out her hand to me. I didn't move. I could taste blood in my mouth and it wasn't mine, I could hear the sound of the battlefield all around me and the sound of my own blood rushing in my ears. My arms ached from the weight of a sword that was almost as tall as I was. And then I was on the ground, a terrible pain in my side and she was walking towards me, her hand held out.

She held the knife out to me. It was a pretty thing, the hilt encrusted with sapphires and the blade shining. In another world, another life, I would have coveted it, but now I took it in my right hand and hacked the ring finger from my left.

And that noise, that screaming, was me. That blood on the leather coat was mine. The sound all around me was crows and laughter, and I saw for a moment a young man and his wife, saw him catch her in his arms and spin her round and round and they were both laughing.

And then they were gone, although his laughter lingered in the air. My family were all around me. My mother was weeping and my father raging. I looked down and saw that the knife I still held in my right hand wasn't the sapphire encrusted blade the crow woman had offered me, but my own knife with its plain wooden handle and dull blade. My severed finger lay on the riverbank and the ring it wore shone in the first sunlight we had seen for weeks. It was pure, untarnished silver like the moon. On the far side of the river, a young man turned away from me and all the crows took to the sky at once in a great black cloud, all except one, a magpie, that swept down in a flash of black and white, and snatched up my finger and the ring and took them away.

Driving Home for Christmas

Just when I'm driving past the place where my brother used to say there was a water-witch, the wind comes down from the north like it always does. It buffets against the sides of the car and I can hear it howling across the moors. My brother used to say that was the witch howling for her pool. My brother has a crazy imagination.

It's one of those nights when it's best to be tucked up inside – central heating on, glass of Baileys, a video and a big bowl of snacks. I don't like nights like this, and I especially don't like them up on the moors on this particular patch of road. They make me remember her.

But it's Christmas Eve and every Christmas Eve without fail, I drive home for Christmas. Every year, I put on my CD of Christmas songs and leave all the shimmer and shine of London behind and drive north, up the motorway and then across the moors. And every year I say to myself that this will be the last one. Each year that goes past I'm another year too old to be spending Christmas with my mother and my brother.

Most years, I don't leave it so late to set off. I leave in the bright, early morning light and I'm up by lunchtime. This year, there was the office party last night and then drinks again at lunchtime today and, to be honest, I shouldn't really be driving. I was careful on the motorway – checking my mirrors and sticking to the speed limit but I know these roads like the back of my hand and besides there's not likely to be anyone out on Christmas Eve looking for drunk drivers. I've gotten complacent, but you'd think I'd have learned after what happened that other Christmas Eve when I drove home drunk. Truth is, I need a drink to get me there, especially in the dark, especially along this stretch of road where it's pitch-black save for the headlights and the moon that's so often obscured by fast-moving clouds. It was windy that night too, the same icy wind battering across the moors, twisting trees into wraiths and screaming at the windows like a banshee or a water-witch. A wicked wind, my mother calls it, safe in her farmhouse kitchen with all the hatches battened down and the tree blazing light.

Any moment now, I'll come to the bend where the little roadside shrine remains. It breaks my heart that someone still comes up here to the middle of nowhere to remember her. Missing her.

Tonight, it's as if I can feel her. As if she's in the car with me, sitting on the back seat with her red coat and pompom hat, her blond hair. I never found out her name – never wanted to – or what she was doing alone in the road in the middle of nowhere, dressed like some sort of winter princess on Christmas Eve. I can feel her, but when I look in the rear-view mirror, there's no one there, just darkness behind me to match the darkness in front. My headlights hardly break it.

I'm coming up to the bend now and I know I'll feel better once I've passed it and the little shrine. I'll be almost home then. I remember that there are always Christmas roses laid there and one of those miniature football strips people hang in their cars is hung up on the fencepost, the red and white almost festive. That's my team too, and Christmas roses have always been my favourite flowers. It's like she's mocking me, but of course, she isn't. She's dead and I killed her.

There's the tree; black shadowy branches pointing like fingers against the moon, whipping in the wind as if the tree is in a rage. It was windy that night too – it's always windy up here. I remember that I was looking at the tree against the moon and thinking that it would make a good photograph. And then I saw her from the corner of my eye, too late, a flash of red and a desperate attempt to swerve.

She died, and it was my fault. I could blame her for being on the road. I could blame a patch of ice or a particularly strong gust of wind, or the darkness, or my clapped-out old car for not reacting fast enough, but ultimately, I'd had too much to drink and I drove all the way from London on no sleep and I killed her.

Don't think about it, don't think about it. Don't think about her. It happened, it's done. That was 1997 and this is 2017. Twentieth anniversary. Don't think about that either. Just drive, round the bend, past the tree and the shrine and then home for Christmas.

But I can't not think about her. There might as well be two of us in the car. I can almost see her: her red coat and blond hair and how there was something strange about her. It wasn't just the strangeness of her being there on Christmas Eve dressed like that. It was the look in her eyes as the car hit her. It wasn't fear. It was something else. Triumph maybe, laughter perhaps. It wasn't right.

She wasn't right. She was like something my brother would have made up. But that's hindsight and maybe it's me trying to justify what I did.

You drive here in the summer and it's just beautiful. The sweep of the moor all ablaze with gorse and heather, with the hills all around you and the white dots of sheep, the hugeness of the sky. Down there somewhere, there's the pool where my brother said he saw the water-witch and where he tried to terrify me with stories about how she'd come out of the water, all straggling hair, green skin and fangs to steal your soul away. I never believed it, not even as child, but still I wouldn't go near that pool on my own. My parents drained it to make way for holiday chalets that were never built – something to do with planning permission. My brother once asked my mother where a water-witch goes when her pool is gone. My mother and I laughed and said there's no such thing as ghosts or ghoulies. Right now, I wish I believed that.

I slow right down to take the bend. *Don't think about it, don't think about it.* I reach forward to turn up the volume on the CD and the car fills with the sound of Nat King Cole singing *O Holy Night*. It was playing in the car that other night, too. I remember singing along to it, laughing at how tuneless my voice was but enjoying every moment of it. I sing along at the top of my voice, almost shouting out with defiance:

'O holy night,
The stars are shining brightly.'

I ignore the witchy branches of the tree. I don't look at the moon. The shrine is nothing to do with me. It's sad and unfortunate, but it was twenty years ago. People should move on.

'The thrill of hope, the weary world rejoices,' I sing, 'For yonder brings a new and glorious morn. Fall on your knees.'

And she's there. Standing in the road just like before. It can't be, it can't be...

I slam the breaks on, turn the wheel but it's too late. I hit her hard and fast and for a brief moment, as the car spins out of control towards the tree, I can see her face and she's laughing. Her eyes are blazing and she's laughing. Or screaming, I can't tell.

Then she's gone, and the car hits the tree and for long moments, there's nothing but silence and pain. Such pain that fills every part of me, turning everything to white and light. Then it's gone, and everything is dark again. Clouds speed across the moon, the wind howls and Nat carries on singing about angel choirs and nights divine.

I'm OK, I think, *I'm OK*.

I remember her – another girl in a red coat standing in the road and I don't understand. Once was strange enough, twice is something else. I can't quite believe it and I wonder if I hallucinated her, but I know I didn't, and I know there's only one girl.

I'm shaking. I can't get my thoughts in order. I try the door on my side of the car and it won't open, just like it wouldn't that other night. I crawl over to the passenger side and manage to open the door and almost fall out. The wind is screaming now and there are flakes of snow in it. I wonder briefly and stupidly if we'll have a white Christmas.

The headlights are still on, lighting up the mangled remains of my car. It looks almost cartoonish. I look for her. She can't be far even if the impact hurled her away from the tree, but I can't find her.

I sit down suddenly – it's the shock, I think – and put my head in my hands. I can feel blood sticky against my palms, but it doesn't hurt. That must be the shock too. The first time, I remember thinking: how can I get away with this, how can I explain it so that it isn't my fault? And I'm ashamed, but that's what I'm thinking now: how can I get away with this, how can I hide it?

I stand up again. I'm not far from home so the first thing I can do is walk there. Suddenly, I want my mother and my crazy mixed up brother with his superstitions and the rattle of the talismans strung around his neck. I want to be in the kitchen, drinking hot chocolate with Baileys in it, telling ghost stories, not being in one.

I have a torch in the boot of the car, so I walk back towards it and *O Holy Night* is still playing. The impact must have damaged the CD player and now it's on some sort of loop. As I get closer, I can see that there's a shape in the car on the driver's side, something bent and broken over the wheel. But that can't be, it can't be. It's too dark to see properly, so until I'm right up close, I think it must just be a shadow, a trick of the light. But when I'm close, I can see black hair and the twisted legs of broken spectacles. I reach up and touch my own broken glasses and I feel my breath catch in my throat. I'm the one in the car, but I'm the one out here in the wind and the snow. It can't be, it can't be…

The world is fracturing around me, shattering, splintering into ice and snow and Nat King Cole tells me over and over to fall on my knees. I stumble to the roadside, to the shrine and stare at the red and white of the football strip pinned up like a sacrifice, the Christmas roses wilting. My flowers, my team, my photograph fading in the weather. The world spins and begins to fade and I see her standing on the roadside in her red coat, a water-witch without a pool become a haunt of the roadside. And as the world begins to vanish around me, I know that this is all there is for me now: Christmas Eve and this stretch of road, the bend, the tree and the shrine. The same Christmas carol played over and over. I have been here before, every Christmas Eve for twenty years. This is all there is.

And then I'm gone, lost in a swirl of snowflakes and the blazing laughter in her eyes. Gone until next Christmas Eve and the next one and the next one...

Cosmic Ordering for Vampires

Almost thirty years after I murdered his girlfriend, it's the video footage that brings Solomon to my office. You might have seen the video – it went viral for a while. It's just a few moments of CCTV footage, grainy and difficult to see quite what's going on, but if you look closely enough, you can see a man walk through a wall. That man is me. Of course, it's widely believed to be a hoax. A few people have tried to work out how it was done and why, but most people watch it once, acknowledge it as a hoax and don't think about it again. I am quite happy with that. I didn't walk through a wall to get sixty thousand hits on YouTube. I did it because it was New Year's Eve and the pub I was in was crowded, and the people I was with were becoming increasingly loud and more obnoxious, and I was bored. There were crowds between the table where I was sitting and the exit, and it just seemed too much effort to get through them, to make my excuses for leaving without hurting anyone's feelings. So, I went to the corridor beside the kitchen and walked through the wall and went home.

This was New Year's Eve 2016 and it's autumn 2018 now, so I'm surprised it's taken Solomon this long to track me down. I thought he was more tenacious than that. Last time I saw him, he was twenty-three years old, backing away from me, stumbling over the body of his insipid little girlfriend and begging me for it.

My secretary tells me that there's a Mr Davies in reception asking to see me. I do not know who she means. I have a pile of contracts to check and sign, and my diary is supposed to be clear of meetings today. I am not expecting anyone. It's only when she says his first name that I remember.

Solomon Davies. I always knew him as Solomon Hollowman.

I spin round and round in my desk chair while I wait for my secretary to bring him up from reception. I know he will be impressed by my office with its three glass walls and views across the river to the Shard and City Hall, almost straight down to the Tower. I could tell him that I remember when the Tower was surrounded by countryside. I could tell him about the time I saw

Henry the Eighth and how he looked nothing like his portraits, but I won't because Solomon doesn't care about those things and nor do I.

Solomon has aged well. He is still tall, handsome and well-dressed, his black hair artfully streaked with grey at his brow, laughter lines round his eyes. Expensive suit, tasteful tie, polished shoes. If anyone was to guess, they would say he was the vampire, not me.

He walks all round my office, pausing to admire the view before turning to grin at me.

'Look at this place,' he says, 'look at you.'

In truth, I am not much to look at. Nondescript, just the right side of attractive but not so much that anyone would look twice at me.

'You haven't aged at all,' he says.

'Well, no,' I say, 'obviously.'

But actually, I could age if I wanted to. I can rearrange the molecules and particles I'm made of into something different, something that can walk through walls. I can look like whatever I want to look like, but I have always known that it does no good to draw attention to oneself. So here I am – black hair, grey eyes, modest attire.

'I saw you,' he says, 'you're the person in that video.'

'What video?'

'You know. Walking through a wall. New Year's Eve 2016. It's you.'

I don't deny it. I sit down behind my desk and nod towards the spare chair. He sits for a moment and then stands up and begins pacing round and round my office. He was always a ball of energy. At home and at work, he could never sit still for long. I can remember him pacing up and down the length of the long open plan office where I first met him, shouting into the first enormous mobile phone he owned, flirting with colleagues, arguing with everyone.

He opens the office door to read the name plate.

'Matthew Askew.' He grins. 'Head of Corporate Compliance. Wowzers. I remember you when you were Matt, the one who did the photocopying and made the tea and answered the phone. I made you, didn't I?'

I raise an eyebrow. 'You made me?'

'Yeah,' he said, 'you remember. It was me who said you needed to get qualifications, wasn't it? And I said, ask the universe for what you want, and the universe will give it to you.'

Summer 1995 and we're in Solomon's mother's back garden in a housing estate in Milton Keynes. There's a barbecue going on and Solomon has invited everyone from work, regardless of their place in the hierarchy. The work people mix with the other guests and it's a noisy, chaotic hell. The sun hurts my eyes and the beginnings of a thirst is burning at the back of my throat.

I'm sitting in the shade with Solomon and his girlfriend, Lucy. Solomon has not stopped talking and neither Lucy nor I have made much of an effort to get a word in edgewise. So far, Solomon has soliloquised about Blur versus Oasis, the Conservative party and the possibility of a general election, the Milton Keynes grid system and whether cats are better than dogs. Now he's talking about how to get ahead in business.

'Cosmic ordering and the laws of the attraction,' he says. 'Have you heard of all that? It's this thing – it's been proven and everything. Peer reviewed by scientists and all that shit. It's legit. So, what it is, is you think of the things you want – doesn't matter how big or how small it is, and you ask the universe for it. And the universe delivers. Of course, there's a lot more to it than that – you've got to believe in it to the extent that you act like you've already got it – but that's it in a nutshell.'

In the olden days, we used to ask God for what we wanted. We used to pray and invariably God did not deliver. I wonder if this is the same, but I don't mention it. I know there's no point in attempting to interrupt Solomon, much less change his mind about anything.

'So, I just ask for anything I want, and it will be delivered?' Lucy asks.

Solomon nods. He grabs a couple of chicken drumsticks from someone else's plate and grins.

'Yeah. I'm asking for immortal life,' he says. 'Don't laugh. Scientists are working on it. There are drugs for everything and they're getting better than ever, so you mark my words, in twenty, thirty years, I'm going to be living forever. And get this – I asked for you, Lucy. I saw you across the office and I asked the universe for you and even though you were engaged to another guy, I got you, didn't I? I said to the universe, *I want that girl, please can I have that girl?* And I got you.'

Lucy laughs. Only someone as stupid and bland as her could laugh at something like that.

'OK,' she says, 'so what should I ask for?'

'Anything you want. Aim high or aim low.'

She smiles and glances sidelong at me. 'OK, I'll start small. I have a horrible desk at work. Right next to the fax machine, where everyone dumps their papers and empty coffee cups. I want a new desk, a bright sunny desk at the window. Maybe where Matt sits.' She smiles sweetly at me to show it's a joke and Solomon claps his hands and roars with laughter.

I laugh too. I run my tongue round the inside of my mouth and I am growing fangs. My body is readying itself for the drink I will have to take soon.

'You should be careful what you wish for. Wishes have consequences,' I say and then pull my sunglasses down over my eyes.

Needless to say, two days later I have to change desks with Lucy. She has the grace to look apologetic and she buys me a paper cup of coffee as a peace offering and sets it down on my new desk beside the fax machine.

'Sorry,' she says, 'I didn't think it would work.'

'She asked the universe, didn't she?' Solomon blares, 'and the universe delivered.'

It is undoubtedly true that Lucy asked the universe for my window desk, but she also asked her manager who saw that in the hierarchy of the office, a trainee marketing executive was much more deserving of that desk than a lowly filing clerk.

I really wish it wasn't the case, but it's a fact that I am petty and small-minded enough to kill someone over a desk.

I watch Solomon walk round and round my monster desk and I wonder if he even remembers that. He picks up my ceramic coffee cup, fiddles with the stapler, rearranges post-it notes. He opens and shuts the desk drawers and I don't know what he's looking for. He's just moving because he's worked up about something and he's never liked staying still.

'Why are you here?' I ask, when I can't bear it any longer.

'You know. You remember I asked the universe for eternal life?'

I nod.

'Well, here I am.' He sits down momentarily and then jumps up again.

I sigh. 'I am not the universe, Solomon.'

He carries on as if I haven't spoken. 'I said twenty or thirty years, didn't I? I thought I had to wait for science and medicine to catch up, but then I saw that YouTube video and I remembered it's you who's going to give me it.'

I suppose I should ask him why he wants it. I should say something about it not being a gift but a curse and tell him of the agony of watching your loved ones die time and time again. I should say something about the moral dilemmas involved in the killing and blood drinking. But I don't. There's a lot of things I should do that I don't do. The truth is, I have never loved anyone and watched them die. I care for nothing. It's just a life and survival is all.

'What do you do now?' I ask him.

'Logistics,' he says, 'haulage. I got me a fleet of trucks going up and down the motorways. Even Europe now.'

'Are you married? Do you have children?'

'Three wives.' He laughs. 'Not all at once. Two divorces. Six kids. God, they bleed me dry, the lot of them. Hey, don't you be getting any ideas. They're not for you. I haven't forgotten what you did to Lucy. That was messed up, man.'

'Well, if I give it to you, you will have to do that messed up thing over and over again,' I say.

'I know,' he says, 'I've thought about that and I don't care. I can do it.'

'Are you sure? What you see in the films is a myth. Those two neat little puncture wounds in the neck, don't exist. There's always a mess and a body to dispose of. You know – you saw Lucy.'

'I know,' he says, 'and I can do it. I'm a psychopath. A psychopath, man.'

'You are?'

'High functioning, of course.' He grins. 'I'm not going to fry up your liver and eat it for dinner with a nice glass of wine. No, I've used it to get ahead instead. I don't care who I trample on to get what I want, do I? You saw me in action twenty years ago. I got to the top fast, didn't I? I had to push through the dead wood to get there. Hell, I had to burn the dead wood down. And I didn't care. I could see that I should have cared, that other people would have cared, but I didn't. I took the risks, I burned through the dead wood without a care, and here I am.'

I am not entirely sure I know what he's talking about.

'You too, man,' he says, 'you're the same.' He waves an arm round my office and the view beyond. 'Look at this place. Look at what you got. When I first knew you, you were earning the minimum wage and living in my mother's spare room like fucking Harry Potter.'

'Solomon,' I say, 'I got here because I worked hard. Do you remember? You brought me university prospectuses and told me to get a qualification. Well, I did. I got a law degree and I worked hard, and this is where I've ended up. I haven't trampled over anyone to get here, I've just applied for promotions. I have filled in countless application forms. I have practised interview techniques. I haven't asked the universe for anything. I haven't cheated or lied or schemed. I've just worked hard.'

For a moment Solomon is silenced. 'But why?' he asks. 'Why would you want this when you're— when you're what you are? Why would you want this – nice though it is – and why would you have wanted to be a filing clerk back then? You were nothing. You were the lowest of the low.'

'Because there's nothing else,' I say, 'because back then I just needed a roof over my head and a little money while I worked on something. I needed a safe place. The world is empty, Solomon, it goes on and on and nothing means anything. Nothing new happens. The faces change, but the people beneath them are the same over and over again. I can be here in my corner office signing million pound contracts or I can be cleaning toilets or waiting tables or fixing washing machines or anything. It doesn't matter. It's all the same.'

Solomon shakes his head. 'I don't believe that. There's always new stuff to see and new stuff to learn. You're just jaded and old. You need me. I can make you young again. I can show you stuff you won't believe.'

'Really? You are not young anymore either.'

He laughs. 'Rude. What were you working on then, back then in my mum's spare room?'

'I was teaching myself how to do this.' There's no harm in showing him. He's seen me do it before. It was how I got him to believe in what I was after I killed Lucy. He knows I can walk through walls. I lift up my arm and slowly turn my hand into vapour, letting it creep over my wrist towards my elbow before I stop it and make my arm back into flesh and bone again.

Solomon grins. 'That's so cool. You can show me how to do that, and I'll show you the world. Hey, can you get away from here? I want to show you something.'

'What?'

'Come with me and see. You can get away, can't you?'

I nod. I can always get away. It doesn't really matter to me if I get disciplined or fired for not being at my desk. I reach for my jacket.

'Where are we going?' I ask.

'A little trip down memory lane,' he says. 'I'll drive.'

His car is a monstrosity: bright green, huge and ugly and parked on a double yellow line blocking the tradesman's entrance to a restaurant. He tears the parking ticket from the window and tosses it away.

'I'm not going to worry about that,' he said, 'you don't worry about parking tickets, do you?'

'No,' I say, 'but only because I make sure not to park where I'm going to get one.'

'What do you drive, anyway? Something boring, I bet. You used to have that old banger, didn't you? It was more rust than car, as I remember. It leaked. It smelled bad. Didn't you find a rat in it once?'

'I have a company car now,' I say. 'It's not that important to me.'

Solomon drives exactly as you would expect: fast and careless and dangerous, although he tells me that he is a very safe driver as he skips the red lights and screeches round corners, pushes the car well beyond the speed limit as we join the motorway north. He puts music on too loud, a Britpop compilation that makes me think of that summer again.

Lucy and I are following Solomon along a dusty hot street and onto one of Milton Keynes's many cycle paths, redways as they are called. Solomon's whistling to himself while Lucy and I walk in frosty silence. I have not forgiven her for the incident with my desk. I care about it because it's small and petty, and I have to care about something or I'll lose my mind. I am sick with the need to drink, the last of the sunlight hurts my eyes and I have a headache. My teeth hurt, and I am not at my best. I cannot be bothered with this, with them.

Solomon is enjoying the tension between Lucy and me. He walks with a kind of bounce in his step that reminds me of the roosters I used to watch circling one another in the cock-fighting pits not so many centuries ago – all strut and swagger and a nasty end up ahead. I pitied those roosters and I pity Solomon. He's tense and excited and happy all at once, and I wonder if he's taken something, but I'm pretty sure he hasn't. This is just the way he is.

The redway slopes down to an underpass between housing estates. Traffic rumbles above us and Solomon gropes in his pocket for his mobile phone. It's one of the latest models and has a torch attached to it. He uses it to light up the mural graffitied on the wall of the underpass.

'Look at that,' he says gleefully. 'Look at that, guys.'

The graffiti depicts a vast white and gold figure with wings and a halo. At its feet, trampled into the dust is a twisted bat-winged creature with fangs and red eyes. It's actually quite good. I look at it and then at Solomon.

'What is it, babe?' Lucy asks.

'The archangel Michael trampling Satan underfoot and eradicating evil from the world. It's from the Bible.'

'And you're showing it to us because...?'

Solomon's grin stretches wider and he moves his phone to light up the bottom corner of the picture where the artist has signed it in tall spiky letters: Hollowman.

'I did it, didn't I?' Solomon says. 'It's mine, my art. Hollowman's my tag. Solomon Hollowman, that's me.'

'It's brilliant, babe,' Lucy says.

While she's extolling Solomon's genius and he's basking in the glory of it, I lean down and look at the twisted face of the devil. I used to do this when I was young. I'd go into churches and cathedrals and look at the faces of the devils and demons painted on canvases and altarpieces to see if there was some trace of me in their features. There never was. Solomon's devil is no different.

Lucy's voice whines on and on. I walk away from them and along the redway a little way to where it branches off into Linford Wood. The wood is networked with paths, and I follow one without much thought as to where it leads. Solomon and Lucy follow me, Lucy still praising him while he pretends to be modest.

My head hurts and although the sun is going down, it's still too hot. Tomorrow, I will sit down at my desk next to the fax machine and all day it will makes its annoying noises and my head will ache, and when it breaks down people will expect me to fix it. When it runs out of paper, they will expect me to fill it up again. They will talk to one another over my desk and leave their plastic coffee cups there for me to throw away. They will borrow my pen and my ruler and not give them back. When I go for lunch, I will undoubtedly come back and find ten or twenty faxes taken off the machine and dumped on my desk for me to distribute, or else someone will be sitting on my chair chatting to someone else, and they'll look up at me and apologise for sitting in my chair and then not move for another five minutes, while I stand there pretending I don't mind. And all the time, none of them know that I am growing fangs and a bloodlust so strong I can hear the blood in their veins, I can almost taste it.

Another path leads off between the trees and I take it. It's narrow and the gravel soon peters out into a dirt track. I know that eventually it comes out in a secret clearing, and that on the way, if you look hard enough, you can see carvings in the trees. I don't look tonight. Even the first light of the moon makes my eyes hurt.

'Hey, Matt,' Solomon calls, 'where are you going?'

I don't answer. I am not really thinking anymore. I am just walking, leading them to the clearing where the trees stand tall and black against a perfect sunset. There's a tree stump that someone has carved into a monster. During the day, it's friendly and benign. Children climb and play on it. In the twilight, its white stone eyes burn with malevolence.

'I don't like it here,' Lucy says. 'Let's go home, Solly.'

It's not how I would have planned it, but when the end result is always going to be the same, what's the point in making plans?

'Cosmic ordering,' I say.

'What?' Lucy says. 'What's he talking about, Solly?'

'Consequences,' I say.

I grab her shoulders and pull her to me. She cries out and Solomon shouts at me to take my hands off her. I ignore him, lean forward and sink my teeth into Lucy's neck and drink. Solomon shouts again. I can feel his hands on my shoulders trying to pull me off her, but I'm strong and I jab an elbow into his stomach and he falls back. He tries again, but by then it's too late. I let Lucy drop to the ground and turn to him, wipe my face with my hand and smile.

'She used to call you Solly,' I say as we roar up the motorway in the middle lane all the way. 'I bet you hated that.'

'What are you talking about?'

'Lucy,' I say. 'She used to call you Solly.'

'I did hate that,' he says.

'Do you ever think about her?'

'No.'

'I do,' I say, 'she was the last blood I drank. I was getting sick and her blood made me well. Maybe I'm the only person who ever thinks of her now. I didn't like her. I don't think good things about her.'

'She was dull,' Solomon says, 'I can see that now. My first wife – she was like me. She was never dull. Gorgeous, too. I couldn't live with her, though. We were going to murder one another if I didn't leave.'

He rambles on about all his wives. I don't listen. We pass the junctions for the M25, for Luton and Dunstable.

'Are we going to Milton Keynes?' I ask.

'Yeah. I want to show you something, so you'll understand about me. So that you'll give it to me.'

'Do you still live in Milton Keynes?' I ask. 'Do you still live with your mother?'

'Yes, I still live in Milton Keynes. No, I don't live with my mother.'

I frown. 'I don't know why, but I thought you'd have moved away. London, Paris, New York. Somewhere else.'

Solomon shakes his head. 'It's a great place. City of the Future and all that shit. What's not to like – no traffic jams, house prices on the up, roundabouts, municipal artworks, redways, green spaces, lakes, big businesses moving there from London. Ley lines, man, there's a ley line going right through it if you believe in all that shit. There's a fucking forest in the middle of the city. Why would I want to live anywhere else?'

'I just thought – because of the things you said after Lucy died, after what you asked of me, that the whole world wasn't big enough for you.'

Lucy's body hits the ground with a soft thud.

'Fuck!' Solomon shouts. He drops to the ground beside her and stares at her. Her eyes are open but she's not breathing. I know her heart has stopped because I felt the moment when it stopped. He shakes her and then looks up at me, his face is white, and his eyes are huge. 'She's dead. You fucking killed her. Fuck, fuck, fuck.'

I don't say anything. I can feel Lucy's blood in my veins and I feel better. Solomon reaches inside his jacket for his phone.

'Don't,' I say. I walk towards him and he scrambles backwards away from me.

'I need to call the police. An ambulance.'

I move fast and snatch the phone from his hand. 'No.'

He stares at me and then moves towards the path. I move faster, blocking his path.

'You fucking killed my girlfriend,' he says.

'I did,' I agree.

Solomon sinks down to his knees on the grass. 'You tore her throat out. You drank her blood.'

'I did.'

'Fuck. What the fuck?' He starts to gather strength. 'I'm going to fucking kill you.'

'No, you're not.'

'Why not? Give me one fucking good reason why not.'

I wish he'd stop swearing. It's ugly and I've never liked it. Words like that just don't form in my mouth even after seven hundred years.

'What if I told you that I'm not what you think I am at all? I'm not just an administration clerk earning the minimum wage and driving a bad car and wearing cheap clothes. Here's what you should know about me. I don't like bullies and show offs. I didn't like Lucy, but somehow, I do like you. I don't like people much, but I do like animals. I was five years old when I became what I am – it was a time of war and plague. The first blood I drank was from my best friend, the little girl who lived next door. I killed her and ran away, and they hung a man for both our murders. And maybe there was a moment when I could have chosen a different life, but I don't remember that. I just remember the thirst came over me all at once and I drank with a child's greed and a child's need and after that I was this – this monster. What else? I've never been drunk. I've never been in love. I have worked countless meaningless dead-end jobs. I have never died, never grown old. There is no word for what I am, but the one that comes closest is this one: vampire.'

Solomon gapes at me. 'You're nuts,' he says. 'I'm calling the police.'

'No, you're not,' I say. 'Look.'

He looks at me and slowly, effortlessly, I lift up my arm and turn it to vapour, starting from my fingertips and working up towards my shoulder. Solomon stares, silenced, his mouth falling open. I can see him trying to work out the trick, looking for an answer that makes sense. When he can't think of anything, he sits back down.

'Fuck,' he whispers, 'fuck.'

I smile. 'I am very old. I could live forever.'

Solomon stands up and starts pacing round and round the clearing. He pauses in front of Lucy's body and then starts pacing again. This is more like the Solomon I know and love. I can see that he's getting pumped up again.

'I want it,' he says. 'What you have, I want it. Give it to me.'

'No.'

'Fuck, man,' he says, his voice rising with excitement. 'You and me. Think about it. We could be magnificent. We could change the world.'

'No.'

'Why not, man?' he's grinning now. 'This is destiny. This what I asked the universe for. I asked it for eternal life and I thought it would be medicine and science and all that shit, but the universe brought me you. This changes everything. How does it work?' He rolls up his sleeve and offers his wrist to me. 'You drink from me and I rise from the dead, right? Lucy, too? Fuck, I don't care about her. I don't need her round my neck like a millstone.'

'That isn't how it works, anyway,' I say. 'Lucy's dead and she'll stay dead. Tell me why you think you deserve this.'

'Because I'm me.' He grins. 'Come on, Matt. I'm your friend. We can do this together. You're boring. I can make you interesting. We can go round the world over and over, we could be rock stars, millionaires. We'll be alive when they put men on Mars, when they cure cancer and the common cold, when the nuclear war comes. It'll be ace. Come on – you and me – together we can shake up the whole world. I need this. I deserve this. It's what I was born for. Me, Solomon Hollowman. I was made for this. Don't tell me you don't get lonely. I know you – you don't have any friends except me. You stay in your room at my mum's that's really just a big cupboard and you don't go anywhere or see anyone. Well, now you've got me. We can do this. The world is ours.'

I stare at him and for a moment I wonder what it would be like not to be alone in this but to have a companion. I shake my head and start to walk away, leaving Lucy there in the grass with the monster and the night-time trees watching over her. Solomon starts to follow me. He's still talking. The words roll out of him in an uncontrolled stream of thoughts and ideas. He is happy, I realise. His girlfriend is dead, and I am on my way to get all the things I need to dispose of her, and he is happy. He doesn't for one minute think that there will be any outcome to this except for the one he wants.

'No, Solomon,' I say, 'no, I am not going to give this to you. I am not lonely. I don't need friends. I don't need you.'

He pauses for a moment. I walk faster, joining the main path through the woods again. After a moment, I hear him behind me again.

'Not now, then,' he says, 'but another time. Another day. I asked the universe and the universe always delivers. Cosmic ordering for vampires.' He laughs, and his laughter follows me all the way out of the woods.

He takes me back to the underpass where his graffiti angel is still visible.

'The angel of Milton Keynes,' he says. 'They tried to paint over it, but it came through the paint. Now they keep it nice. Still looking good, isn't it?'

I examine the painting.

'Why are you showing me this again?'

'Because it's me, isn't it? Hollowman was my tag back then. I'm still the Hollowman. I'm a psychopath, man. I'm hollow. I got nothing inside. No feelings, no emotions, nothing. You and me, we're the same. We're both empty. This picture is me.'

I frown. 'It's an angel, Solomon.'

'Exactly.' He grins. 'I can be good, I can be bad. It's all the same because I haven't got any conscience, have I? So, I choose to be the angel. I choose to be a good man. I could just as easily choose to be the evil one, but instead I choose to trample evil and badness underfoot. This thing – this *gift* that you're going to give me – I'm going to use it to spread good. Like Superman.'

I suppress a smile. I am immeasurably fond of him. 'Solomon,'

I say, 'you are not a superhero. You are a middle-aged, twice divorced father of six. You are the director of a haulage company. You are loud and annoying, but you are ordinary.'

Solomon's smile falters for a moment, but then it's back, bigger and brighter than ever. I am coming to the conclusion that he's not entirely sane. 'I can be anything I want to be,' he says. 'I'm the Hollowman.'

I start to walk along the redway towards Linford Wood. He follows me.

'Where are you going? I don't want to go there.'

I ignore him. Trace our footsteps from all those years ago, along the main path and then along the overgrown dirt track to the clearing where the monster still lives. It's broad daylight; anyone could come upon us, but I don't care.

'Come on, man,' Solomon says, 'I don't want to be here. I don't like it here.'

I whirl round, grab his shoulders and for the first time I let him see my fangs, my monster face. For the first time, he is afraid of me.

'You say you're a psychopath,' I say, 'but you're not. You're just an idiot. You track down a hungry vampire, you follow him into the woods.'

He tries to wriggle free, but I am strong. All those years ago, Lucy's blood made me strong and I am still strong now.

'Are you going to kill me?' he asks. For the first time I can see the doubt in his eyes, the painful realisation that he is not going to get what he wants.

'Yes,' I say. I lower my mouth to his neck and I can almost taste his sticky red blood. The wind rustles the leaves, a bird sings higher and higher and the monster watches us with its stone eyes. I open my mouth to bite, to drink, but I don't.

I don't know why. Maybe I'm just not hungry enough. I push him away from me and turn away.

For once, he is silent. I can feel his presence behind me, his fear being replaced by bewilderment.

'Matt?' he says at last, his voice little more than a whisper. 'Are you all right?'

I'm not all right, that's the truth of it. I have never been all right. I am all wrong.

'Go,' I say, 'and if in forty years, when you are on your fifth or sixth wife and you have many more children, when you have grandchildren, great grandchildren and all the other things you have amassed – if you are still the Hollowman then, come to me and I will give it to you.'

I walk away from him, through the woods and onto the redway. Past his angel. I walk towards the city centre and the railway station where I'll catch a train back to London. After a while, I hear him behind me and he's laughing.

I sigh and let him catch up with me. He seizes my shoulders and kisses both of my cheeks.

'You didn't say no,' he says. 'You're going to give it to me. I'm not ready for it now – I can see that. But one day. You and me, man. We're going to light up the world. I asked the fucking universe and the universe isn't giving up on me. Cosmic ordering, man, cosmic ordering for vampires.'

I chuckle all the way to the station, smile to myself all the way back to London. I sit in my glass office and admire the view and laugh when I think of him. I wonder if one day he will turn up here again, grey and bent and insufferable in his old age. I hope so, I really, really do.

Just Another Day at the Office

The Lottery Lady

A few weeks after Edward Carter joined the lottery syndicate, I realised I was going to have to kill him.

I've been treasurer of the syndicate since 1994. Back in the day, we took it more seriously than we do now. Mark Walton was the secretary and Nigel Morton was the president and the three of us chose the numbers between us. Every member who was in the original syndicate had a copy of the numbers. There are twenty of us. People have come and gone since those early days; Mark went to work for another company and left the syndicate, and Nigel – bless him – had a heart attack and took early retirement. He died a few years ago. People's lives change – they have children, they change companies, they retire – and some stay in the syndicate and some don't. But some things have stayed the same – there are always twenty members, I buy the tickets and I always use the original numbers.

Edward Carter was the twenty-first member.

No one's that interested in the syndicate anymore and nobody cares who's in it and who's not, so I choose new members myself whenever someone leaves. I have a look round, decide who seems like someone I won't have to chase for subs every pay day. I wouldn't have chosen Ed Carter even if there had been a vacancy for him.

He was young, for one thing. He had heavy rimmed glasses and floppy hair like Jarvis Cocker back in the 1990s. He was nervous and jittery, and his eyes darted everywhere, as if his body couldn't keep pace with the speed of his thoughts. I had a bad feeling about him right from day one when David Slater introduced him to me. Sometimes, I can just read people like that. David's one of the old school – a bit slower than the younger underwriters but more meticulous, more cautious. Bankers have a bad name these days, but it wasn't men like David that gave them that bad name. I've always had a soft spot for David. He says what he thinks but I don't mind as long as he stays respectful. Over the years, I've done a bit of his admin and some of the younger girls tell me off for it, say he should be doing his own record keeping, but I like to do it. I do the same for some of the other oldies. It's how we used to work back in the day before it was all about targets and bonuses.

When David introduced Ed to me on his first day, I was on my lunch hour. I was sitting at my desk working my way through a sudoku and eating my sandwiches.

'This is Paula,' David said. 'She's one of our stalwarts. Paula this is Ed, our new large loans underwriter.'

I swallowed down a mouthful of cheese and pickle and Ed leaned over my desk with his hand extended. It was a big hand, cold when I shook it, and his wrists were bony.

'Hi,' he said, all teeth and grin.

'Paula's been here even longer than me,' David said. 'She knows everything.'

Ed grinned. 'I'll remember that.'

I didn't like him, but I really didn't think much about him after that. Youngsters like him don't last long here. They get a bit of experience and then move on to Barclays or HSBC or one of the other big ones. I've seen enough change over the years to know that nothing's constant and you can't hold onto anything. You can't get attached to a particular way of working, a favourite desk by the window, even people, because these things are beyond your control. Processes change, someone else higher up the rankings makes a claim for your sunny window desk, people get new jobs and move on.

We pay £9 into the syndicate each month and that covers the Saturday draw. We used to do the weekday draw too but when ticket prices went up, I decided we'd just do the Saturday one.

'Good decision,' Karen said when I bumped into her in the canteen. 'It's not like we ever win anything. We must be due a big win soon.'

'We had a couple of tenners a week ago,' I pointed out.

Karen laughed. 'A couple of tenners between twenty people. I keep thinking I should come out of the syndicate. They do a bonus ball draw thing in my new team and I could enter that. But you know what'll happen – the week I leave will be the week you finally get your big win.'

I smiled and nodded. 'Fingers crossed.'

£9 a month isn't much. An experienced underwriter takes home something between £30K and £40K a year, a mortgage sales advisor can double their basic salary in commission. Even for an administrator like me £9 isn't really very much.

I collect the subs on pay day and I have a spreadsheet to record who's paid and who's owing. I'm super-organised when it comes to the lottery. Once I've collected everyone's dues that's £180 a month, a nice round number. £189 just didn't feel right.

There's a bunch of underwriters and mortgage sales people who go to the Wetherspoons across the road every Friday. I get invited but I don't often go – only if someone's leaving or there's something to celebrate. The banter makes me uncomfortable and I'm not one of those mortgage sales girls with their loud laughs and flicky shiny hair. And besides, I like my sudoku and a quick browse on the internet at lunchtime. Sometimes, I'll pop out to M&S for a sandwich. I like my routines. I sound like I'm a hundred years old, but actually I'm forty-five, divorced with two adult children. It's just that I've worked at Winslows since I was sixteen. I feel like I'm a hundred sometimes.

So, soon Ed was going to the pub with David and the other underwriters. From an underwriting point of view David had taken him under his wing. I think there was a mentoring arrangement between them, one of Human Resources' many new initiatives. Socially, Ed had fallen into Liam Baker's clique. Liam's in the syndicate too. It took me a while to make up my mind about him; on the surface he's a typical sales person – loud and brash and always something witty to say – but I noticed that there was never anything cruel in the banter and when it got round about my ex and That Woman, he bought me some chocolate to cheer me up. Apart from on lottery pay day, though, I'm pretty much invisible to Liam. But either Liam or David must have mentioned the lottery to Ed because about two weeks after Ed started, I got an email from David saying that Ed had mentioned the syndicate, and could I add him and buy an extra line next Saturday.

Just like that. No please, no thank you. And I knew it wasn't a big deal. But still it rankled.

That afternoon, Ed came to my desk with his money. 'What are the numbers?' he asked.

'The numbers?'

'The lottery ticket numbers.'

'Oh,' I said. 'I don't have them here. I've got them written down at home. I do it all online and the system just remembers the numbers from one week to the next. I'll have to set it to do an extra line now.'

'Oh, I'm sorry,' Ed said. 'David said it was no trouble to add another line.'

'It's not,' I said.

'The syndicate's a waste of money,' Lucy Frost said from across the partition between our desks. 'They've never won anything more than a tenner.'

'We won £75 once,' I said.

'Wow, £75 between twenty people. What's that? Two pounds each?' Lucy laughed.

Lucy has bouncy corkscrew curls and wears fluffy pink sweaters. She giggles and gossips and is not in the syndicate.

'That's what's fascinating,' Ed said. 'Maybe it's not the syndicate that's unlucky. Maybe it's the numbers. If you give me the numbers, I can do some analysis and maybe find some luckier numbers. I love stuff like that. Probability and risk. I guess that's why I'm an underwriter.'

'Nerd city,' Lucy said, but she was smiling at him.

'I don't want to interfere or anything,' Ed said, 'but if you send me the numbers, I'll do a bit of analysis. Find us some luckier numbers.'

'OK,' I said. 'I'll try and remember and email them to you.'

Of course, I had no intention of doing that.

No one but me knows what the numbers are anymore. The syndicate trust me – no one else needs to know.

I know what you're thinking. You're thinking that one week we won the jackpot and I pocketed a cool £20 million without telling anyone else. But that's not it.

It's this. Every month I collect £180 (£189 for the few months Ed was in) from the twenty people in the syndicate and most months I just don't bother buying the tickets. In a year, I collect £2,160. It's not much – it doesn't even add up to what an underwriter takes home every month. It's not fraud on a grand scale, but it pays for a few careful treats – first-class tickets on the train, a weekend in London in a five-star hotel once a year, hardback books, a decent bottle of wine and a Radley handbag. Little things that no one notices.

Maybe another two weeks went past, and I didn't send Ed the numbers. I saw him every day because he'd taken to stopping at Lucy's desk for a chat and a flirt. Liam sat in the same pod so there was a lot of banter, a lot of loud forced laughter so that everyone could see how happy and witty and clever they were. I'd join in with the laughter sometimes, even make a little comment of my own now and again just to keep relationships good.

Ed had unsettled me though, and I bought the tickets two weeks running. The first week we won £20. The second week nothing at all.

The Monday after the second week I was coming back from the canteen after a late lunch with Karen. I'd gone to the Ladies near the service lift because it's quieter there than the main loos and when I came out, Ed was lurking in the corridor.

'Hi,' he said. 'Look at this.'

He pushed open the door to the stairwell.

'What am I supposed to be looking at?' I asked.

'There are stairs here. I've worked here for six weeks and I've never noticed these stairs before.'

I smiled politely. 'It's just the stairs.'

He peered up into the stairwell. 'What's up there?'

'Human Resources on the second floor and the executive suite at the top.'

'Come on, then,' he said.

'I've got work to do.'

'Live dangerously,' he said, 'I read somewhere that you should have a little adventure every day. This is my adventure for today and you can come with me.'

There was something infectious about his excitement. I even felt a little flattered that he'd chosen me to share this ridiculous mini-adventure.

'You never sent me the lottery numbers,' Ed remarked as we climbed up the stairs.

'Sorry,' I said. 'I forgot.'

'Well, there's no rush,' he said.

The stairs ended on a small landing outside the door that led to the executive suite. Instead of walls, there was just glass and, through the glass, we could see the whole town beneath us and around us. It made me catch my breath, seeing it all there – the office blocks and roads, the tops of trees, cars and people in the streets below, pigeons patrolling officiously on the rooftop opposite. I stood as close to the glass as I could, and I could see the walls of the building falling away beneath me, down to the branches of the plane trees growing up from the pavement.

'Can I ask you something?' Ed said.

'What?'

'It's a work thing. A process thing.'

I tore my eyes away from the glass. His hands fluttered nervously but his face was still.

'I don't like to ask the others too many questions. I don't want to seem stupid. I think I can ask you. You seem like you wouldn't laugh at someone for asking something really stupid.'

'Go ahead,' I said.

'I'm just trying to get my head round the whole process,' he said. 'So, what happens is, I agree to a mortgage and I put it into the system that I've agreed it, yes?'

'Yes.'

'The system sends a message to the admin team – your team – and you send out the mortgage paperwork to the customer. Yes?'

'Yes. We produce the mortgage offer and add in any special conditions. It's just a process. Nine times out of ten it's the same process.'

'OK,' Ed said, and I noticed that his hands were still now. He was looking at the view, but he didn't seem to be seeing it. 'What if there was no customer? What if there was just a mortgage but no customer?'

'I don't understand.'

Ed smiled. 'What if I, as the underwriter, agree to the bank paying, say £250K to begin with, to a non-existent customer. What happens then?'

'There are checks,' I said. 'There are checks and systems in place. The admin team make the checks before any money is released. There has to be a survey, we have to check the customer's identity. We check that there is a customer.'

'Uh-huh,' he said, 'and who makes those checks? Who pushes the button that transfers the money from us to the customers' bank account?'

'It doesn't go into a customer's bank account,' I said. 'It goes to a solicitor's account. The bank has a list of approved solicitors.'

Ed smiled. 'That's OK. I know one of those approved solicitors very well. Who pushes the button to release the money?'

'I do,' I said.

I can remember being called into Nigel's office before he left, being told that it had been agreed that I'd be given this responsibility. It was a promotion, of sorts, though there wasn't any extra money. I was so proud of myself for being entrusted with it. There were weeks of training, weeks when I wasn't allowed to release any money without it being counter-checked. But that was years ago. No one checks anymore.

'The bank trusts me,' I said.

Ed nodded. 'And the lottery syndicate trust you too, don't they?'

'I don't know what you're talking about,' I said. I tried to make myself look and feel bigger, but my heart was pounding and there was a weird rushing sound in my ears. I was suddenly very aware of the long drop below us to the pavement and how much bigger than me he was, how he wasn't so much skinny as lean, now that I was seeing him as he really was.

He turned away from me. 'Funny how one little fraud can lead to another great big fraud, isn't it?'

And then he was gone, loping down the stairs two at a time and I was left at the top. I stayed there for a long time – much longer than my lunch hour should have been – looking at the view and thinking.

I thought about it all afternoon as I input mortgage applications and answered customer queries, as I checked paperwork and pushed the return button on my keyboard to release the money to the solicitors' bank accounts. I typed out a couple of letters for David and agreed to let him transfer his calls to me because he was so busy. My mind wasn't on the work and when I saw Ed get up and head towards the vending machine, I got up and followed him.

He was standing at the machine feeding 2p coins into it.

'Hi,' I said.

'Hi,' he said. 'Can you believe they make you pay 20p for this dishwater? And you know what? 2p of that is for the plastic cup. A plastic cup that the recycling police make you give back at the end of the day.'

'Which solicitor?' I asked.

'What?'

'I want to know which solicitor is involved.'

'John Horwood from Greyson, Sharp and Parry. Why?'

I talked to John Horwood on the phone almost every day. He reminded me of David in some ways. I'd thought he was old school – dependable and honourable like David. Every telephone conversation we had, I'd ask him about his kids and he'd ask me about mine before we got down to whatever mortgage related business we had to discuss.

'OK,' I said. 'I want in.'

The machine started spitting out coffee. It looked thin and watery, unappetising. I always go for the hot chocolate myself.

'What do you mean?'

'If you want me to be involved, I want my share.'

He took his drink from the machine, sipped it and grimaced and then had a quick glance round to check no one was near. 'You get your share. You get to keep your little lottery scheme and the respect of your colleagues.'

'It's not enough.'

'Too bad.' He started back towards his desk.

I put some money in the machine so that it wouldn't look suspicious. I must have been on edge, because I pressed the wrong button and got something that claimed to be a cappuccino instead of my hot chocolate. I walked back to my desk and sat down. I processed a few more applications and I listened to Lucy's incessant chattering and all the time I was watching Ed and I knew he was watching me back. He'd already formulated his plan and I was just beginning to formulate mine.

I badgered Ed constantly over the rest of the week. Every time he got up to go to the coffee machine or the photocopier or the filing cabinets, I was there. I didn't even have to say anything – I was just there. I'd smile at him, ask how he was getting on and maybe mention that I'd spoken to John Horwood, the solicitor, about one of his cases. I could tell that I was getting to him. People started to notice, and I knew he didn't like that. Apart from anything else, it was embarrassing for a young lad like him to have someone like me pursuing him so obviously.

'D'you fancy him or something?' Lucy asked one morning. She had that sly glint in her eye that told me it wasn't that long ago she'd been the queen bee at her expensive girls' school.

'What?' I feigned innocence. 'Don't be ridiculous. He just brings out my motherly side. He looks like he needs someone to cook him a square meal.'

That's the thing, you see, people like Ed thrive on being invisible and non-threatening. They grow powerful because no one thinks about them the moment they've switched off their computer and left the office. The worst thing for someone like Ed is to be the source of gossip. Me? I found I quite liked it.

He gave in on Friday afternoon. It must have been after some considerable ribbing in Wetherspoons at lunchtime. We spoke at the photocopier as it churned out twenty copies of the new underwriting policy that I'd agreed to print out for the underwriting team.

'Following me again?' he said loudly.

'No, just keeping an eye on you.' I raised my voice too, but no one looked up from their work and I was pretty sure no one could hear us above the noise of the photocopier. The person sitting closest was a temp whose name I couldn't remember. She had earphones in and was nodding along to the music.

'OK,' he said. 'You're in. I spoke to John and we've agreed that you can have a fifth of what we make.'

'A fifth?' I asked. 'Why not a third?'

'Because all you do is press the button. Anyone could do it.' He cast his eyes round the office, coming to rest on the temp girl. She glanced up and he smiled at her. 'Anyone.'

I didn't tell him how long I had had to work here before they'd trusted me to release the funds, and I didn't tell him about all the training I had had to do. I just nodded.

'I want to discuss how it will work properly,' I said, 'not here in the office with everyone watching us. Let's meet somewhere outside of work.'

'OK.'

We agreed to meet at a nature reserve not far outside the town. There's a lake and reed beds and some kind of rare bird lives there. During the day it's busy with dog walkers and families and bird watchers, but at night there's no one there. I know this because it's where my ex-husband used to take That Woman. I followed him once, confronted them both, and there wasn't a single person there except the three of us. It was pitch black save for the headlights.

I finished copying and took the papers back to my desk to collate. My mind wasn't on the task. I was doing sums in my head, just to make sure. With Ed's scheme, I could make £50K on a mortgage fraud of £250K. That was more than ten times what I was making on the lottery and for a moment I did consider it. I pictured myself treating my children to a holiday in the Caribbean or getting a state-of-the-art kitchen fitted or a zippy little sports car, and I knew it was too much. People would notice. They'd talk, they'd speculate, and I'd have to leave. I like it here and I don't want to have to start again somewhere new. The treats I buy myself from the lottery money are small. No one notices. And it was never about the money anyway, not really.

I passed out the underwriting policy I'd spent all afternoon copying and collating and half of them didn't even look up from their computer screens, didn't even say thank you. Ironic, really, that the only one of them who seemed truly grateful was Ed.

I kept it simple: used a knife from my own kitchen, wore dark-coloured clothes and walked so that I wouldn't leave any distinguishable tyre tracks. It was a few miles' walk and I took the bridle way and then a footpath. It wasn't easy in the middle of the night, and I had to use the torch on my mobile phone. I wasn't scared, though; I was single minded. I had a job to do and I was doing it. And actually, doing the deed wasn't hard. I was worried that I'd falter when it came to the bit, but I didn't. I just went for it and it didn't take much, not really. I think he was surprised, but I didn't give him much time to think about it.

Afterwards, when he was on the ground, I stood over him and recited the numbers until I was sure he was dead, then I started walking home again, went back three times just to double check, and then walked all that way back home in the darkness. At home, I put the knife in the dishwasher and all my clothes, even my trainers, in the washing machine and set the dishwasher and washing machine going and went to bed. The next day, I made up a bag for the charity shop and put the clothes and trainers I'd worn in it along with some books and some other bits and bobs I didn't need anymore. I left it on the pavement outside the Oxfam shop that morning.

By Monday, it was all over the news. Everyone at work was devastated. Lucy cried, and David looked grey and even Liam didn't have anything to say. I sat at my desk and cried a little too and David bought me a proper cappuccino from the coffee shop, not a 20p-one from the machine. I was touched.

The police came and took away his computer, but no one looked twice at me. I went about my work: inputting applications, answering the phone, pressing the button to release the funds.

'Terrible,' John Horwood said when I spoke to him. 'Shocking. And the police are no further forward with their enquiries?'

'I don't know,' I said. I don't know if Ed had told him about me or if he just said that he'd found some silly faceless drone to do their dirty work for them. If John did know, I knew he had too much to lose from speaking up. Sometimes, after that, I'd put his calls straight through to voicemail or transfer them to the latest temp. Mostly, now we communicate via email, but that's the way of the modern office.

The lottery money was due three days ago and there are a couple of people who haven't paid up yet. Just yesterday, I saw Liam standing up to go to Wetherspoons with Lucy and some of the others and I thought I'd grab him for his subs before he left. As I was walking towards his desk, I heard Lucy say: 'Here she comes, the Lottery Lady. She needs to get a life. All she's got is the bloody lottery.' I took the money and pretended I didn't hear. None of them know. All they see when they look at me is poor, lonely dependable Paula, pandering after more senior staff, doing her sudokus and eating her sandwiches and collecting the lottery money regular as clockwork. They don't know that I've killed a man and it was easy and now, maybe, I have a taste for it.

So, we go on. I collect the lottery money and we never win anything. I've booked myself and my daughter into *The Ritz* for a night and afternoon tea. My treat, I told her, I've been saving up.

The Last Days of the Jesus Star Mission

After we sent Trevelyan spinning and whirling into the blackness of the galaxy, we said prayers and lit candles. We prayed that his body and the SOS message he carried with him would be preserved in the capsule and that if someone found him, they would treat him with respect – not as their next meal, not as another piece of space trash. We dared to believe that they'd come in ships that flickered with lights and were full of food and precious oxygen. We dared to hope that they would be good people, whoever they were, wherever they were from.

People who have never been on spaceships think that they're all hi-tech with lights and computer screens that plot the ship's journey through the stars. And maybe there are parts of the ship that are like that, but the first time I saw the navigation deck, I was disappointed. There *were* computer screens mapping our coordinates, tracing our pattern through the emptiness, but it was boring. We weren't about to hit an asteroid belt, there weren't unidentified alien objects ahead and no one was trying to blow us up with laser beams. We were just travelling slowly and steadily through nothingness. The crew were standing around drinking vending machine coffee. There were carpet tiles, like in the office back home, and some of them were stained. On Tom's desk there was a coffee ring beside a sheaf of papers and one of them was a list of holiday cottages in the Cotswolds. When I saw that, I thought I might just as well have stayed at home with my cat and my boring job.

After things started to go wrong, we stopped calling each other by our first names and we all became surnames and titles. So, George became Trevelyan and Tom became the Captain. It was how we showed we knew things were serious and this wasn't fun anymore. The only ones who stuck rigidly to their first names were the god-botherers. They were still Mary and Joy and Raymond. My papers say that I signed up to this trip with the Jesus Star Mission, but I lied on the application form when I said I was a devoted Christian.

That was just a way in and a way to get away from my old life, where nothing ever happened or changed. I'm good at lying. I have lied my way onto this ship in exactly the same way I've lied through job interviews and dates and all the other tedious things you have to endure. And even though we're free-falling in space and the food and the oxygen will run out soon, I'm glad I did this.

There was a woman who worked in the kitchens; they said she was a witch. No one knew much about her. She didn't sign up through the Jesus Star Mission, and she wasn't part of the regular crew. She was a contractor from an agency but none of the other contractors had worked with her before. Truth be told, she looked like a vampire from some cheesy film and she kept herself to herself and that, I think, was the only reason they picked on her. She didn't appear to care when they called her a witch and accused her of cursing the ship. She just looked right through them and carried on with whatever she was doing. They said the food she prepared tasted wrong and Mary, Joy and Raymond refused to eat it.

The first thing I did when things started to go wrong was get down on my knees before the altar. It wasn't about belief or faith; it was about fitting in. It was so that no one could question why, although I had joined up to be a missionary, I was never in chapel? I've worked in offices for years and being on a spaceship is similar. The same four rules apply:

1. Fit in
2. Keep your head down
3. Be useful
4. Be nice even when you want to throttle someone.

It doesn't matter where you are, but if you want to survive, you don't go around looking like a witch and not talking to anyone, because as soon as things start going wrong, they'll start looking for someone to blame and you'll be the first one they notice.

The mission was supposed to be seven months long: three months travelling out and then a month converting aliens and space monsters to the glory of Jesus. After that, we'd head home glowing with holy zeal and smug self-satisfaction. The sad truth is: there were no aliens. We saw no strange planets encircled with dust rings flourishing beneath the light from two suns like in the glossy brochures. We saw the occasional asteroid, the behemoths of other ships passing silently by, and a myriad of stars in the far distance. Some people made a big thing of looking back at the Earth, sighing and marvelling at how beautiful and blue it was. I didn't do that. I couldn't quite understand why it mattered. The only thing I missed was my cat.

Anyway, two months in, the engines stopped working. Just like that, they stopped. At first no one was bothered. The astronauts went out in their space suits to perform a spacewalk just like we'd seen in films. There was a lot of technical talk at that time, but I didn't pay much attention, although it was around then that I started making more of an effort to go to the chapel. I stopped hanging around with George and the other crew quite as much. I can't say that I knew things were going to get bad. I can only say that it seemed like a good idea to start taking precautions in case they did. Soon after that, everyone started praying, but I don't think any of us believed the prayers would make any difference.

Three weeks after the engines stopped, Raymond said he saw an angel. He said he'd seen a strange man on the observation deck wearing a business suit while he watched the stars.

'Doesn't Death always wear a suit in the movies?' Trevelyan asked.

Raymond had no sense of humour. His personality had been swallowed up by his faith. He didn't even bother to respond.

'When I asked him what he was doing,' Raymond said, 'the man turned round and looked at me with an expression of such love and pride, I could feel God all round me. I could feel his love shining on me.'

'Hallelujah,' Trevelyan muttered, and I had to look away, so they couldn't see I was smiling.

'Then, do you know what happened?' Raymond addressed us as if we were a children's story circle at the local library. 'The man stepped through the glass and out into space. I saw him walking through the stars, and you know what?'

Trevelyan rolled his eyes. 'You realised you shouldn't have eaten that cheese you found under the sofa?'

Raymond ignored him. 'He was walking through the stars all the way up to Heaven.'

I wouldn't say that Trevelyan and I were friends exactly, but he was the one person on the ship whose company didn't drive me insane.

Again, it's like being in an office: you're stuck day in and day out with people you have nothing in common with and who, nine times out of ten, are wrong about everything. But you have to make an effort to get on with them, to be civilised. You pretend you like them, you pretend to be supportive of them, and, all the while, you're secretly relishing every mistake they make, every pay rise they don't get. Their misfortunes are the only things that make you feel good about yourself and you hate feeling that way, but you don't do anything to change it. So, when someone like Trevelyan comes along who makes you laugh and shares your outlook on life, it's a bonus, a little something to get you out of bed in the morning.

It was horrible how he died. We knew we were all going to die, but we were expecting it to be slow. Trevelyan died in the canteen. He choked on one of the peppermints they give you at the end of a meal. We tried everything: first glasses of water, then slaps on the back, then the Heimlich manoeuvre, but nothing worked. He went purple and his eyes bulged. His death was fast and brutal, and it left us staring in horrified disbelief as the last life twitched out of him. I looked away and, for a moment, I thought I saw a man in a grey suit standing by the door, but when I looked again, no one was there.

They cast the girl from the kitchens out. Raymond wanted to burn her, but the Captain pointed out it was against health and safety rules, so instead they made her get in one of the capsules like the one they put Trevelyan in and they sent her out into the void. She was crying and protesting that she wasn't a witch. She said she was shy, and she said we made her nervous and anxious and that was why she didn't say much. She said she was sorry. Raymond said she was wicked. He'd found some books about hedge magic and paganism in her cabin. He said the day before he died, Trevelyan had been talking to her and she'd cursed him. The girl said they had been chatting about a band they both liked. They'd been talking about gigs. She cried when they cast her out. There was no food in the capsule and just enough oxygen for a couple of hours. She floated away. I watched until the capsule was nothing but another speck amongst all the other specks that could have been suns or planets or rescue ships. I felt bad for her, but she should have made more of an effort to fit in.

Today, the Captain said that we have perhaps one week's worth of oxygen left. If we're careful, we have enough food to last until the oxygen runs out. The food was supposed to run out first, but no one's been hungry. Everything tastes like dust. The Captain assures us that he and crew are still doing everything that they can and that of course there is still hope. Raymond says the same, but in Raymond's version it's God and his shining angels who will rescue us. These days, everyone has been seeing the strange man in the business suit. They've seen him in the mess hall, in the labs and floating outside the windows of the navigation deck. I don't know, but I think Trevelyan might have been right about him.

The Captain says he has some pills. There aren't enough for everyone, but he'll start giving them out on a first come first served basis to anyone who wants one. As soon as he said that, I went to him and asked for one. I keep it hidden in an envelope tucked between the pages of my Bible. Raymond and the others say that suicide is a sin. They say whatever happens, God loves us and though his ways are mysterious, they are always right.

I don't spend much time with anyone now. I've taken to lying on my bed watching a little video clip I took on my mobile phone before I left. It's of my cat; just a minute and a half of her pottering round in my flat. I lie on my bed and imagine the warm soft weight of her on my lap. I don't miss my family or my friends, I don't miss home, but I miss my cat. One of the crew says he knows how to connect my phone to a projector, so I can project the video on a loop onto the white wall opposite my bed. Tomorrow I'm going to ask him to do it and then I'm going to take my pill and lie down and watch my cat over and over again until I can't see her anymore. And when the man in the grey suit comes, I'll take his hand and step out into the stars and whatever else happens, it won't be boring anymore.

We Are Not Who We Think We Are

'We are not who we think we are,' Gemma said and then she started screaming because she'd seen something in the mirror in the Ladies. She was going to throw herself down the stairwell, but Ian and Jack held her back and managed to calm her down.

That was on Day Four when there were only five of us left and there wasn't much to eat, and the water had started to taste funny, though it was better if you went upstairs to the canteen on the fifth floor to get some, but no one wanted to go up there. No one wanted to go anywhere if the truth be told. We were camping out in a meeting room on the fourth floor, not looking out of the window at all the wrong things that were out there, and not looking at anything much inside either.

I don't know why I'm writing this except that it's something to do. The computers work, so I've been writing a lot of stuff. There's a comfort in the movement of my fingers over the keyboard, the little clicking noises the mouse makes and the way the words appear on the screen in front of me. I've been writing down some theories about what's happened, what I think might have happened, because I don't know what happened, but something did. And it's important to me, somehow, I think it's important to write it down. It's something to leave behind, isn't it, something for whatever else is here to find and read. And if it happens again – whatever happened – maybe someone will find this and have a head start.

This is Day Six, and there are still five of us, so that's good. But there are footsteps upstairs all the time now. We can hear them walking back and forth, back and forth. Shadows move on the other side of the glass walls of our meeting room and behind the double doors. Where we thought we were safe, the shadows move. The lift goes up and down, but it never stops on our floor. Thank God it never stops on the fourth floor. Not yet anyway.

Jack goes out from time to time, but even he's stopped going upstairs or downstairs. He wanders the long length of our floor opening desk drawers and rifling through their contents looking for anything to eat, anything we could use to defend ourselves. I don't like it when he goes out of sight behind the tall grey filing cabinets and I don't like it when he whistles — it grates on my nerves — but I like it even less when he stops.

The food's running out. There's plenty of food upstairs in the canteen and downstairs in the coffee bar. We should go — all of us together — and get some, bring it back down here where it's relatively safe. But no one wants to go upstairs where those footsteps walk back and forth, no one wants to step out of the open plan office and into the stairwell where there are always footsteps going up and footsteps going down.

There were twelve of us on Day One. There are five now.

Day One

It was just an ordinary Wednesday in November. Rain coming down in sheets outside, hot and fuggy inside. Traffic moving up and down on the street, people walking past on their way to the shops for Christmas shopping. I was drinking black coffee to stay awake and bored witless and wondering if I could get away with doing two hours overtime and claiming for three or even four. There were a group of us doing overtime that night, trying to earn a little bit extra for Christmas. It was just an ordinary day.

I don't know what happened. I don't know when it happened. The lights didn't flicker — the lights have remained remarkably stable throughout this — the ground didn't shake, alarms didn't sound. We were working away at our desks inputting data, approving loans, filing and archiving a backlog that should have been dealt with weeks ago.

A few people went home, and someone started talking about phoning for pizza or us all going to the pub afterwards for drinks and dinner, which I didn't want to do because that would eat into my overtime money.

Dale left and then came back saying that the main entrance was locked up and there was no one on the security desk, which was weird because there was supposed to be someone there all night because of the 24-hour call centre on the first floor. But no one paid much attention and Dale went off to leave by the side entrance. He was the first victim though we didn't realise it until maybe Day Three. We found his bag and his security pass outside the Gents on the ground floor, blood spattered on the wall.

About eight o'clock, I became aware that there was a tapping at the window. The vertical blinds were closed, and I opened them and saw… nothing. There should have been streetlights and traffic moving up and down the road towards the city centre but instead there was nothing but darkness outside. You could see a little way because of the light shining out from the office and all I could see was trees. The tapping noise was twigs against the window. I say there was nothing but trees, but that's not true. In the distance there was a light. It flickered and guttered in the darkness and something about it made me feel sick, made my heart start pounding, made me want to scream. Because even then, when we thought this was a mistake, an elaborate joke, I knew there was nothing good where that light was.

'What the fuck?' Jack said.

'I don't know.'

We weren't scared then. Or we weren't scared enough. We all of us stood at the office window where we must have been silhouetted against our garish fluorescent lights for the things out there to see. And see us they did.

That little white light started moving closer.

Here are some of the Day One theories:
o It was a practical joke
o It was some kind of weird elaborate team-building event
o The trees were a painting, or a huge advertising hoarding dropped down from the roof to cover the whole front of the building.

Josh, Tricia and Megan went downstairs to see if anyone in the call centre knew what was going on, and Ian and David went down to the main entrance where the security desk is. Ian and David were back before long.

'Everyone's gone home,' Ian said. 'Did we miss a message or something?'

Everyone agreed that they hadn't seen an email about the building closing early. Ian checked the managers' intranet page, and I looked through the news stories on the intranet home page and there was nothing. Upstairs, there was a creak, and something fell over.

'Someone's up there, anyway,' Ian said.

David was standing at the window peering out into the darkness.

'It's raining,' he said. 'I'm not in any hurry to go out there. Who's up for the pub when the doors open again?'

I went to stand beside him, and it was pretty obvious that the trees outside were not paintings. I tried to look sideways, up where the street should have been, to where the pub was supposed to be. It was curry night and my stomach rumbled.

'They can do gardens really quickly,' Ian said. 'You've seen what they put together for the Chelsea Flower Show. I took the missus in the spring. It's amazing what they can create in a few hours. Trees and sheds and all that. That's what's going on here.'

'Why would they do that here?' I asked.

'Fuck knows,' Ian said.

'You're the manager,' Jack said. 'You ought to know.'

There's history between Jack and Ian. They both applied for the team manager job and Ian got it. Jack's my best work friend, but he can be an asshole sometimes.

I went back to my desk. I figured if we were going to be stuck here, I might as well do some work and get paid for it. I had a half packet of custard creams in my drawer and I offered them round. We didn't know then, you see, that we should be saving food.

There were footsteps upstairs and the wind outside rose. Twigs tapped on the glass and I was glad when Ian closed the blind and shut them out. That little light had moved closer and stopped. I didn't like to think that there was someone out there in the dark who we couldn't see, but who was watching us.

'Josh and Trish and Meg have been gone for ages,' David said.

They didn't come back. We thought they'd got out. Maybe Trish and Meg did, but now it's Day Six, we know for sure that Josh didn't.

Day Two

We spent the night sleeping in our desk chairs or, in the case of Arvinder and Claire, under a desk at the far end of the office, where they could get up to in peace what everyone had been rumour-mongering about them for weeks.

It was a mark of how unafraid we were, that we slept at all and all of us at the same time with no one keeping watch. Jack and I took ourselves away from everyone else and camped out near the vending machine and sat up late just talking and talking. There were rumours about us too, but as neither of us was married to other people like Arvinder and Claire were, we weren't such a subject of gossip. Despite everything, it was good to spend that time with him, just the two of us. There's nothing going on between us, but no one makes me laugh like Jack does.

All night, we were aware of noises around us. Some of them were just the noises you'd expect in an office late at night. Lights ticking as they cool down, the vending machine humming and gurgling like a fridge, a phone ringing somewhere along the length of the office and the murmur of people talking and laughing. But there were other noises: the lift going up and down all night, footsteps on the floor above, tapping at the windows and a noise – I don't know what it was, but it sounded a bit like the dry papery noise you get when you peel an onion.

In the morning, I was aching from sleeping on the floor, but Jack was sleeping as soundly as you would at home, so I left him to it and wandered back along the office to where our desks were. The others were camped out under desks or in their chairs and some of them looked like they'd stayed up all night chatting. The vertical blinds were still drawn, but Ian was standing at them looking through the gap between the strips.

'What's out there?' I asked. I was hoping he was going to look at me as if I was crazy and pull the blinds apart to show me the road and the office blocks across the street, the cars and buses and people all going up and down.

'See for yourself,' he said and stood aside so that I could see what was outside. And what was outside was trees. Just trees and nothing more. They were winter trees with branches that stretched towards a grey sky. On the ground the grass was brown, scattered with broken branches and dead leaves.

I stared at it and felt my heart start to flutter too fast in my chest. I waited for Ian to say something, to explain, but he didn't say anything.

'There are things in the trees,' Gemma said behind us. 'Look.'

I couldn't see them at first, but after a moment I saw what she meant. There were scraps of cloth and bundles of what looked like twigs and bones and feathers hanging from the trees, swaying gently in the breeze.

'It's a bit Blair Witch,' I said.

'What's going on?' Gemma asked. 'It's a prank, isn't it? Some team-building crap?'

Ian was our manager, so if anyone was going to know what was going on, it was him. But he shook his head. 'I've no idea,' he said. 'I'm not in on it, whatever it is.'

Gemma linked her arm with mine – she's sweet like that, always touching people and hugging them. She's only eighteen, the youngest person on our team. She's only been temping here for a couple of weeks. I bet she regrets taking that assignment now.

'Do you want to go and raid the coffee shop for breakfast?' she asked me and then looked at Ian. 'That would be OK, wouldn't it?'

Ian waved a hand. 'Sure whatever. Get me a coffee. A flat white.'

I stared at him. 'You really think someone's going to be in the coffee shop to make your flat white? Surely, you don't think I know how to use the machine?'

Ian smiled, but he looked worried, which worried me. Ian is capable and sensible and a little bit humourless. He's the exact opposite of Jack, which is why Ian got the manager job and Jack didn't.

'Just do what you can,' he said.

The coffee shop is one floor up. We walked to the stairwell, past where Jack was still sound asleep near the vending machine and pushed open the double doors and stepped out into the stairwell. It was cold out there and it smelled strange. Not unpleasant exactly, but of leaves and wet soil. The lifts were next to the double doors and we could hear the lift coming up. It made a cheerful dinging noise when it stopped on our floor and then carried on up.

'Does the lift just go up and down all night?' Gemma asked.

'I don't know. I don't think it normally does, but I'm not usually here all night.'

The toilets are out on the landing, too, and Gemma pulled me into the Ladies and stood at the mirror staring critically at her reflection. She's a pretty girl with long brown hair and big brown eyes.

'So, you and Jack?' she asked. 'What's going on there?'

'Nothing,' I said. 'We're friends.'

'Really? Because I think he's kind of cute,' Gemma said. 'But I don't want to step on your toes.'

I was pretty sure that Gemma hadn't a hope with Jack. She's eighteen and he's almost thirty. I couldn't see it happening, so I was happy to give her my blessing to go ahead and have a try.

'Go for it,' I said, 'but I think he's a bit old for you.'

'I like older men,' Gemma said. 'What do you think is going on here? Do you think it's team-building?'

'I don't know. Maybe.'

The truth was that I had a bad feeling about the whole thing, but I didn't know what to say. I didn't have an answer that made any kind of sense. Something about the silence in the huge building was creeping me out, but the silence was better than the noises that shouldn't be there. There was a ticking sound from one of the lights, as if a moth was fluttering against it, but there was no moth.

'Come on,' I said, 'let's go and find breakfast.'

The coffee shop was empty. Usually, it's full of people queuing for their morning cappuccino or latte, buying blueberry muffins and croissants, lining up to make overpriced toast in the toaster. Today it was empty and silent. We got a tray and filled it with cellophane wrapped muffins and flapjacks and Gemma piled on several bags of crisps and a couple of apples from the bowl that I'd never seen anyone buy from.

'All the major food groups,' she said cheerfully.

I wandered over to the coffee machine and stared at it, wondering how to go about using it. In the shiny chrome of the machine, I could see my reflection distorted out of shape, and close behind it, something moved. I whirled round and there was no one there. Gemma was standing a distance away rearranging the contents of her tray so that she could fit more on it. But I'd seen... I shook my head. It was impossible what I'd seen, but it had looked like the shape of a man – not bent and distorted by the curves of the machine as it should have been, but standing straight and tall, a man with a broad-brimmed hat and a long coat, pale hair blowing about a face that was all shadows.

'Come on,' I said. 'Let's go back.'

'What about Ian's coffee?' Gemma asked.

'He can get it himself or get it from the vending machine downstairs.'

'OK,' Gemma said, 'Do you think we should check and see if anyone is up here? What's on this floor anyway?'

The thing about working in really big offices is that you only go to the places you need to go to, and you only really know your immediate team and a few people whose jobs touch yours. So, I knew my way to my desk, the coffee shop and the canteen, to a few meeting rooms and the post room and that was about it. I didn't know what was on the other floors or what the people who worked there did.

'I don't know,' I said. I wanted to get back to the others. I couldn't get the image of the man standing behind my reflection out of my head. I didn't know if he was still there. 'I think it's marketing or human resources, or something.'

Gemma set her tray down on one of the tables. 'I'm going to check in case there's someone up here.'

I followed her back out onto the landing and then through the double doors and into another open plan office laid out much like ours downstairs. We could see the whole length of the office and there was no one there. I heard that papery peeling noise again and shivered.

'There's no one here,' I said. 'Come on.'

'OK,' Gemma said, 'but we should check out the top floor. It's probably higher than the treetops. We'll be able to see what's out there.'

'OK,' I said, 'but later.'

There were footsteps on the stairs below us. Slow and steady and moving upwards. I knew it wasn't anyone or anything good, but Gemma didn't seem to feel it.

'Hey,' she called, 'who's there?'

The footsteps stopped but no one answered. The smell of leaves and wet soil had intensified, and the air felt cold, all of a sudden. Gemma leaned over the bannister and stared down. I went over to join her. There was nothing to see. Just the white bannister and the puce carpet, the long fall down to the basement below. Then, almost too fast to see, a glimpse of a booted foot, the ragged hem of a grey coat, and the footsteps started coming up.

'Fuck,' Gemma said.

I grabbed her arm and pulled her back. I started dragging her back towards the coffee shop, but then I remembered that shape reflected behind me and I knew it wasn't safe. In the open plan office, there was the papery noise, so that wasn't safe either. That's how I've managed to make it to Day Six – by knowing right from the beginning that it wasn't safe. I stopped, my heart racing, and those footsteps kept on coming up and up and I knew – just knew – that if we saw whatever was coming up, if it saw us, we were dead.

I pulled Gemma into the Ladies' toilets and pushed her into a cubicle with me, locking the door behind us. Pipes gurgled, and Gemma's breathing was as loud and fast as I knew mine was. The fluorescent light began to tick just like the one downstairs had ticked. Even though it should have been impossible to hear through the door, we heard those footsteps coming steadily up the stairs, reaching the landing and walking across it, pausing outside the door of the Ladies. Gemma made a little whimpering noise and I put my hand over her mouth, though I knew that whatever was outside knew we were in here. A silence stretched on and in the cubicle next to where we were hiding, there was a dry papery sound, like an onion peeling.

Neither of us moved. We could feel the presence outside on the landing. Something rotten, something utterly malevolent. I thought of those bundles strung up in the trees outside and knew that whoever was out there on the landing was the one who had put them there for whatever twisted reasons.

Something scratched at the wall of the cubicle next to ours and Gemma clung to me so hard I knew I'd have bruises, but finally whatever was outside on the landing moved away. I felt the presence recede and heard the sound of footsteps moving slowly and steadily up the stairs.

I didn't think – I should have thought, it's only luck that The Walking Man or the Peeler didn't get us there and then – but panic had got a hold and I grabbed Gemma's arm and pulled her with me, out of the toilets and down the stairs as fast as we could to the first floor where the others were.

And that's when the screaming started.

These are some of the Day Two theories:
- o It was a team-building event to see how we would cope as a team whilst persons unknown tried (and eventually succeeded) in terrifying us
- o We had been hypnotised into believing the office was in the middle of a forest full of murderers
- o It was nightmare
- o It was bad trip
- o It was all going to be all right, somehow.

It was Anisha screaming. She and David had found Arvinder and Claire under the desk where they'd crept away to conduct their not-so-secret affair the night before. Anisha wouldn't stop screaming and David just crawled under his desk and wouldn't speak or come out. Jack wouldn't let me look, but everyone was talking about it, so I didn't need to look to know what had happened. They were dead, and it was horrible. I didn't need to know anything else.

Later, Jack stood beside me at the window with his arm round my shoulder, holding me just a little too tight.

'Those aren't bits of cloth in the trees, are they?' he said, 'They're skin.'

'The bodies weren't real,' Ian said. 'They're fake. Made of rubber and latex. It's amazing what they can do with special effects nowadays.'

'Do you think so?' Gemma asked eagerly.

Ian nodded. 'It's the only possible explanation.'

'I can think of another,' David said from under the desk where he was still hiding. It was almost comical, because David was properly fat, and it couldn't have been easy for him to get under there. I wondered if part of the reason he wasn't coming out was because he was stuck. I stored the thought up to mention it to Jack when we were alone. I thought it would make him laugh.

'What's that?' Jack asked.

'We're trapped in a building with a homicidal axe-wielding maniac,' David said.

'It wasn't an axe that got them, that's for sure,' Jack said, and Anisha started whimpering.

'Shut up,' Ian said, 'both of you. I'll tell you what this is. It's a game. It's some sort of team-building or strategy type thing and the last person standing gets the prize. Like paintball, only grizzlier.'

'Grizzly?' Jack said. 'You're calling this grizzly? This is sick and twisted.'

Ian forced a smile onto his face. 'It's fun,' he said. 'Just remember, Arvinder and Claire are in the pub, probably with Josh and Trish and Meg, having a laugh about all this.'

Jack shook his head and made a noise of contempt. 'You're insane if you believe that. How do you explain the trees outside? And bodies made of latex and rubber don't smell like meat.'

It's true that Ian and Jack were never going to agree with one another, but I agreed with Jack on this one. I really, really wanted to believe Ian, but I don't think even Ian believed what he was saying.

We talked about trying to go outside. Ian and David had already checked the exits and they were all locked, but we could have tried breaking the windows and getting out, but for the moment at least, it felt safer to stay in the building. Jack and Gemma had gone up to the top floor and looked out to see that the trees stretched away into the distance. There wasn't anything beyond them.

I opted to stay on the first floor with David, while the others decided to have a look round the rest of the building and at the very least get Gemma's tray of goodies from the coffee shop. It was agreed that David shouldn't be on his own. I foraged around in the desk drawers closest to where he was hiding and managed to amass quite a hoard of chocolate bars, crisps, teabags and cup a soup. I sat down with David and shared a bar of chocolate with him. I could hear the footsteps of the others on the floor above and the trees tapping against the windows but other than that, it felt safe. I was so bored, I even contemplated doing some work.

'Do you think—' David began and then the phone on Ian's desk started ringing.

We stared at each other and I stood up.

'Don't,' David said, 'don't answer it.

But there was still a chance, wasn't there, that Ian might be right, and this was some kind of game, some sort of team-building exercise. The phone call might give us a clue, instructions, and who better to call than our team leader?

I picked up the receiver. 'Hello?'

'Hello,' a woman's voice said, 'can I speak to Ian? Is he there?'

'He's away from his desk,' I said and felt like an idiot because despite everything, I was still using office speak.

'This is Charlotte,' the voice said, 'his wife. Can you ask him to call me when he's got a minute? It's not urgent.'

Relief surged through me. I couldn't speak for a moment, I was so happy to hear her voice.

'He's here,' I said, 'he's just gone upstairs. Something weird's going on. We're stuck in the office and— can you call the police, please? Tell them, tell them—'

Something rustled behind me, and I whirled round, dropping the receiver and saw...

Something of red and black and grey. Two eyes, one higher than the other, the red slash of a mouth. Pale hair and too many teeth, too many fingers. A broad-brimmed hat and a coat of rags, boots splashed with red and a stench of leaves and soil and rot. Far away I could hear the tinny sound of Ian's wife from the phone receiver, but there was also the sound of the trees tapping on the glass, and

I swear they sounded more like claws, they were closer than before and one of those bundles banged and bumped on the glass. Something made a dry rustling peeling sound and David started whimpering under the desk.

'The Walking Man,' he sobbed, 'the Walking Man. Please God. Please God...'

The man's mouth opened, but no noise came out. One long arm reached out and closed on my arm, squeezing and I screamed and wrenched myself free.

'Take him!' I screamed. 'Take him not me. He's fat and juicy and...'

I ran, just ran the length of the office and out into the stairwell and down the stairs to where the exit door was shut and wouldn't open and the trees outside were closer than they should have been. I hammered on the glass nevertheless and it wouldn't yield, so I crept into the cleaner's cupboard under the stairs and hid there amongst the buckets and mops and industrial-sized bottles of detergent until Jack came and found me.

'It's all right,' he said. 'It's all right.'

I crawled into his arms and he held me, neither of us speaking until we heard the dry onion skin sound just round the corner and we fled up the stairs to the first floor where the others were.

David was still under the desk. He was alive, but he wasn't talking anymore, just rocking himself back and forwards and muttering to himself. The others were cobbling together a meal of soup and instant noodles and blueberry muffins, washing it down with some wine they'd found in a shopping bag under someone's desk. No one was hungry, but we ate anyway.

'I'm sorry,' I told David, but he didn't react to me.

'Sorry for what?' Gemma asked.

'Nothing,' I said.

And that, pretty much, was Day Two.

Day Three

I woke in Jack's arms, under his desk and lay listening to the soft sounds of the others sleeping. I was pleased that we hadn't lost anyone during the night. We had intended all to take turns keeping watch, but David was no good for anything and Anisha and I weren't much better. Then Jack and Ian went into a battle of machismo and ended up doing the watch themselves, vying to stay awake the longest. Ian must have won, because Jack was asleep beside me.

We had breakfast and tried again to figure out what was happening. Ian was especially encouraged by his wife's phone call.

'Contestants always get one phone call,' he said.

'Contestants?' Jack said

Ian nodded. 'Don't you ever watch reality TV? There's always the episode with the phone calls home. Obviously, something went wrong, and it should have been me who picked up the call.'

'You're crazy,' Jack said. 'We're not on TV. None of us signed up for this. And don't you think, if this was a TV show, or a team-building event, or an elaborate hypnosis event or whatever, that someone would have seen the state David's in and intervened?'

'Not just David,' Anisha said, 'I'm not far behind him.' She looked up at the ceiling as if she was looking for the hidden cameras. 'I've had enough. I want to go home.'

Almost on cue, we heard the lift give a jaunty little ping and this time it stopped long enough for us to hear the sliding sound of the doors opening.

'Fuck,' Gemma whispered. 'Did someone get out of the lift?'

'No,' I said. 'The Walking Man takes the stairs and the Peeler... I think the Peeler just materialises.'

'The Walking Man?' Ian laughed nervously, 'the Peeler? Is that what we're calling them?'

I was feeling brave. Maybe it was surviving another night, maybe it was the normality of hearing everyone bickering, maybe it was because the Walking Man had almost got me yesterday, and I'd got away. Whatever it was, I was feeling braver. I stood up and pulled Jack to his feet.

'Let's go and see what fresh hell the lift has brought us,' I said.

I really wish I hadn't made that joke now, because what the lift had brought us, what had been going up and down and up and down for the last two days, was our colleague, Joshua. The Peeler had got him.

We decided to leave the first floor and set up camp on the fourth after that. On the first floor there were the bodies of Arvinder and Claire not far away and none of us wanted to be there when they

161

started to smell even worse. Ian said that the fourth floor was where Payroll and IT were based. There was a big meeting room with glass walls that we decided was the best place to camp out. It was also about as far away from the lift as you could get. Jack, Anisha and I stayed up there while Gemma and Ian went back to the first floor to try and get David to come out from under his desk. We decided to try and make the meeting room homely, so we walked round the fourth floor, raiding people's desks for nice things, for normal things. We filled the meeting room with toy trolls, wind-up toys, stress balls, pot plants and children's drawings and photographs. Lots of photographs – all those smiling strangers and pets – the wedding photographs, the children in school uniforms, the photographs of mountains and trees that didn't look like an army of the walking dead. We made up stories about the people in the photographs to pass the time. Ian and Gemma came back and said that David wouldn't move, and I asked if that was because he was scared or because he was too fat, and we all laughed. God forgive us, but we laughed.

The day passed, and we saw nothing. We heard things; the inevitable footsteps and rustlings and tappings, the dry peeling sound, but we dared to believe that by being together, by surrounding ourselves with these things that other people cared about, by telling stories and laughing, we had somehow made ourselves safe.

At around six o'clock when we were thinking about finding something to eat, we decided to go back downstairs and try again to get David to leave his desk and come and join us. We would make him, we decided, through bullying and cajoling, we would make him come up and join us.

But when we got downstairs, he was gone. It didn't take long to find him. He was on the floor at the bottom of the stairwell, blood spreading out from the back of his head, his eyes staring back up the stairwell, where something walked steadily and relentlessly up and down. We didn't know if he jumped or if something drove him to fall. We didn't talk about it, there wasn't much to say.

When we got back to our sanctuary on the fourth floor something had been in the meeting room and had turned all the smiling family photographs face down on the table.

And that was Day Three.

Day Four

I know what's happened. We've fallen between, into a crack, a fissure, between realities. We are somewhere that doesn't exist. We don't exist. We're not who we think we are.

Gemma saw it first in the mirror in the Ladies' toilets on the fourth floor where she'd gone to try and wash her hair in the sink with hand soap. She came out screaming: *We're not who we think we are.* She said it over and over again and it made no sense until I found the courage to go in and look in the mirror myself. I was expecting to see my own reflection replaced by the Walking Man, to catch a glimpse of what the Peeler was and what it was that it was peeling that was most certainly not an onion. I was ready for that.

Instead, I saw...

...an open plan office and people working at their computers. I saw someone walk past with a paper cup of coffee from the coffee shop. I saw Joshua standing up while he talked to someone on the phone, and Meg and Tricia were giggling behind the filing cabinets. I saw Dale tapping away at his computer and David shambling up the office with an armful of files, saw Claire at the photocopier and Arvinder watching her from his desk. I saw Ian sitting at his desk at the window, staring at a screen full of spreadsheets, his brow furrowed with concentration. Anisha was gathering up papers and her notebook and hurrying to a meeting, and Gemma was surreptitiously texting someone, with her phone hidden on her lap under her desk. And I saw myself and Jack, leaning together and laughing about something. I could see my overtime claim form was half completed on my computer monitor.

And outside, clouds were scudding across a November sky and there were no trees except those planted by the city council. Cars and buses and people passed by on their way to the shopping centre. Everything was as it should have been, and we were all there. We were all safe.

The others came and stood beside me at the mirror. We watched and waited for something horrible to happen, but it didn't. There was no Peeler over there, no Walking Man. It was safe over there. It was real over there, and the people there were real, were us. And we were – I don't know who we are, I don't know what crack we have fallen into, but that was Day Four, and Day Five, and now it's Day Six, on and on until the end.

It's the End of the World...

A Tale from the End of the World

For a long time, the sea had been crossed only by screaming gulls, but one evening as the sun began to set, a small boat with a white sail drifted between the rows of needle-sharp rocks and into the shadow of the towering cliffs. A man stood tall like a prophet in the prow of the vessel, his silvery blond hair billowing about him. He gazed up at the crumbling remains of a vast city perched on the cliffs above the sea and smiled to himself as he drifted with the wind, but his smile was cold. His eyes were as grim as the choppy waters but when the city had passed and he spied an old crooked house not far down the coast, he laughed out loud. This must be the place.

It seemed as if Cliff House stood at the end of the world. This was the way of things now: cities, towns and villages had become isolated, as separate from one another as countries and continents. The city along the coast from Cliff House was ancient but had almost been forgotten by the outside world. The houses and tower blocks had crumbled to ruins and the sea was slowly eating up the cliffs from one side while the wilderness crept steadily in from the other: a riot of carnivorous trees, nettles and briars with thorns like blades that grew over streets and parks and roads alike until all that was left habitable was a few houses clustered round the harbour where the last of the city folk struggled to make a living out of what was left. One day, the rusting fairground had fallen away from the land and now it reared monstrously from the waves. Over time, seaweed, salt crystals and barnacles had covered it, turning the sad, corroding merry-go-round horses into magnificent, magical sea creatures, steeds for Neptune and the mermaids.

The Blood family had lived in Cliff House for centuries. They were a family who, at one time, had been notorious for their wealth, their history of insanity and the twins they produced in every generation – always a boy and a girl. Although the world was falling apart around them, Gabrielle and Raphael Blood continued to live in the manner to which they believed their ancestors had become accustomed even though this meant foraging for treasures in their attics and back rooms to sell to the peddlers and other traders who sometimes passed by.

Cliff House was surrounded by hedges of rose briars, nettles and barbed wire. The twins had two black hounds with red eyes and slavering tongues to protect them from outsiders. Their garden was wild and crooked, falling into the sea. It was a madness of mutating topiaries, statues, wind-chimes and curious little summerhouses and gazebos. It was an uncanny place, filled with eyes. Raphael kept cats and they yowled and prowled around the gardens claiming one-armed, decapitated statues for their own, waging war on the rooster and his ever-growing harem of scrawny wives that the twins kept for eggs and Sunday dinners when they could be bothered to catch and cook them.

Through the maze of statues and topiary there were great banks of lupins and daffodils; hogweeds and briars; shimmering masses of pink willow herb; ponds choked with lilies and acid green algae and herb gardens neatly planted with sage, marjoram, valerian and all the other herbs Gabrielle thought would give her sweet dreams. The garden was strange, all askew. Even the kitchen gardens which the twins kept from necessity other than any love of horticulture, were full of the strange shapes of vegetables gone feral: giant pumpkins collapsing in on themselves, cabbages gone to seed and potatoes to fat poisonous berries.

The house was the same; a perfect reflection of the twins' combined personalities: a place of dark, ugly furniture; strange empty rooms; cobwebs; twisted candelabras; burnt-down candles; antique lace and moth-eaten, velvet draperies. There were wasps' nests in the back rooms, and the cellars were filled with vintage wines and rats. The twins let flowers die in cracked vases until the petals turned papery. They kept butterflies in glass jars and painted contorted, dark portraits of one another. They played peculiar, old stringed instruments and left archaic books face down on the floor with their spines bent and broken. The long corridors stretched away into perfect, inky darkness. Sometimes there were only two candles burning in the whole house.

The twins lived mainly in the attics. Here, they thrived with the darkness and dust. They breathed it in and then out onto everything they touched.

Gabrielle and Raphael Blood were named after angels and they looked almost like their namesakes; golden-haired, blue-eyed and perfectly turned out in dark silks, velvet and lace. They went everywhere together, as if bound by some invisible chain. Gabrielle was the leader and she led her quieter, perhaps more dangerous brother through numerous indiscretions and escapades.

They had no family. As far as they knew, they were the last of their line and now it seemed the Blood family was destined to be swept forever from the world. And yet, in the dusty old books of family history, they had read of ancestral relatives who had left Cliff House in order to marry into other families, to fight in the War or to make their fortune in some far-off city. Someone, somewhere, might have survived to generate a second great dynasty of Bloods. Often, the twins talked of finding these people, but they were afraid to leave Cliff House. Beyond it, lay the wilderness where the roads were overgrown. Only outlaws and peddlers travelled there and even they were becoming fewer and fewer. The forests and wild animals were creeping back. The land was wild and the people who haunted it were wilder still. The world was full of wicked folk; victims of the War. It was better to stay at Cliff House where it was safe. And besides, the twins were secretly proud of the tragedy of being the last of their kind and happy to ponder the mystery of whatever it was in their blood that meant they had been blessed with their good looks and good health in such a savage world.

They lived alone, save for Hump, their hunchbacked servant. Sometimes peddlers rested overnight on their wanderings between settlements, but they never stayed for longer than one night. The twins made other people uncomfortable. Raphael watched them unblinkingly, while Gabrielle asked incessant questions, demanding to know if the peddlers had ever met anyone else by the name of Blood, anyone else who might be part of their family. Sometimes it was as if the twins could talk to one another without opening their mouths.

When they left and reached safety, the peddlers were always eager to tell stories of the twins. They believed talking of it cleansed them of whatever poisons the Bloods had breathed onto them. The twins were so beautiful and golden. They shone while everyone else in the world was bowed down by poverty and sickness, old and grey before their time, like tarnished silverware growing dusty at the back of a cupboard. It was unnatural. When Gabrielle wore Raphael's clothes, the peddlers could not tell which twin was which.

One man had stayed in Cliff House on the night the twins' parents had died. He had heard movements in the night and barred his door. In the morning, he had found the twins standing dry-eyed over the bodies of their parents, dead in their ornate bed with blood splashed on the walls in elaborate swirls and patterns. The twins told him a wild animal must have gotten in, they couldn't imagine what else could have happened and they had smiled identical smiles that chilled his blood. It was their birthday, they said. They were sixteen now and had grown up. They would be quite all right on their own. His dreams were still haunted by the way they had stood in the doorway to watch him leave, shovels in their hands to bury their dead.

So, although the twins knew almost nothing of the world beyond, there were those who knew about them.

And one morning, watching from their garden, the twins saw a boat drifting slowly across the sea towards them. A single figure stood tall in the prow. The twins observed in silence. They believed in sea gods and mermaids and in lost kingdoms beneath the waves. They believed there really was a better place.

Raphael chewed his bottom lip in suspicion, while Gabrielle leapt up and called to the black hounds. She leashed them and set off for the cliff path. Raphael followed her, cats twining round his legs.

The twins made their way down the treacherous, crumbling cliff path to the shore below. The hounds growled threateningly, hackles raised, while Gabrielle waved a hand at the little boat. The man at the prow began to guide the vessel towards them.

Gabrielle turned to her brother. 'What if...?' she breathed, but did not finish her sentence, for the man was walking through the water towards them. He was tall and slender, his face cold in its eerie perfection. He was like a man made from stone, ice and metal. Different from them, different from the poverty-stricken, plague-ridden people who lived in the remains of the city and the wind-lashed villages up and down the coastline.

Gabrielle drew back, uncertain. No one spoke, but the twins were suddenly aware of the cobwebs in their hair and the worn patches on the elbows and knees of their clothes.

'Good morning,' the man called.

The twins did not answer. They gazed at the man and smiled

nervously as he advanced towards them. His feet did not seem to touch the ground and the sea water had hardly wet his robes. He looked at the twins and then at their home on the clifftop. 'I wonder if you might help me,' he said.

The twins exchanged glances. They waited for the man to continue.

'I am looking for Cliff House and the Blood twins.'

'Who wants to know?' Raphael asked.

'I know of their family,' the man said.

'We have no family,' Gabrielle replied.

The man smiled benevolently. 'No, you are wrong. In a city in the south, there are other Bloods.'

The twins' hearts leapt and then fell again. This made everything different and they were not sure how they felt about it. The stranger was as tall and fair as they were. His beauty was eerie and familiar; he looked almost like them. They were frightened, yet fascinated too, filled with a strange kind of yearning.

'Are you one of us?' Gabrielle asked.

The man smiled. He held out his hand to her and she shook it tentatively. 'My name is Nathaniel,' he said. 'Nathaniel Blood.'

'We are Gabrielle and Raphael Blood,' Gabrielle said.

The man smiled broadly. He swept his arms wide as if to embrace them. 'I have been searching for you everywhere and by coincidence the sea has cast me up here.'

The twins did not believe in coincidences. Everything had a purpose. Otherwise it meant that the chaos and anarchy in the world beyond the city was all for nothing. It meant that there was no reason for the demise of the human race, no reason for its ever having existed. The twins believed in magic, and, to them, Nathaniel looked like a magician.

They took him up to the house. As they walked, Gabrielle talked nervously, her voice high and excited, the hounds fighting on their leashes before her. Raphael walked a little behind, stooping now and then to pick up seashells or pieces of coloured glass worn to opacity by the sea. Throughout the day, they showed Nathaniel around the gardens and the house.

They sent their servant, Hump, to the city with a purse full of old coins, to trade for fish for supper. As the sun began to set, they had him cook them a meal of fried fish, potatoes and herbs from the garden, which they spread out on the scratched oak table in the dining room. Gabrielle lit candles all around the room, and Raphael threw the windows open wide to blow the dust and cobwebs away.

The twins drank too much of the sweet berry wine they had made themselves the autumn before. They laughed at secret jokes they could not share with Nathaniel, for all that they tried. Cats jumped up on the table and spilled the wine. Giant ghost moths fluttered and crackled in the candle flames. The twins shone with a vibrant, frenetic beauty: Gabrielle flushed and eager to please; Raphael brooding and quiet, his eyes bright with unasked questions.

Nathaniel studied the twins intently and did not drink the wine. His eyes remained cold throughout the meal, and he flinched when the cats touched him.

As the candle stubs flickered in the late evening breeze, Gabrielle said, 'What do you do in the city, Nathaniel? Are you an artist, a musician, an architect?'

Nathaniel shook his head. 'I am a scholar,' he said. 'I study people like you.'

'Like us?' Gabrielle asked, frowning.

'Yes,' Nathaniel said. 'Those special people who are not twisted or deformed. Where I come from babies are born deformed; two-headed, Siamese twins or hermaphrodites. Many have diseases we cannot cure and die.' He leaned towards them a little. 'In my city, we need people like you. We have to find out what makes you different.'

The twins smiled at the thought of two-headed hermaphrodites. Raphael reached across the table for the wine and refilled the glasses. The wine spilled over the rim of Nathaniel's glass and splashed on the table.

'But our family have always been mad,' Raphael said.

Gabrielle looked dreamy. 'Yes. Our mother believed...'

Nathaniel interrupted her quickly. 'If my people could be beautiful once more, I assure you, they would risk insanity.'

'You *are* beautiful,' Gabrielle said. She bit into an apple. 'Beautiful and clever. We like you.'

Nathaniel laughed his strange, cold laugh. 'Unfortunately, I wasn't always like this.'

Gabrielle put her head on one side. 'What do you mean?'

Nathaniel paused for a moment, then said, 'My bones have been straightened and reinforced with metal. I have had surgery...'

The twins looked at one another. Raphael fiddled with the

buttons on his shirt and Gabrielle opened her mouth to speak, then closed it swiftly as if to silence an importunate question. Both twins shifted in their seats, smiled nervously at one another and at Nathaniel. He seemed false now, a lie superimposed upon some deformed, hunched reality.

'*You* don't need us, then,' Raphael said at last.

'The process isn't always successful,' Nathaniel said in a measured voice. 'Nine times out of ten it results in death. I was lucky to survive. Also, the operations are very expensive, as well as painful and time-consuming. Sometimes they go horribly wrong and produce only monstrosities. That is why we need people like you.'

'But what would you do to us?' Gabrielle asked.

'Simply run some tests on you, isolate the things that make you different.' Nathaniel smiled. 'It wouldn't take long...'

'Are *all* our family like you?' Gabrielle enquired. 'Metal and plastic not flesh and blood?'

Nathaniel nodded. 'They need you. You will be their salvation.'

Gabrielle smiled. It appeared she liked the idea of that.

'Tell us about them,' Raphael said.

Nathaniel began to talk. Raphael's eyes were fixed upon him, considering everything he said, half smiling.

Gabrielle listened, entranced. 'We must write all this down in the family history books,' she said. 'We mustn't drink much more tonight, or we'll forget what you've told us.'

Nathaniel nodded. 'Very wise.' He paused. 'You will come with me, won't you? You would be with your family. We could look after you and make sure that you want for nothing. After all, what is there here for you, at the end of the world?'

The twins were indecisive. The thought of the city and all its splendours frightened them and yet Nathaniel himself was fascinating. They wanted to be with him, hear his stories. He knew, and had experienced, so many things. He was a magician who might save them, just as they might save him. If only he would remain here, at Cliff House. If only he did not want them to go away with him.

'We must carry on the bloodline,' Gabrielle said.

'Exactly,' Nathaniel agreed smoothly. 'And if you don't like the city, you can always come back here.'

'Good,' Gabrielle said. She rose from the table, took Nathaniel's hand and led him out onto the terrace, Raphael following. Both twins still carried glasses of sticky wine. Outside, the purple half-light was perfumed with jasmine, roses and the scent of the sea. Nightbirds called among the trees. The garden was beautiful and dangerous, full of dark corners and weird shadows.

The twins and Nathaniel sat down at a weathered table beneath a tangle of briars. Gabrielle lit candles.

'Once I've shown you the city,' Nathaniel said, 'you'll realise you live like savages here.'

The twins nodded vaguely and became silent in the narcotic air. Moths danced around the candle flames and settled on the rims of the wine glasses. Their feet stuck in the sugary liquid, their wings flapping frantically until the cats swiped them into oblivion with delicate, clawed paws. Gabrielle set out a game of solitaire on the table and Raphael lay in the hammock nearby, swinging gently and reading the family history books. From time to time, he looked up from his page and glanced sidelong at Nathaniel.

When the twins' wine glasses were empty, Nathaniel produced a package from inside his robes. He unwrapped it and showed the twins its contents. In a bed of crisp tissue paper lay a stick of something. It looked almost like cinnamon, but with a silvery-grey, crumbly appearance.

'This is silvertree,' Nathaniel said. 'It comes from the bark of a special tree. Let me share its secret with you. Bring me some clear water.'

Raphael went inside and returned with a brimming jug, from which he poured out three measures into the empty glasses. Nathaniel broke the silvertree into three and dropped a piece into each glass. The substance began to dissolve, turning the water to a silvery iridescence.

'What is it?' Gabrielle asked. 'What does it do?'

'It is good,' Nathaniel answered. 'It shows you things.'

'What things?' Raphael asked suspiciously.

'Things you wouldn't otherwise know,' Nathaniel smiled. 'Perhaps you'll see my city.' He offered them two of the glasses. 'Try it.'

He watched the twins swill the liquid round in their glasses to dissolve the last pieces of silvertree. Colours drifted through the mixture and faded away. The twins sniffed it, exchanged glances and frowned.

Then Raphael put down his glass. 'No,' he said politely. 'No, thank you.'

But Gabrielle was less cautious. She hoped the silvertree would show her Nathaniel's city and her family. She wanted to know these things. Without further pause, she lifted the glass to her lips and drank deeply. 'Go on,' she said to her brother. 'Do this with me.'

Raphael waited until he saw Nathaniel drain his own glass, then drank from his.

After a while, the twins climbed into the hammock together. With eyes half-closed, they began to float, to drift away.

Nathaniel, who had taken silvertree so many times it barely affected him, watched them curiously. He thought of Adam and Eve in their magical garden, founding the human race. He stared at Gabrielle's slender, elegant body, the curve of her breasts against dusty velvet, the tiny waist encased in silk. Dreaming, the twins seemed to have become a single person; a graceful tangle of arms, legs and blond hair. Their eyes were heavy-lidded, their whispers slurred, as they shared identical visions. Nathaniel considered them objectively. In the house, he had watched them laugh at their hunchbacked servant and entice hapless insects into the candle flames. He had recoiled from the strange paintings they had daubed. The crooked house itself, with its fecund, untended gardens and startling statues, chilled his blood. And yet, he was intrigued by the twins' twisted innocence and amoral purity. In their innocence, they would become his tools.

Tomorrow, he would begin his journey home. Now, he was sure the twins would come with him, that he had enchanted them.

Nathaniel leaned back in his chair and sighed in contentment. It was almost too good to be true. He had scarcely believed it when travellers had told him of the twins and their cruel perfection. He had heard about their desire to find others of their strange tribe, and if they believed he was of their blood, they would surely go with him. Nathaniel had already made plans.

The boy would be killed, his body frozen and studied to isolate the precious genes that made the twins unique. Eventually, his pure blood would be decanted to fill the twisted veins of an eager recipient. His clear eyes would look out from a new skull. His skin...

The girl they would breed with. And if his people were lucky, the twins might never discover that there were no other Bloods in the city. As far as Nathaniel knew, there were no other Bloods in the world.

The twins were dreaming. They saw wide city streets filled with dancing people who applauded as they passed. Their feet did not touch the ground and their bodies were caressed by the finest silk. Around them, the city was white and silver in the sunlight. There were palaces and mansions, shady parks, galleries and museums. The twins knew that, in this place, they could have anything they desired. The people clamoured to touch them, as if a brief contact could heal them. The twins felt loved, needed and – almost – happy.

But there was something dark behind them. They heard it slithering and creeping, the hiss of its darting forked tongue. It whispered their names, tried to entice them and it reached out to crush them in its coils. *Beware the serpent: it tells lies. Lies. It is not what it seems.*

The next morning, Nathaniel awoke in his seat on the lawn. The twins were having breakfast: camomile tea in a cracked, willow-patterned teapot; sizzling hermaphroditic fish from the poisoned sea and thick slices of home-baked bread. There were cats on the table again; flies buzzed around the food. The twins were wearing thin, white, summery clothes that looked alien on them. Nathaniel thought they must be trying to emulate his appearance. Gabrielle fed the hounds and chattered amiably, while Raphael read an ancient, paper-backed book, its title obscured by coffee and wine stains. He cut an apple into neat slices with a long-bladed knife.

'It was nice in the city,' Gabrielle said. 'We liked it, but how do we know it's really like that?'

'Trust me,' Nathaniel said.

'In the dream, everyone loved us,' Gabrielle said.

Raphael did not look up from his book. 'Not everyone.'

'No.' Gabrielle frowned. 'Something was after us. Something dark. It wanted to hurt us.' She smiled. 'We should stay here, and you should stay with us. It would be better.'

'I don't belong here, and neither do you,' Nathaniel said. 'You'll see that when you come to the city. What about meeting your family?'

'We're not sure we want to meet them now,' Gabrielle said. 'We don't need them really. We have each other.'

'You are being silly. There's nothing to be frightened of.'

Raphael glanced at Nathaniel. 'We are not going to your city. The thing that followed us in the dream: it was you.'

Nathaniel laughed. 'Me?'

'You're not part of our family at all,' Raphael said. 'Are you?' He laid down his book and stood up. 'You're a scientist.' He spat out the words as if they poisoned him.

'I told you: I'm a scholar.'

'Who studies people,' Raphael said. 'Yes... we know. We understand.'

Nathaniel spoke calmly. 'I think you're overreacting. You're alone too much.'

'Then stay here with us,' Gabrielle said. 'We want you to. We really do, but we can't go to the city with you. The visions showed us that.'

Nathaniel looked around at the twisted house and the sprawl of the gardens, nothing beyond them but the desolation of the ruined city and the wilderness. He realised how alone he was in this place. When he looked back at the twins, it seemed as if an unspoken communication passed between them. Raphael's hand closed around the knife on the table top.

'Please, don't go,' Gabrielle said. 'Say that you'll stay.'

'We're not going to your city,' Raphael said. 'And neither are you.'

'If we let you go, you'll tell others about us,' Gabrielle said.

'They'll come for us...'

'Strap us to tables...'

'Stick needles in us...'

'Scientists...'

'Serpents...'

Gabrielle smiled. 'So, you'll have to stay with us.'

Nathaniel's laughter was uneasy now. 'You're being ridiculous! You can't stay here for ever, and I certainly can't!'

'Please, don't say that.' Gabrielle's voice was almost a whisper, pleading, desperate. 'Say that you'll stay.'

Nathaniel shook his head. 'I'm sorry. I have to go back.'

Again, a silent message passed between the twins. Nathaniel began to feel uneasy. He did not like the way the twins stared at him, with their identical blue eyes; unreadable expressions on their flawless, heart-shaped faces. The hounds and the cats were looking

177

at him, even the dead moths on the table. Only then did Nathaniel realise the twins did not mean to let him leave.

The knife glittered coldly in Raphael's hand; the hounds growled softly at Gabrielle's feet.

Nathaniel rose slowly from his seat. He had to tear himself away from the cage of eyes.

He ran down through the labyrinth of the gardens towards the cliff path, and his boat. He heard the hounds behind them, drawing closer. As the great animals brought him down in the unmown grass, he thought of the twins and their family living here for centuries, isolated and inbred, growing strange and different until they were not like anyone else, until they were barely human at all. Sharp teeth ripped his clothes, his flesh. Fetid breath filled his nostrils.

Then he heard the twins call off the hounds and opened his eyes to see them standing over him. But before he could stand up, and attempt to escape, Raphael lunged forward. Nathaniel felt the long-bladed knife slide between his ribs, slicing through flesh and into his heart. He felt the warm spill of blood that flowed out of him, down onto the grass. Raphael leaned forward to pull the knife out, and Nathaniel saw bright splashes of fresh blood spatter the boy's white summer clothes. The twins looked down at him fearfully, as if they thought he might rear up and bite them. There was blood in their hair, on their faces. As he floated, drifted in his last agony, Nathaniel was glad he would not live to see the twins and their descendants inherit this dying world.

The twins gazed down at Nathaniel's body, and then at the blood on their white, summer clothes. They put their fingers in the blood and licked them. Nathaniel tasted of chemicals and sterile air. They did not like his taste.

'But we did like *him*,' Gabrielle said sadly.

Raphael wiped the knife clean on his shirt. 'Yes,' he said. 'We did.'

'Do you think his bones really *are* plastic?' Gabrielle asked.

'We could open him up and see,' Raphael suggested, but neither twin was really that interested.

That evening, Gabrielle and Raphael walked along the beach with the cats and dogs and even a couple of the chickens following them.

They wore white and in the evening light, they looked like angels.

'What if Adam and Eve hadn't eaten the apple?' Raphael mused. 'What if they had killed the serpent instead?'

Gabrielle nodded, then smiled. 'What if they never ever left the garden?'

He May Grow Roots

There was once a mad scientist. He lived a vast sprawling house in the ruined suburbs of what had once been a great city by the sea. Ivy and briars grew over his house and beneath the twisted roots and snatching branches, the scientist carried out unspeakable experiments on anyone or anything that crossed his path. He seldom ventured out and the few people who remained in the city, clustered in their little hovels on the sea front, were afraid of him. They shrank away from him, as they shrank away from all people who they did not know or understand. He alarmed them in countless ways; he was a fat man in a town where there was never enough to eat; his hair and beard were wild and flaming red and his voice was loud and full of smug arrogance. He jeered at them and their pitiful lives, scraping out an existence at the edge of the world. They watched him in the distance with his butterfly nets, catching birds and fish for his experiments. After he passed through their streets, they would find cats and dogs missing, and once a baby was gone from its cradle, though there was never any proof that he took it.

The scientist knew about medicines and he knew how to make electricity. He could have helped his neighbours to become as strong and healthy as he was, but he had no interest in the well-being of anyone but himself, and no interest in anything except his experiments and how far his knowledge and his strange machinery would take him.

That's how he came to create a monster

There was a library of ancient books in his big, old house. The books were written in the golden years before the city began its long slow decline into ruin, before the Wilderness took over the rest of the world and began to creep into the edges of the city, where there were once long streets of white houses and gardens and parks. These were books of a type that no one wanted to read anymore: books about anatomy, books about tampering with nature, books about magic and harnessing the power of the earth. There were old storybooks about vampires and werewolves; about the walking

181

dead and flesh-eating trees; and about monsters stitched together from bits and pieces of dead people. They were stories to turn the blood to ice on winter nights, when the wind was tearing around the shells of houses and angry waves crashed against the shore.

But these books were sustenance to the scientist and from science, magic and miracle and his own unlimited imagination, the scientist created his monster and named him after the first of all men: Adam.

Years passed, and the scientist and his monster continued to live in the house in the suburbs until a plague swept in from the Wilderness and took the mad scientist and most of the townspeople. After that, the survivors saw Adam from time to time. At first, they only saw him in the distance, wandering by the shoreline towards Cliff House where the Blood twins lived their reclusive lives, but gradually he crept closer to them and they saw that he was not a hideous creature stitched together from the old body parts that sometimes swept up on the shore. Instead, he was beautiful and fey with long slender limbs and ebony hair and eyes that shone like jewels. There was so little that was beautiful in their lives that they fell in love with him. They fell so much in love with him that they stopped noticing there was something insectile in his stare, that the veins that twisted beneath his perfect white skin were green and not blue. They didn't notice that he never ate, that he grew wilted and more fragile in the winter, while in the summer months he burned and shone with passion and excitement.

The townspeople watched him stand on the broken pier and stretch out his arms to catch the last of the evening sunlight and they loved him and yearned for him and forgot how he had come into being.

Adam still lived in the sprawling house in the suburbs, where no one else dared to go for fear of the giant insects and flesh-eating trees that the scientist had boasted of creating. He read the scientist's books and learned about medicine, alchemy and chemistry. The words spun and twisted through his brain and they wove a strange and confusing spell in his head. When he slept, words he did not understand patterned his dreams.

He wrote formulae on the sand with pieces of driftwood and the townspeople gathered round trying to understand, although only Raphael Blood, making a sudden and unexpected visit to the city, seemed to have any comprehension. Adam drew designs for machines to harness the power of the waves and the wind. He sketched automobiles, clocks and flying machines and more and more when he looked up from his sketches, he would find one or the other of the Blood twins watching him. The twins pretended indifference, but their cold impassive eyes would suddenly flash with amusement or widen with surprise or pleasure, as they too fell reluctantly in love with Adam.

So, it was inevitable that Adam soon became Gabrielle Blood's lover. She liked him because he was different from every other person she had met. He talked about things she and her brother did not understand and although she was not interested, she liked the way his eyes shone and seemed to lighten and darken as he talked. And Raphael did not seem to mind. He lay in his hammock, gently rocking, and pretending to read his coffee-stained novels while Adam talked, and from time to time he would smile at Adam and ask a question that showed that, just for once, he was interested in something beyond his books and his sister and their small insular lives.

Adam's touch was like silk; soft and gentle but strong. He stroked Gabrielle's skin and wrapped her in his long limbs. When they made love, Gabrielle felt as if he was lifting her up and away from their home to some higher better place she might never return from.

He always woke before her in the mornings. When she came downstairs, she would often find him in their kitchen drinking sugared water and talking to Raphael in his soft lilting voice, while Raphael pretended detachment. Or else they would be playing cards or cutting back the straggling topiary in the kitchen garden. Adam chatted to them about things they didn't care about – the latest town gossip he had heard from the fish wives: who had had a baby, who was sleeping with who, who had died, who had dared to brave the Wilderness and wasn't expected back. He teased them and laughed at them, calling them both staid and eccentric, mimicking their mannerisms until sometimes they laughed too.

Although none of them had been anywhere else, Adam widened their lives. When he left them and went back to his house in the suburbs, they wandered around their house and gardens like lost souls, saying nothing, their yearning almost tangible until they fell into one another's arms on Gabrielle's wide bed that smelled of flowers and leaves and Adam.

One day, they walked along the treacherous cliff path towards the harbour where the streets where the people still lived were. Adam occupied the privileged position between the twins. He was as bright as a butterfly compared to their dark dustiness. His clothes were patched with bright scraps of cloth and he wore a wide-brimmed hat to protect his eyes from the sun. The twins wore black, moss green and grey and one of their huge inbred dogs padded by Gabrielle's side.

Halfway to the harbour, Adam stopped suddenly. He frowned and put his hand to his chest.

'What is it?' Gabrielle asked.

'Something strange,' Adam said.

Gabrielle put her hand over his heart. She could feel its curious double beat inside him, somehow faster and more fragile than a human heart.

'Do you hurt?' Raphael asked.

'No,' Adam said, 'not exactly. Something just changed inside me. I felt something move and change.'

'Perhaps you should go home and lie down,' Gabrielle said. 'We'll look after you.'

Adam shook his head. 'No, I'm all right. Come on.'

They strolled to the few shops that still remained on the sea front. The twins turned their noses up at the fishmonger's and the greengrocer's. They stared distastefully at the filthy misshapen children playing in the streets and smirked at the dwarf child who lived above the only remaining tavern.

Adam took them to the *Curiosity Shop* where he chatted with the shopkeeper, while Raphael fingered ancient encyclopaedias and Gabrielle filled her pockets with necklaces made from seashells and sea glass, which she had no intention of paying for. Adam chatted idly about the weather, the scarcity of edible fish in the sea and the dreadful possibility that the plague might come back.

He stopped talking suddenly, stepped backwards and then swayed and fell against a display of tarnished silverware. The display crashed to the floor around him as he lay there writhing and clutching at his chest. The twins were at his side in a moment.

'What is it?' Gabrielle asked.

But Adam could not reply for there were changes happening in his strange, mysterious body and it felt as if someone was thrusting red hot needles thought his heart and filling his veins with fire.

Raphael picked him up from the floor, his legs buckling beneath the weight, even though Adam did not weigh as much as he ought to have. He lacked substance, as if he were made from gossamer and glass.

The twins took Adam back to their house and laid him on a bed in one of their myriad spare bedrooms. They stared helplessly as he writhed and moaned on the brocade counterpane. His eyes were full of blood and when he blinked, great ruby tears slid down his face. Gabrielle loosened his clothing and cried out when she saw that beneath his skin, bones and veins were moving, pushing out against the skin that enclosed them.

Raphael opened the heavy velvet curtains at the window and sunlight flooded the room. Adam moaned and closed his eyes. Blood spilled down his face from beneath his closed lids.

'Keep him warm,' Raphael said. 'Make him comfortable. I'm going to his house.'

'Why?' Gabrielle asked.

'To see if the scientist left anything to tell us why this is happening.'

He took an old double-barrelled shotgun and two of the black dogs on a double leash and strode out through the city, beyond the harbour and the safe areas to where the streets were blocked by fallen rubble and vines snaked in and out of the empty windows of the ruined shells of high-rise buildings, where cars rusted to dust and things scuttled unseen in an undergrowth of nettles, hogweed and banks of fireweed. Out in the far suburbs, the remains of the plague victims had withered and desiccated in the sunlight and ivy grew over dry bones and cold stone alike and crept unstoppably through cracks and in windows and doorways. Giant banks of rhododendrons drooped lacy lilac blooms to attract enormous butterflies and bees. Trees reared up – rowans, birches and ancient crooked oaks – and from their branches vines dropped down to caress Raphael's shoulders and snatch at his hair. There were faces in the bark, grimacing and screaming. The ruined shapes of the city that had once been there were stark and bleak amongst the straggling vegetation.

Raphael followed a narrow path through the vegetation, the very path that Adam must have followed every day when he went to and from his house. The dogs strained on their leash, angry and ready to kill or maim anything that crossed their path. Raphael was almost as tense, his finger on the trigger of the gun, ready.

At last, he came to the mad scientist's house. Ragged scarecrows flapped in the herb garden, and honey bees buzzed about a row of hives. The air smelled sweet, like lilac, lavender and roses, and Raphael felt his heart surge with affection, an emotion that was almost unknown to him. He wished that he and Gabrielle had not been afraid of the suburbs and had come here before.

The house was unlocked and, despite the ivy and briars that had colonised it, it was full of light and fresh air. Raphael walked through each room, opening and closing doors, until he found the laboratory. Here, he stood gazing at glass bottles and tubes, crucibles, test tubes, burners, bottles and pots of strange smelling things, all labelled in Adam's neat hand.

He went to the bookshelf and stared at rows and rows of books, took down a few and read through their contents pages before letting them drop to the floor, not understanding them.

He carried on through the house, opening drawers and raking through their contents for anything that might tell him how the mad scientist had created his beautiful monster. He found Adam's bed neatly made with a scarf of Gabrielle's wound round the bedpost. On the window ledge was a huge bowl of white roses buzzing with bees. The petals were edged with a scarlet that bled into the white petals in places, staining them like blood.

In the drawer by the bed, he found a slim leather-bound volume. Inside, there were words and figures scrawled in a hand too untidy to be Adam's. There were pages of diagrams and chemical formulae. Raphael sat on the edge of the bed to read, his forehead creasing with concentration as he struggled to understand. He knew that on these pages the mad scientist had scrawled the secrets of Adam's creation. He read of experiments with birds and animals strapped to tables, with babies stolen from their cradles. He read of cultures grown in test tubes, of substances lovingly mixed and heated and bonded with other substances. And he read of plants, always roses, torn apart and crushed and divided into ever more miniscule parts and then combined with other parts; human parts, butterfly parts, feathers and fur and bone. The house seemed to echo with the agonised cries of dying animals and birds and the frenzied clicking of insects: ghosts and roses and something that was not yet finished.

And there on the last page in a script more legible than the rest, the words: *He may yet grow roots and burst into bloom.*

Raphael thought of how Adam's veins were moving beneath his skin like vines. He sat still and thought about what he had read and was sure that even if he did not understand the method of the experiment, he understood its final outcome.

His eyes fell on the roses on the window ledge and he snatched them from their bowl, ignoring the thorns that tore his fingers and the blood that ran over his knuckles and inside his sleeves. He shoved the notebook into his pocket, picked up the shotgun, whistled for the dogs and set out for home again.

Adam lay on the bed and did not move. He felt strange. There was no pain now but a curious floating sensation. He felt as if he had become a colour, a scent, something ephemeral that was caught up and blown about on the sea wind. His skin was turning thin and papery and his veins and arteries were shifting and rearranging and breaking through his skin, glistening and green like new shoots in the spring sunlight. His heart felt enormous and precious as it swelled and pushed against the fragile bones of his chest. He felt it push and push until his breast bone and rib cage shattered and gave way, but still it did not hurt. The sun shining through the open window caressed his body and the wind that blew from the sea felt wonderful, full of salt and flower-scent. The particles that made up the air flowed into his body giving him all the nourishment he thought he would ever need.

Through a film of blood, he saw Gabrielle in the doorway, her mouth forming a scream before she stumbled backwards in horror. He tried to speak, to tell her it was all right, that everything was going to be exactly as it was supposed to be.

'Don't go upstairs,' Gabrielle told Raphael when he returned. 'Don't look.'

Raphael unleashed the dogs and laid the rifle down on the tabletop beside the roses he had brought back. He handed Gabrielle the notebook and she flicked through it without really looking at it.

'I brought him some flowers,' Raphael said.

'Don't go up there. Don't look.'

Raphael ignored her and walked through the house and upstairs to the bedroom where Adam lay. Gabrielle followed him reluctantly. The whole top floor of the house smelled of roses. Gabrielle stood in the doorway and watched as Raphael walked over to the bed. He seemed unsurprised at what he saw there. The notebook must have told him what to expect.

'It's beautiful,' he said at last.

'It's horrible,' Gabrielle said, thinking of nights wrapped up in Adam's arms.

It looked as if someone had wrapped Adam in vines and leaves, but these stems and leaves were part of him, growing from the veins that had burst through his skin. In the centre of it all where his heart should have been was a huge rosebud. The bedspread was stained with greenish blood that smelled of perfume. Adam looked at Raphael and smiled slightly.

'I brought you some flowers,' Raphael said.

'I can smell them,' Adam said. 'Roses from my garden. My favourites.'

Beyond in the garden, the million buzzing, flickering insects sensed the sweet pollen-filled centres of the roses and hummed closer to the open window. A bumblebee flew in and buried itself in the white petals and a butterfly flittered in and settled on one of Adam's hands.

'That's nice,' Adam murmured. 'Tiny little feet.'

'Does it hurt?' Raphael asked.

'Not now. Feels strange. I wish I could share this with you. The sun feels so good.'

That night the twins lay one on either side of Adam. Giant ghost moths settled on Adam's body and the air buzzed with insects. The night scents of jasmine and stock could barely compete with the scent of roses. The twins held hands over Adam's body. They knew they smelled musty and dusty and cobwebby, the way moths ought to smell.

Adam did not sleep. He lay gazing at the ceiling and waiting for the first rays of the sun to fall through the window. The twins slept on, but Adam felt his leaves begin to unfurl and reach towards the dawn sky. The giant rosebud that had once been his heart began to swell.

Later the twins carried Adam outside into their garden. They laid him in the hammock and trails of stems and vivid green leaves fell over the sides. Adam closed his eyes and drank up the sunshine. He drifted off into ecstatic sun-washed dreams.

Townspeople began to come to Cliff House with gifts for Adam. The twins were reluctant to let them into their enchanted garden, but they liked the gifts they brought and knew they would keep them for themselves when all this was over – wildflowers, seashells, driftwood and wind-chimes made from washed up things. Everyone who visited tried to talk to Adam, but he was too far away, drifting somewhere strange and beautiful and scented with roses, lilac and sea winds. His rosebud heart swelled in the sunlight.

Raphael brought more white roses from the house in the suburbs. The twins arranged them around the hammock in buckets, vases and old cracked jam jars. They watched the insects flutter around them as they pored over the scientist's notebook, identical frowns creasing their foreheads as they tried to understand.

On the seventh day, the bud opened. White petals rimmed with scarlet unfurled and turned towards the sun, opening wider and wider to show the pollen-laden centre to the bees, wasps, butterflies and moths and to any other insect that came calling. Adam moaned and stirred with delight as the petals opened. The scent of the giant bloom drifted as far as the ruined city and made the people forget their struggles for a few hours, made them want nothing more than to lie on the warm sand, soaking up the sun and never move again.

The bees were heavy with golden pollen, the butterflies drunk on nectar, and as the day wore on the petals began to turn brown and crisp at the edges. The twins rushed to fetch water, but the petals began to drop off, one by one, and the leaves began to shrivel and curl.

'Go to bed,' Adam whispered as the sun began to dip. 'Don't worry about me.'

That night the twins lay in one another's arms. Gabrielle wept into Raphael's shoulder and he held her, staring at the ceiling and biting his lip until sleep took them both.

In the morning, the dawn light woke them early and they hurried out into the garden in their flimsy nightclothes. The hammock was empty save for few tattered leaves and rose petals, save for a large brown seed.

'No,' Gabrielle whispered. 'No.'

Raphael said nothing. He picked up the seed and held it, and it was warm and full of life. He put it to his lips and kissed it and for a moment his eyes, usually so detached and dispassionate, flashed with tears.

They planted the seed among the untidy topiary trees and they made a scarecrow with angry glass eyes and clanking wind-chimes attached to its outstretched arms to keep away all their jealous cats and dogs. They watched as year after year a rosebush grew from tiny shoots to a tall elegant bush with scented white blossoms edged with scarlet. They waited and waited to see what would happen for they knew that one day, perhaps many, many years from now, Adam or someone very like him would stand in their doorway, dropping soil and leaves on the step, laughing and teasing them and making them feel alive.

Ginevra Flowerdew

Ginevra Flowerdew's family lived in a rusty, cold caravan on the waterfront opposite the village tavern. There were six children, and Ginevra was the youngest. She was a tall, pale child with huge colourless eyes and hair an unfortunate shade between blond and brown that was almost grey. Her veins showed through her thin, pale skin, the very tracery of her being. She wore no shoes and all her clothes were hand-me-downs from her older brothers and sisters. They hung off her body like rags. She did not have the strength or the inclination to work the land for whichever of the farmers were hiring, as her brothers and sisters did as soon as they were old enough. The fish wives would not have her near them for she unsettled them with her unblinking eyes and her silence. Some of the villagers whispered that she was a witch-child who would sour the milk and bring ill luck.

Ginevra wandered the few streets of the village and sometimes ventured out onto the moor towards the mansion house where the lord of the village lived. Often, she wandered along the shore collecting sea shells that she piled into cairns and threaded into necklaces. She watched the sea sweeping endlessly up the shore and eating into the cliffs and she combed through the strange things it cast up with every tide. She left feathers, wildflowers and scraps of cloth behind, in exchange for what she took.

Some days, she walked down the shore to the rocks at the very edge of the sea and sang to the waves, and to the seals and dolphins who hid amongst them. She knew there was a kingdom under the waves – a beautiful, coral city populated with mermaids, seal people, water horses and sleek, silver-skinned dolphin men. She dreamt of gardens full of waving seaweed and coral of impossible colours and shapes. She sang to the city in the sea and hoped her singing would draw up a silver-blue dolphin man. Her voice was high and tuneless, like weathervanes squealing in a storm. The wind carried it away, carried it far across the waves and under the water.

One morning, Hump, the hunchbacked servant of Lord Winterfrost, was hurrying along the clifftops to the village from his lord's crumbling mansion on some pointless errand, when he saw Ginevra down on the rocks singing to the sea. He saw her, and he was transfixed. She was a fragile thing of light and purity and he was afraid that the sea wind would break her and carry her away from him. He stood on the clifftop gazing at her and he knew that her presence was enough to wash away all his lord's cruel jibes about camels and gargoyles. She would surely see beyond his hump and his twisted features. If she would only notice him, she would love him in a pure, clean way. He filled his arms with wildflowers and the tiny sweet strawberries that grew along the clifftop and hurried down the narrow path towards her.

She smiled when she took the flowers from him and then cast them one by one into the tides. When they talked, she laughed at his nervous jokes and the words that poured out of him. She reached forward to wipe the strawberry juice from his chin with her finger without a trace of revulsion.

For months, he courted her with flowers and precious things he stole from his master's vast unused rooms, with jokes and quaint old-fashioned songs. He listened to her strange tales of mermaids and dolphin men and he thought of her when he served Lord Winterfrost at his table. His lord's cruel demands and mockery washed over him like tides over sand. He thought of her as he lay alone in his narrow bed and something inside him straightened out and grew tall, like a flower starved of sunlight.

Hump didn't notice at first. She filled his thoughts – he thought he knew every tiny part of her, but he didn't notice when her stomach began to swell. Didn't notice until Lord Winterfrost made some passing spiteful comment about the Flowerdew brat being pregnant by person unknown, and Hump dropped the blue and white patterned teapot that had belonged to the lord's family for centuries and barely heard Lord Winterfrost when he started screaming at him.

He ran to the sea's edge and found Ginevra there where she always was. She smiled at him, and he felt his heart breaking into pieces, felt that thing that had straightened out begin to curl up and wither again. They sat hand in hand watching the waves and neither of them spoke. Ginevra put her hand over her stomach and smiled and Hump knew that she hadn't meant to hurt him.

Of course, it wasn't his for all that the village people whispered and nudged one another. Their laughter and mockery and crude jokes did not make the child his, no matter that he wished they did. He and Ginevra were as chaste as the old fishermen who sat outside the tavern mending their nets and yearning for the old days when the harbour was full of boats and the sea full of fish.

Ginevra's stomach grew and grew, and her family cast her out of the rusty caravan, shouting that she shamed them, that she was never to show her ungrateful face there again. Hump gave up his bed in the attic of the mansion house for her, but she never slept in it. Instead, she took her few possessions and slept on the shore at a place where the natural curve of the cliffs sheltered a small bay from the worst of the weather.

While Hump's thoughts were consumed by her, she thought only of a tall, slender man with smooth silvery skin; a man who smelled of saltwater and sea wind and held her in strong arms and wrapped her in the endless, floating threads of his silvery green hair as they made love out amongst the waves. She could taste his breath on the wind and it brought tears of longing to her eyes. She dreamt of sunlight falling through water, glancing off fish scales and impossible towers and minarets of coral. She sang to the sea, but her songs had taken on an ache. When Hump came, her dearest friend, she could find nothing to say to him, nothing to laugh at in his jokes. She picked at the food he brought her, wrapped his blankets and soft eiderdowns round her thin shoulders, but his love washed over her without leaving a trace.

The baby grew and grew. When it kicked, she pictured a turquoise and golden fish swimming inside her, thrashing its tail against the walls of her womb. She laid her hands on her stomach and sang softly to the baby, promising that one day soon its father would come for them both.

When her time came, there were no cool white sheets, no boiling water or fluffy towels. There was only the sand and the sea and bent-over, hunchbacked Hump, as kind as any midwife. The night carried her cries out across the waves and the sand soaked up her blood. As night drew in, the wind rose and candles in the village refused to stay lit. Hump heard whales singing far away, out in the storm. Ginevra cried out to them, believing that they would carry her sea-lover to her.

Hump had nothing to say. His heart had already begun to crack and now he felt it shatter, and the pieces fell away, taking with them all the dreams he had had of the life he would give to his Ginevra and her child.

It was growing light when the baby was born. The sky and the sea were grey, tired out from the storm. The whales had stopped singing and even the sea was silent. The baby wailed with an unearthly despair. Ginevra rocked herself backwards and forwards as she nursed it. She watched the sea but there was nothing there, only gulls and water and the last of the storm clouds.

Ginevra wouldn't take her baby back to Hump's room. She clutched the pale, silver-skinned child to her chest and waited, a blackness filling her thoughts. A creeping suspicion began to come to her that there was no city under the sea, there were no mermaids or dolphin men. All that existed was this place and these people – a cluster of ramshackle hovels on the edge of the land presided over by a cruel and lazy lord. There was no beauty and no magic. She turned away when Hump came to her. His kindness threatened to break her, but his twisted, lumbering body repelled her. She knew she had broken him more than the fates who had given him that body ever had.

On the evening of the third day after the birth, Hump gathered holly and hawthorn for Ginevra in the faint hope that the bright berries and shiny leaves might make her smile again and see beyond his hump and his twisted face and gnarled hands.

As he walked along the clifftop, he looked towards the sea, hating it, and saw a pale figure walking into the water. He cried out and the wind tore her name from his mouth in a scream. She turned round and waved and, for a moment, he thought he saw her smile at him that way he always wanted her to. But then she turned again and continued walking deeper and deeper into the waves.

He began to run, scattering holly and hawthorn behind him, but he was crippled, bent almost double by the weight of his hump. His legs were short and frail, and he was clumsy. He stumbled and fell, and as he lay in the sea grass and thrift, he heard Ginevra's voice for the last time and she was singing in her high, tuneless voice, singing to the sea before it took her and her child away from him forever.

Another three days passed before the sea cast up Ginevra's body with all the other unwanted flotsam and jetsam. She lay on the sand, close to where the bleached bones of a wreck stood half-buried in the sand. The sea had been kind to her. Her body only looked frozen in death, her eyes closed, and her pale hair entwined with seaweed. They buried her on the clifftop above the bay where she had given birth to her child. Hump carved her name on a wooden marker and laid holly and hawthorn on the mound of earth.

The villagers searched half-heartedly for the child, but they found nothing. The sea did not give the baby back, keeping it hidden beneath the waves, and everyone but Hump forgot about Ginevra Flowerdew and her child.

Years later, in a purple twilight, Lord Winterfrost sent Hump out on another of his pointless errands. Hump had become shorter and had grown broader and there was grey in the brown thatch of his hair now. Every winter he felt the weight of his hump more and the pain of her loss never lessened, was always a wound in his heart that failed to heal.

That evening he heard singing, tuneless and pure like wind-chimes or weathervanes in a storm. He turned and looked down to the rocks at the edge of the shore and there was a girl there, a girl with pale skin and silvery green hair who sang to the land as her mother had sung to the sea. She waved to him and called his name and he went to her. He followed her through the waves and when the sea broke over his head, he still followed her into the depths and the sea never cast him up unwanted.

The Plague Doctor

When I give the order, they wall up the dead and dying inside their homes.

We used to paint a symbol on the door and others would come along and do the brickwork. Now we do it as we go along. It's more efficient. There's a lot of things we used to do that we don't do anymore.

We go from house to house. The priest swings his censer, the workmen cover their mouths and noses in makeshift masks. I lead the way. I used to have a fine leather mask, but I don't bother with it anymore.

There's hardly a person left on this street. Plague marks fade on the doors and crows alight on the rooftops and watch with beady-eyed expectation. The stench makes one of the boys vomit. I march on, my coat-tails flapping behind me, my footsteps ringing out.

Near the end of street, stagnant fumes drift from the river and there's one house left untouched. It's a hovel of rotting wood and gaping windows. The door is closed but there won't be a lock. I knock all the same – three loud taps that scatter a nest of rats from the pile of garbage by the step.

No one comes. Of course no one comes. One of the men coughs and a murmur of unease passes through our scant ranks. The priest swings his censer harder, scattering smoke and the scent of churches. He mutters Latin but there's no one left to understand it.

I knock again and call gently. 'It's the doctor. Does anyone need the doctor?'

When no one answers, I push the door open and the stench is overpowering. The priest makes a choking sound and backs away, sweat beading on his forehead. The men hover around the doorway. I ignore them and walk into the room, waiting for my eyes to become accustomed to the gloom and my nostrils to the smell. There's a single room, shapes in the bed that were once people, smaller bundles on the floor wrapped in scraps of blanket. The rats have got in and one stops in the doorway and stares balefully at me.

At first, I think everyone is dead, but there's a movement in one of the bundles on the floor. I step closer and bend down. It's a girl with sores round her mouth that are probably from some other sickness than the plague. People forget, in these dark times, the myriad other ways there are to die. I smile at her, but she doesn't smile back. Death is creeping close. There's a pocket inside my fabulous coat and I reach inside and take out my knife and cut a square of cloth from her nightdress.

After that, there's nothing else to do except have a quick look round for anything worth taking.

'There's a girl,' I tell the priest. 'Not dead.'

Something besides piety crosses the man's face: fear perhaps, disgust, disappointment. All things a man of God should not feel. He doesn't move.

'It makes no difference whether you do anything or not,' I say and that's enough to shame him. He places his mask over his face, ventures into the hovel, swinging his censer vigorously and speaks Latin words. Last rites, I suppose. I would have known once, I would have cared.

One of the men taps my shoulder. 'Is there anything?' he asks.

'No,' I say, 'but see for yourself.'

I step aside so that he can see that there's nothing worth taking. He curses quietly, and I walk away to let the priest finish and the men go to work sealing the house to keep the contagion inside. It used to be harder than this. People saw the doctor and the priest, and they'd have hope, or they'd be angry. There would be tears or threats. Back then, we had the king's men to keep us safe, but plague doctors were still murdered by the people they tried to heal. But the takings were better in those days. Now – now there's nothing left but death.

And here's the thing: death isn't a pale rider on a pale horse. Death's a red raw rash and a swelling that won't go down; it's a rank taste in the water; it's when the rich leave and the market stalls are empty, and people fight for the last mouldy loaf of bread. It's rats the size of cats, and carrion birds on the rooftops. Death is bricked-up houses with the living still screaming inside and me and my band of merry men roaming the streets, taking our wages where we can. Death is when it all goes silent and there's no one left at all.

Except for me. I don't get sick. I don't die. Death casts its baleful eye over me and passes on.

We go out to the big houses where the countryside is edging back, taking over gardens with banks of fireweed and packs of feral dogs. The boy with the cough says there are wolves, and we all laugh because the last wolf died centuries ago.

'But what if they come back?' he asks. 'What if the things that were gone start coming back?'

We do our work. The men make jokes about the dead and the dying that aren't funny, but we laugh all the same. Even the priest laughs. In one house we find a ragdoll on the window ledge and the priest takes it. I don't know why. He stands clutching the toy to his chest and staring at nothing and once I might have asked. He had a daughter, perhaps, a niece whom he loved. It doesn't matter. The men make gentle jokes about the priest and his dolly, and the priest tucks the doll in his bag. In the bedchamber, I cut squares of cloth from the nightclothes of dead children and then go to wait with the priest while the men work.

'Is there any point?' the priest asks.

'Probably not,' I say. 'Probably, there's no point to anything. Never has been, never will be.'

'You're a godless man,' the priest says but there's no censure in his words.

Once we would have argued for or against God and science. I would have asked what God meant by this, and the priest would have told me some lie.

'The boy with the cough,' the priest says, 'he's got it, hasn't he?'

'I think so.'

'He'll pass it to the others.'

'Yes.'

'Do you think you have it?'

'No. It doesn't touch me. I've been coughed and sneezed on. I've breathed in the breath of the dying. Pustules the size of apples have burst all over me, but I don't get sick.'

The priest sighs. 'I have an itch in my throat,' he says, 'a bruised feeling under my arms. You'll excuse me if I'm not at work tomorrow?'

'Yes.'

'I'm not afraid,' the priest says. 'I'm more afraid of not dying.

Of being the last one left. May I borrow your knife?'

I frown but give it to him. I don't want him to make any dramatic gestures. Suicide is a sin, even if you'll die anyway. But instead of stabbing the knife into his chest or slashing the veins in his arms, he cuts a square of cloth from his robe and passes it to me.

'For your coat,' he says.

My house is on a street where all the other houses are bricked up. We were happy here amongst the bustle of traffic and shops and people talking and laughing all day and night. Now the only footsteps are mine. My house glitters with stolen treasures: glassware and carved boxes; wooden toys; sacks of flour and spices; chests of linen; bottles of oil and perfume; books and pamphlets and portraits of people whose names I don't know. I have become a rich man.

I stand in the hallway listening and my breath catches in my throat, my heart beats uneasily.

'Please,' I whisper.

I had a wife once, and although she's gone, I still listen for the sound of her footsteps and the swish of her skirts. I pull my patchwork coat tight around me and touch the square of blue cloth that I cut from her wedding dress and stitched to the breast of my coat on the night she died. And next to it, a white patch cut from a christening gown and around it, patches and patches stitched from the clothes of the dead: my coat of many colours. My coat of death.

'Please,' I whisper again.

And then I hear her: the sound of a toy being set aside and the clatter of footsteps on the stair. And she's in my arms, my daughter, with her yellow hair and her blue eyes. I hold her, listening to the babble of her voice and she's alive. She's always alive, just like me.

Every night I stitch patches to my coat and we talk. Then, before we go to our beds, we stand at the window and look into the darkness. The city sprawls around us, still and silent and full of pestilence, but now and again a light flickers, and we know someone is there, looking out and seeing our light. And there is hope. As long as she is alive, and I am alive, there is hope. When the plague has run its course and the world is new again, we can start over, stronger, richer and immune to all the horror in the world.

And death? Death is just a clown on a bloated horse: impotent, useless, achieving nothing.

The Walking Man

He did not have much, just one change of clothes, a large knife and a very large dog. He carried the knife tucked into his belt and the clothes in a knapsack and the dog padded in an easy loose-limbed lope at his side. They called him the Walking Man, and they said that to see him was bad luck, and that if he saw you, it meant death. He had had another name once, but whatever it was, no one remembered anymore, and he did not care. The Walking Man was as good a name as any to him.

He knew that as long as he had the dog, he did not need the knife, but he kept it because it was a pretty thing with a bone handle and the word 'endure' engraved on the blade. The Walking Man could not read anymore, but he like the feel of the letters beneath his fingers when he stroked the blade, as he often did.

The dog had no name, not even one that had been forgotten. It was always angry. It didn't chase sticks or wag its tail. It growled and slobbered, and its muscles rippled beneath its thin white fur. The Walking Man thought that it was biggest, nastiest dog he had ever seen, but they got along well together. There was an unspoken agreement between them that they were equals, companions on the long empty road across the Ash Plains. There would be no baby-talk, no stroking or patting from one side, and no biting, growling or killing from the other, no matter how long it was since either of them had had their last meal.

Something had happened a long time ago and the Walking Man was not really a man anymore. He was a thing, a spirit – perhaps a ghost – of the dead landscape he and the dog walked. His memories of the event were hazy, but there had been a conflagration so great that the sun had been swallowed up by smoke, and ash had fallen like snowflakes. The very fabric of existence had shimmered, and time and space had turned strange and feral and neither were to be trusted out here in the depths of the Ash Plains. Ever since then, the Walking Man had worn a long, patched coat and a hat with a broad brim to shade his eyes from the sun. Sometimes, when people looked at him, they saw a monster with a face so mangled by scar tissue that it was barely human, and other times, they saw an angel, with violet eyes and delicate features. The Walking Man shapeshifted his way through the centuries and across the plains, and only one thing was sure: to see him was bad, but to have him see you was the worst kind of luck.

The Walking Man and the dog walked the vast broken expanse of the Ash Plains that stretched from the crooked ruins of the old walled cities in the west to nowhere. As they walked, the Walking Man talked to the dog. He told it about the war and the plague and the very bad thing that he couldn't remember but which had destroyed the world for once and for all, that had destroyed all the things that had once been where the Ash Plains were now. The dog knew all about ghosts and vampires and ogres from the Walking Man's tales. It knew there were very likely other huge dogs wandering the Plains, but it was not afraid of anything.

Often, the Walking Man told the dog about a mythical city called Haven that it was said (by whom the Walking Man could not remember) lay in the east beyond the Ash Plains.

'The buildings are made of white marble and shine silver and gold in the sun,' he told the dog. 'It's always summertime. Everyone is happy and healthy in Haven, and everyone is welcome no matter who you are or what you've done.'

The dog padded on silently, angrily.

'And of course,' the Walking Man said, 'it doesn't exist.' He knew this because he had walked all the way across the Ash Plains from one end to the other several times, and he knew that the only cities were as weird and twisted as he was and that the land ended in jagged rocks and a grey empty sea. He had looked over the edge of the cliff and seen bodies broken on the rocks below. If he had given them any thought, he might have supposed that when you gave up everything to find a mythical city, the only thing left to do when you realised it didn't exist was to throw yourself from the clifftop.

They had followed the narrow line of the road across plains ankle-deep in ash, dust and what was left of the last great army: feathers and bones, melted glass and metal. They had walked through countless ruined towns and cities and had not seen another living thing. And now they had come here.

'The end of the world,' the Walking Man told the dog. 'The end of all things.'

There was a city here at the end of the world. Not the white city of Haven with its gleaming marble towers and pennants flying in the summer breeze. There were no wide gates thrown open to admit weary travellers. The city that stood here was concealed behind an insane and impenetrable maze of briars and ivy, barbed wire and metal spikes. There were booby traps set up inside the tangles. While everything around it was dead, the city was alive, dark and green against the grey of the plains, as if all the life that had been sucked out of the world had been twisted and pulled apart and regurgitated here. The hedge of thorns had grown so high and impenetrable that little was visible of the city within, just a few broken towers standing black against the sky.

The Walking Man and the dog had been here before. The first time, they had seen thousands of birds, making fantastic shapes in the sunset above the city. The second time, they had seen a cat sliding through the bushes and the dog had taken off after it, disappearing into the undergrowth and returning later without the cat but with thorns longer than the Walking Man's fingers stuck in its flanks. It bore the scars to this day. The third time, they had seen the trees walking, creaking and rearranging themselves all the better to keep people out.

All those things were strange and terrible, but they were not what disturbed the Walking Man the most. What frightened him, was the way this place made him feel, the memories that pushed through his thoughts when he saw the tips of those towers.

'I've been here before,' he told the dog.

The dog looked at him with contempt. It was sniffing around the trees looking for cats. It had not forgotten the cat that got away from it, nor would the dog forgive it.

'I don't mean with you,' he said, 'I mean... before. There was— I think there was a school. I remember— I don't remember.'

The city tottered at the edge of a cliff. Its wall of thorns protected it on three sides, and the cliff and the long fall to the jagged rocks below protected the fourth side. Birds sang inside the vegetation, and something rustled tantalisingly in the leaves. The dog growled with frustration.

'A bad place,' the Walking Man said. 'There are people inside, bad people. We should go.'

But they didn't go. The city was like a lure. It drew them, and they walked round and round it. The dog was looking for a way inside. It knew there were cats and birds and other things inside and it wanted them, wanted to sink its teeth into juicy cat-flesh and tear and break and feast. A light burned at the top of the highest tower, flickering and guttering as the night fell. The Walking Man watched it and felt... something. Memories pushed through his thoughts. There had been a red van with a trailer attached to the back, all their worldly possessions packed into it. People had laughed, called him crazy.

'An angel fell from the sky and I knew it was time to go. It was a sign,' he told the dog. 'I saw it. Other people said it was a falling star, but it was an angel. It was a sign of the end of the world.'

He remembered walking through streets that were noisy and crowded, people talking and laughing, brushing against him, streetlights and traffic, seeing in the patch of sky between two skyscrapers a light tumbling through the air. He remembered people stopping to look, pointing at the sky, the click of cameras, and he remembered that he was not alone. There was someone with him, there was a hand in his, a tiny star-fish hand holding his as they watched an angel falling.

'Who?' he asked the dog. 'Who?'

But the memory was fading into the fog of his mind. All that remained was the feel of that little hand holding his, the sight of the angel falling and the panic that had mounted in his chest.

'They said I was crazy,' he told the dog, 'they said it was just a shooting star, but I knew. I was ready. It was the sign I was waiting for.'

They walked a little further, turning towards the sea. A gull cried somewhere in the night and the dog growled softly. The Walking Man laughed with sudden delight as he remembered something else.

'You were there,' he said. 'I was going to leave you behind, but the children – how many children did I have? – they wouldn't go without their puppy.' He laughed. 'You were a puppy.'

The dog did not grace him with a response.

'Children,' the Walking Man said, 'I had children. One, two, more... I don't remember. Where did I take them? What happened to them?'

He tried to summon more memories, but it was no good. There had been children and he knew that must mean there had been a woman once, but no matter how hard he tried he couldn't remember anything of her, could not see her face or the faces of his children. All that remained was the feel of that tiny hand holding his.

'Well,' he told the dog, 'it doesn't matter anyway.'

By morning they had reached the cliff's edge. The air tasted of salt and ash and chemicals. The sea had begun to reclaim the land and parts of the city lay broken on the shore. The thorns and ivy were crawling down the cliff and over the rocks. There were bodies and bones down there, and the Walking Man supposed that they must be the remains of those who had set out looking for the white city of Haven and found this monstrosity instead.

The dog growled, hackles raised, and the Walking Man frowned, turning round to look back. There was a figure behind them moving closer. The Walking Man reached for his knife, but he was not really afraid. People were afraid of him, he was bad luck, he was cursed. To see him was unlucky, to have him see you meant death. He was used to people running away from him.

But this person kept on walking towards him. As she drew nearer, the Walking Man saw that it was a woman. She was wearing travel-stained clothes and there was a rifle strapped to her back. Long black hair framed a face that was all angles and edges. The woman was still young, but there was a feeling of age and gravity around her, as if she had seen every awful thing it was possible to see and was not quite sure how she had survived to tell the tale. Coming face to face with the Walking Man did not appear to frighten her.

She nodded towards the city. 'Are you from there?'

The Walking Man considered the question for several moments. 'Yes,' he said at last.

'Do you know how to get through the thorns?'

The Walking Man felt vaguely insulted that she was speaking to him like this, so directly without any introductions or niceties. He was used to inspiring fear in people.

'There is no way through,' he said.

The dog growled. It appeared to be insulted as well. The woman looked at it and then bent down to its level and held out her hand to it. The dog growled and turned away disdainfully. The Walking Man was surprised and a little shocked and disappointed that it had not torn her arm off.

'He bites,' he told the woman. 'I can't control him.'

The woman smiled. 'I used to have a dog once,' she said, 'and a cat and a talking bird.'

She began to walk round the wall of thorns, pausing to pull a long, curved knife from her pack and using it from time to time to swipe fruitlessly at the vegetation.

'You can't get in,' the Walking Man said, 'no one can. There are only bad people in there.'

'My family is in there,' the woman said.

'No one goes in and no one goes out.'

'I went out,' the woman said. She kicked at a tree trunk and jumped back with a laugh when the tree dropped down a long vine onto her shoulder.

They walked in silence for a few moments and then the woman turned to the Walking Man. 'I know who you are. You're a legend. A bogeyman. The Walking Man. They say you lure travellers off the road and murder them. They say to see you is bad luck and if you see someone, it means they'll die. I guess I'm screwed, then.' She laughed. 'They told me about you, but I didn't believe it.'

She stopped and wiped her hand on her shirt before holding it out to him. 'Pleased to meet you. I'm Eliza Starling. What do I call you? Walking Man or by your name?'

The Walking Man took her hand and shook it, feeling again the memory of that other little hand in his.

'I don't have a name,' he said.

'Yes, you do,' Eliza said. 'The Walking Man is a name of sorts. But also, before you were the Walking Man, you were Ethan James Hunter.'

The Walking Man stopped walking. There were more memories, a whole wave of them pushing like waves against the cliffs but failing to break through. He was afraid that if they did, they would take him over and shatter him into thousands of pieces.

'You know who I am?' he said.

'Bits and pieces,' Eliza said. 'It was an awful long time ago that you were Mr Hunter. We all knew about the Walking Man in there. It was just a story. A sad story.'

The Walking Man gripped the hilt of his long knife. He imagined sinking it deep into Eliza's chest. He was not sure what he was, but he did not want to be a sad story, a thing to be pitied and whispered about. Better to be a monster.

'Tell me,' he said.

'You were a survivalist, one of the crazy people prepping for the end of the world,' Eliza said. 'This was before the end of the world came and no one believed that the world would really end. I don't really understand what it was like then, I wasn't born. I don't really know what cars and aeroplanes and phones are, but I think they were good things that we used to have. The story is that you took your family out into the countryside, where you'd bought some land and built a hiding place under the ground and you hid out in there. And it turned out you weren't crazy. The world did end.'

'I saw an angel falling,' the Walking Man said. 'I knew it was time.'

'The world didn't really end, though, did it?' Eliza said, 'I mean, space and time went weird and almost everyone died, and there's nothing much left of the world but ashes and ruins, but it's still going on. Maybe you weren't crazy when you left the city, but you went crazy hiding out all alone in your bunker.'

'But I wasn't alone. I had a family.' He felt again the hand in his but this time it felt cold and limp. 'Where are they? What did I do to them?'

'You didn't do anything,' Eliza said. 'They left you. I don't know why. Maybe you'd been holed up there for a few months and the world hadn't ended yet and they got bored, or maybe you had a fight. I don't know. But they left you with just the dog for company and came back to the city and then the world ended.'

The Walking Man didn't speak. They walked round the city in silence for a long time. The dog padded restlessly at the Walking Man's side and from time to time it looked towards the west, where the sun was beginning to sink. It was ready to move on.

'You said that you're from in there,' the Walking Man said at last. 'Why did you leave? Why do you want to go back? There are only bad people in there.'

'I left because I wanted to see the world. They didn't want me to go, they said there was nothing outside but monsters and ashes. But the more they told me not to go, the more I wanted to go. So, I left. Packed a bag and went to see the world.'

'And what did you see?'

Eliza laughed. 'Ashes and dust and ruins mostly. Some very bad things. Some good things. The people in there are not bad people. They are strange and a little inbred and they don't like strangers much, but they're my family. Your family, too. There could be people in there who are descended from your children.'

The Walking Man nodded and did not speak. An image flickered across his mind: a woman standing with her back to him at a window, flowers in a blue vase on the table, children laughing in another room.

'Help me get through the thorns,' Eliza said. 'All the time I've been away, I've missed this place, the people inside. I realised that all that matters is family. Come home.'

The Walking Man tried to picture it, tried to see himself living in this city of ruins and briars, but he couldn't see anything except ashes and dust and the road stretching relentlessly on before him.

'No,' he said, 'and you'll never get back in. You can come with me if you want.'

They looked at one another and then Eliza turned and hacked at the mess of thorns and leaves.

'No,' she said.

The dog made an impatient growling sound and looked towards the west again. They had been north, south, east and west and all the places in between, they had been everywhere but inside this city countless times. They walked. It was what they did, it was what they would always do.

'Well,' Eliza said, 'maybe when you change your mind, I'll see you again.'

The Walking Man smiled. 'Maybe I'll come back and find your bones caught in a thorn bush. It's bad luck to see me, and if I see you it means death.'

Eliza laughed. 'Well, what do you suppose it means if you talk to the Walking Man? Maybe that's good luck.'

'Maybe,' the Walking Man said and for the first time in a very long time, he smiled.

They walked westwards, just the two of them, through ruined cities and past lakes of poison and acid, through strange villages where the people hid from them and the bones of travellers hung in gibbets at the crossroads. They walked with the same steady pace, through day and night without resting. The dog growled and hunted feral sheep and deer, and the Walking Man walked and remembered what it had felt like to have a child hold his hand. Sometimes, he thought of Eliza Starling and smiled.

The Census-Taker's Daughter

This is the world: The Ash Plains, the labyrinth and the city. There is nowhere else. And these are all the people in the world, as noted in the Census-Taker's notebook. There is no one else:

- Human beings – 15
    - men – 3
    - women – 5
    - children (male) – 3
    - children (female) – 3
    - children (indeterminate) – 1
- Angels - 22
    - fallen – 6
    - not fallen – 12
    - in process of falling – 1
    - half-angels – 3 (2 x male, 1 x female)
- Talking animals – 4
    - dogs – 1
    - cats – 2
    - crows – 1
- Clockwork people – 7
- Dream Lords (asleep) – 1

Totalling 49, including the Census-Taker himself and his daughter, Maya, who was also his apprentice.

Of course, there was some disagreement between Maya and her father as to what made a person. The crow, for example, was perhaps just a very good mimic and not sentient in the same way that the other talking animals had proven to be. There was a great deal of argument as to whether beings whose hearts and brains were clockwork, and who could be switched on and off, could be counted as people at all. And none of this touched on the interminable debates and disagreements surrounding angels and falling angels and what they were and why they were.

'All part of the plan,' the Census-Taker would say happily, but he never alluded to whose plan it was, and Maya had given up asking.

And, of course there were the others.

There were ghosts, some more persistent than others, who haunted the overgrown alleyways and drifted between the burnt-out shops in the mall, but it was generally believed that they were not conscious. They were just phenomena, memories, flickers of a time when things had been different.

And there were the heads in jars, stacked up in a horror show in what had once been a laboratory. Maya and her friend Fenella had found them not long ago while exploring a thatch of thorns and thickets on the east side of the city, looking for nests and eggs. Maya still had nightmares about them, seeing the way one particular head, which might have belonged to a girl not much younger than she was, twitched and blinked as if trying to say something. In her dreams, the girl spoke but the words were tangled and confused and circled round Maya like strangling vines until the soft, calm voice of the Dream Lord spoke, saying *it is safe, it is safe...* and she woke up, sweating and tangled in her bedclothes, but safe.

There were the Possible People to consider as well. They were the people who might live in the labyrinth that circled round the city in an impenetrable maze of vines and briars and barbed wire. They were maybe real, but most likely not, and even if they were real, no one knew who they were or how many they were, so they were not counted.

On the first day of June, as they did on the first day of every month, Maya and her father took the census. They stood on the top step of what had once been a bandstand in a grand park. The steps were cracked now, and ivy grew up the walls. Where there had once been neat lawns and flowerbeds full of carefully-planted municipal flowers, there was now seeding grass, poppies and buttercups, all dusted, as everything in the city was, with a fine coating of ash.

Maya and her father counted the people assembled before them and ticked off names in their notebooks. They did this every month, but no one was sure why, except that it made them feel safe to know that everyone was in their place and everyone was accounted for.

'Forty-nine,' the Census-Taker said and frowned for this wasn't right. There should only be forty-eight assembled, for the Dream Lord was too busy sleeping in his house to attend, so they always counted him in absentia. It was Maya's job to go and check up on him afterwards.

They counted again.

'Forty-eight,' the Census-Taker said with satisfaction. 'I must have counted an ordinary crow as well as our Cracker, the crow.'

Maya nodded, but she frowned to herself, for she had also counted forty-nine the first time round and had thought that she had seen, for a moment, a stranger at the back of the crowd, a shadowy figure with a long coat and black flags of hair. But when they counted again, the figure had gone and there were only the shadows of the vine-hung trees dancing against the wall. There were ghosts enough here and Maya knew that she and her father were far from the first to mistake the living for the dead, but all the same, there was something that made her uneasy.

After the census was taken, Maya's father and the other adults always went to the tavern and drank wine or whatever else had been salvaged from deep within the city and they congratulated themselves on the passing of another month without mishap or death. While they did this, Maya and her friends, went to check on the Dream Lord so that she could tick him off in her notebook and make note of the fact that he was still sleeping.

This time, only Fenella and the angel Azriel, came with her. Fenella went first, only the tip of her tail visible in the long grass as she began the pursuit of some small creature before giving up and doubling back again.

'Lucy's pregnant again,' she said scathingly to Maya and Azriel, for Fenella's favourite thing aside from criticising, was gossiping about her sister, Lucy. 'I swear that cat has been up the duff continuously since she was nine months old. The gift of sentience and intelligence is wasted on her. She might as well have been an ordinary alley cat like the rest of our family.'

Maya smiled. She liked Lucy, who was fat and stripy and appeared to want nothing more than to lie in her basket surrounded by kittens. Lucy laughed at Maya's jokes and was polite and grateful for the titbits that Maya gave her and was quite happy to refer to herself as a house cat and a pet. Unlike Fenella, who complained and opinionated and whose favourite saying was: *You're doing it wrong.*

'How many this time?' Maya asked.

'At least nine, I think,' Fenella said.

'Who's the dad?' Azriel asked.

'Lucy thinks that ginger tom who lives near the old fish market, but she thinks there's also a chance it might a black-and-white from down near the labyrinth. A bit of a weirdo, Lucy said, touched with labyrinth fever, but she shagged him all the same. She's such a slut, my sister.'

'But it's instinct, isn't it?' Azriel said. 'The need to breed, to pass on your genes to the next generation?'

Fenella sniffed. 'I believe there's a higher purpose.'

Azriel rose one perfectly arched eyebrow. 'Really? What is that?'

'You should know,' Fenella said, 'you're the angel. One of God's chosen and all that nonsense.'

'It's not nonsense,' Azriel said but he frowned.

'It's twaddle,' Fenella said, 'twaddle and nonsense and poppycock. Where's God in all this mess?'

'His ways are many and mysterious,' Azriel said archly. 'You cannot hope to understand. As you say, a higher purpose.'

They had come to the house where the Dream Lord was. It was just a house where people had once lived. Like all the other houses in the street, its garden was overgrown and there were tiles missing from the roof. Briars climbed the walls and a poison garden of nightshades, henbane and thorn-apple grew in a riot round the door. Fenella opened her mouth to respond to Azriel but stopped when a scent caught her attention. She sniffed around the bushes and then looked up at Maya and Azriel.

'Other cats,' she said. 'That grey that thinks she's sentient – as if. Foxes. A hedgehog. People. Your father has been here, Maya, and Mrs Bailey. The fallen angels have been here but not recently. And someone else.'

'You have the nose of a dog, Fenn,' Azriel said and then ducked a swiping paw full of claws.

'What do you mean, someone else?' Maya asked.

Fenella sniffed at the broken gateposts and then padded to the door and sniffed round the doorstep again. 'Someone whose scent I don't recognise,' she said.

'Well, that's impossible,' Maya said. 'We just counted everyone. Everyone is present and correct and accounted for.'

But she frowned, remembering the ghost she thought she had seen after the census. The ghost that might not have been a ghost.

The house was still and silent inside. They tiptoed down the crumbling hallway where ivy was twisting up the bannister to the upstairs rooms, and where a particularly persistent briar was attempting to grow up through the terracotta tiles on the floor. Maya's father said that the house had been an executive home once, that a family had probably lived there. Maya didn't know what an executive was, and when her father talked about some of the things they might have owned – a paddling pool, juicer, computer – she had no idea, but she felt something strange and sad open up inside her: a sort of longing for the old days when the city had been home to millions but also a kind of relief that those days were over.

The Dream Lord did not sleep in a bed or a chair but on a long tabletop in what must once have been a dining room. There was a dresser full of old cracked plates standing against one wall, and next to it there was a broken glass door that would have opened out into a garden once. The weight of briars, bramble and ivy had broken the glass. The tendrils of brambles appeared to be prying the cracks apart in their eagerness to get in, to spread over everything. Long unnatural thorns grew on their stems and Maya was not sure that they had ever borne fruit.

The Dream Lord was asleep, as they had known he would be. Fenella jumped up onto the dresser and the three of them stood watching reverently as he slept, noting with some relief the steady rise and fall of his chest, the flicker of movement beneath his eyelids. He wore a black suit and a white shirt with the top button unfastened. His hair was neat with a few strands of grey at his temples. Even though he was always asleep, Maya thought he was the most handsome man she knew. When he was in her dreams, his eyes were open, and they were as green as poison and he smiled as he drove back the nightmares. Fenella said that in her dreams he appeared as a particularly plush and velvety black cat with round green eyes and long whiskers. Angels did not dream, but if they did, Azriel told them, he was sure that the Dream Lord would wear the face of God. It was comments like that that made it clear why Azriel was an angel forever in the process of falling.

Maya took out her notebook and pen and placed a tick next to where it was written 'One Dream Lord, asleep'. All was right and well with the world.

Except that when they turned to leave, the floorboards upstairs creaked as if there was someone up there. They froze and listened but there was only silence.

'Tree roots shifting,' Fenella said, and they all nodded in agreement. But nevertheless, they ran back to where the others were and told them about the smell of the stranger at the gate.

Old Ben and several of the adults went back to the house. Ben had the best nose in the city. and he sniffed about in the bushes round the gate, his long feathery tail weaving from side to side.

'Lots of scents,' he said. 'Most I recognise, one I don't.'

'Human?' the Archangel Michael asked. 'Demon?'

Ben sniffed again. 'Human,' he said, 'or as near as makes no difference.'

Maya felt a shiver run down her spine. 'Who?' she asked.

'How?' Fenella asked.

No one answered. The Archangel Michael, Hunter and Jack the Religious went into the house. Hunter had his gun and his long killing knife. If there was anything up there, it wouldn't be alive for long once Hunter found it.

The others waited in the evening shadows at the gate. Maya watched the adults and tried to work out if they were worried or afraid. Ben sniffed around a bit more.

'There's a trail,' he said. 'It ends here but it started somewhere else. You want me to follow it?'

'Tomorrow,' Maya's father said, 'in the full daylight.'

They were all relieved and even more relieved when the Archangel Michael and the others came out and said that the Dream Lord was sleeping peacefully and that they had searched the upstairs rooms and there was no one there.

That evening, as they always did, Maya and her father sat on the top of their tower and watched the sunset and the moonrise. Fenella and her sister, Lucy, were bickering in the background and Maya's foster brother, Oleander, who was half human and half fallen angel was there. Usually, on these long summer evenings, her father would open wine and sometimes he would let Maya and Oleander have a glass and they would talk about nothing much. Sometimes, when he had a couple of glasses, Maya's father would talk about Oleander's mother who had been sweet and pretty and not a bit like Oleander, who was as poisonous as his name. She had died in childbirth, as was always the case when humans bore the children of angels. They never talked of Maya's mother. That was supposed to be a secret kept from Maya, but she knew because Ben had let slip the secret to Lucy who told Fenella who told Azriel who told Oleander who couldn't wait to tell it to Maya.

Maya's mother had been called Louisa, but her father had called her Lulu sometimes. She had been small with long brown hair like Maya's and heavy-framed spectacles. Maya's father was all rules and regulations, he was a man of numbers and equations, a clock wound tight. Her mother was the opposite. She was fireworks and sparkles. It was said that she had tried to awaken the Dream Lord once, that she had walked a tightrope strung up between Maya's father's tower and the steeple of an old church opposite. She was gone because although the city was huge, it was not big enough for her, and she had gone into the labyrinth and wandered for days before coming back, her long hair torn out and her eyes bloodshot and crazed. She'd seen things inside the walls: people who were not like they were; machines that had real thoughts and not clockwork thoughts; monsters with tentacles and hooked claws and eyes that burned and froze anyone who looked at them for too long. There had been no calming her down and she had gone to the Dream Lord again and tried to awaken him, seizing his shoulders and shaking him and screaming into his face: *Wake up, wake up, wake up.* The Dream Lord did not wake up.

'We're all asleep because he's asleep,' she screamed at Maya's father when he tried to placate her. 'The world has moved on, but we have stayed the same. We're dead because he won't die.'

When he wouldn't wake up, she tried to kill him, putting her small hands round his neck and pressing down. The men dragged her off and Hunter saw to her with his long knife and that was that.

Maya didn't remember her mother, but she saw her clearly and often in her dreams, and she wondered how it was possible to miss someone so much when you had never really known them.

On clear nights like this one, you could see out across the rooftops and the treetops, out beyond the labyrinth where sometimes lights flickered in the blackness, and whenever Maya or one of the others asked what they were, they were shushed or told that they were natural phenomena, something to do with gas and hot springs.

Beyond the labyrinth, jagged against the burning sky, were the ruins of other cities. These were the Oil Cities. They didn't have real names and were just known as Oil City One, Oil City Two and Oil City Three. It was said that in the old days few people had lived in the Oil Cities. They had been giant refineries and chemical plants, full of evil smells and clanking, clicking, whirring machinery. But wonderful things had been made in them: medicine and flying machines and dolls that looked like real babies, to name but three of those things. Although no one much had lived there, every morning hundreds of thousands of people had left the city in cars and buses and on bicycles, to go and work in the Oil Cities, and every evening they all came back again. You could still see the line of the ten-lane highway beneath the black, blowing ash.

Jack the Religious had explained to Maya and Oleander what had happened. This was a long, long time ago and there had been a war between angels and the fallen angels (it wasn't nice to call them demons apparently) and there had also been wars between different factions of men. Some were fighting for one god, and some were fighting for a different god. Some fought for the land that the Oil Cities and other cities like them were eating up, some fought for money and some fought for power. None of what they were fighting for really mattered, because what happened was that someone, or perhaps several someones – no one knew who exactly or why – had walked into Oil City Two with a pack of explosives on their back and blew the city sky-high and the flames spread into Oil City One and Oil City Three and the resulting explosion (cataclysm, Jack the Religious called it, and apocalypse) was so great, it took the rest of the world with it. The Ash Plains were made and almost all of the people and almost all of the angels and fallen angels were killed. There were two versions of what happened next. One was that God was so angry that he turned His back on the world that He had made and loved, and that had been ruined, and went off to make another better world. The other version was that the explosion when the Oil Cities went up was so enormous, it took out Heaven and Hell as well, trapping all the angels and fallen angels that were left here on Earth in the city inside the labyrinth.

'What about the talking animals?' Fenella asked. 'Where did we come from?'

Jack the Religious didn't have an answer for that.

'I think there have always been talking animals,' Azriel said. 'It's just that in the past they knew when to shut up.'

That night, Maya leaned over the parapet of the tower's rooftop with Oleander beside her. The air smelled of cigarette smoke and roses and always of ash. A moth danced in the candle flame, narrowly escaping death. Both cats watched it with lazy twitching tails. The adults talked in low voices and one of the clockwork people was making an odd ratchety noise that didn't sound healthy. The last of the birds were singing out the day. The labyrinth was still and dark tonight, an impenetrable mess of high walls, barbed wire and briars. Everything was as it should be, and yet it wasn't.

Maya dreamt of a man made of ash. He was standing in the street before the house where the Dream Lord slept, and ash blew about him, forming and reforming into the shape of a long coat, a hat, a cloak. The shape of the man changed constantly. Hollows that might have been eye sockets formed in the place where his head would have been. A mouth gaped and laughed and jeered. Beneath the ash the man was burning, glowing red beneath the black ash. Tendrils of smoke drifted about him.

In the dream, the man of ash saw Maya. He nodded at her and dust and smoke drifted around him. A smile, wide and red, formed where his face should have been. Maya was afraid, very afraid, but she knew that this was a bad dream and whenever she had had a nightmare before, the Dream Lord had come and driven the nightmare away.

But the Dream Lord did not come and in the dream the man of ash seemed to know this. He raised a crumbling arm to the brim of his hat and then turned away from her and began to walk, dripping ash and cinders behind him, towards the house where the Dream Lord slept.

Maya opened her mouth to shout but no sound came out. She tried to run but her limbs would not move. Terror surged through her because she knew that the man of ash was going to enter the Dream Lord's house to do one of two things. Either he would kill the Dream Lord as he slept, or he would wake him up. And each was as bad as the other.

And still, as the nightmare stretched towards its inevitable close, the Dream Lord did not come with his soft, calm voice to drive the nightmare away.

Maya awoke with a jerk, her heart thundering in her chest. Her room was silvered with light from the full moon slanting through the open window and she could see the soft shape of Fenella curled up on the end of the bed, tail and whiskers twitching in a nightmare of her own. Outside it was almost silent. There were no nightbirds singing as there usually were, no rustling in the tangles of briars, vines and nettles outside. Just silence.

And then, almost too quiet to hear, the sound of a footstep on the ground outside, and then another and another. The footsteps were steady and measured, the type of footsteps a man made from ash might make as he passed by in the street below. The air smelled more of ash and chemicals than ever. Maya froze, heart pounding, terrified that if she moved the man passing by would know that she was up there listening.

The footsteps passed and there was silence again. Only then did Maya dare to creep to the window and pull aside the curtain. The full moon lit up the street below, silvering the cracked tiles and ruined buildings, the overgrowth of vegetation. Something scurried in the undergrowth and the nightbirds began to sing again.

'What time is it?' Fenella muttered from the bed.

'Late,' Maya said, 'or maybe very early. I had a nightmare.'

'So did I,' Fenella said, and her nose and whiskers twitched. 'A cat made of smoke and poison came. The Dream Lord didn't come.'

'For me, it was a man made of ash.' Maya sat down on the edge of the bed and Fenella settled close to her. 'The Dream Lord didn't stop my nightmare either.'

'Something's wrong,' Fenella said. 'Someone's here who shouldn't be.'

'Bad news, bad news,' Cracker the crow screamed at them when they came down the stairs for breakfast and found almost everyone congregated there, all talking at once. 'Very bad news, very bad news. Bad awful news. Doom. Disaster. Calamity.'

'Shut up,' Fenella said, 'idiot bird.'

Almost everybody had gathered in Maya's father's kitchen and everyone was talking at once, all comparing the bad dreams they'd had. Hunter had dreamt of a man made of blades, Oleander had dreamed of falling from a high tower, Lucy had dreamed that all her kittens were born dead save for one with fur as red as blood.

Maya picked her way through the clamour to the stove where her father was cooking eggs. He smiled sadly at her.

'I dreamed I lost you,' he said. 'You were lost in the labyrinth just like your mother.'

'I dreamed of a man made of ash and fire,' Maya said. 'The

Dream Lord didn't come.'

'No,' her father said, expertly flipping one of the eggs over so that it cooked just the way Maya liked them. 'That would appear to be the one thing all these disparate dreams and dreamers have in common. The Dream Lord didn't come.'

'Is he dead?' Maya barely dared to ask.

'No, Hunter and Ben went to check first thing. He's sleeping.'

'Then, why—'

'Demons coming,' Cracker shouted suddenly. 'Beware, beware. Demon approaching from the west. Danger. Danger. Evil.'

'Idiot bird,' Maya's father said.

But Cracker was right. The demons were coming. Although, of course, it was wrong to call them demons. They were angels, just as surely as Michael and Gabriel and the others were, but they were angels who had fallen, and it was possible, just possible, that one day they might repent of what they had done and be restored once again to God's glory and esteem. The word 'demon' apparently inferred something that was beyond redemption. But, of course, all this was just pointless discussion and argument, because God had been blown sky-high and far away when the Oil Cities blew up.

There were six demons and they lived high up in the ruins of what had once been a high-rise office block. The building was now so overgrown and rickety that no one save the demons dared to set foot inside it. Michael, who could remember when the city had been young and new, said that the building had been the headquarters of a bank and that fortunes had been made and destroyed in seconds within its walls. Michael claimed it was a temple to greed and quite fitting that the demons should have chosen to dwell there.

Demons, Michael had explained, could take whatever form they wished, and it was a mystery to him why any of them would choose to look as they did. The Cherub Twins came first, giggling and chattering and looking for all the world like mischievous toddlers with their blond ringlets and chubby limbs, and their eyes that glowed red and purple and orange. They had terrified Maya since the time when she was very little and had mistaken them for ordinary children and tried to play with them. Next came Spider, the Many Armed, who was, as might be expected, part woman but mostly spider. Then came Sephiron who was tall and handsome and fond of music and singing and frequently came to visit Maya's father to talk about books or to share works of art he'd rescued from the remains of the city galleries. Sephiron didn't feel or look like a demon or a fallen angel. Maya thought that he was less strange than Azriel, Oleander and Fenella who were her best friends. Then came Shuck, who took the form of a huge black dog with eyes that glowed like coals and a mouth full of rotting yellow teeth and a stench of carrion and death.

And last, taking the rear was Hexthalion, the Arch Demon, who had once been an archangel like Michael. Hexthalion, who had fallen hard and fast, refusing to acknowledge God's will or the greatness of His creation, who had broken rules and bedded women and who had built the labyrinth all those long centuries ago, when the world had been younger and different. Hexthalion had shapeshifted his way through the centuries. It was said that when the Oil Cities had exploded, he had laughed and run headlong into the conflagration to bathe in the flames and fumes. Hexthalion wore black suits and white shirts. His black hair was perfectly trimmed and one of his eyes was blue and the other green. His teeth, when he smiled, were perfectly white and even. You might not have thought him anything more than a man, but sometimes Maya thought that she caught a glimpse of another Hexthalion. One with clashing metal wings, horns and talons, eyes that flashed red and teeth that dripped with gore.

'Here comes trouble,' Azriel muttered in Maya's ear.

'Do fallen angels dream?' Maya asked. 'Do they have nightmares?'

'They dream of being elevated back into heaven,' Azriel said. 'That's a nightmare for them.'

Hexthalion sat down at the table. He reached for the teapot and poured himself a cup of tea and sipped it, grimacing. Shuck helped himself to the eggs Maya's father had been cooking, wolfing them down in a few mouthfuls.

'Change is coming,' Hexthalion said. 'All the time while we're eating breakfast and comparing bad dreams, someone is walking closer and closer to our Dream Lord, to place a kiss on his forehead and wake him up. And then what will become of us all?'

'Who is he?' Hunter asked, his hand on his long knife.

'Wickedness,' Cracker announced from the top of the dresser, 'evil. Badness upon badness and doom and—'

'Idiot bird,' Hexthalion said and threw his teacup at Cracker.

The cup shattered on the wall and Cracker clacked and flapped and settled on the Archangel Michael's shoulder.

'Not who is he,' Hexthalion said, 'but who is she? Do you remember, Michael, do you remember who she is?'

The archangel was frowning. It was plain that he did know what Hexthalion was talking about. It was said that once, during one of their interminable celestial battles, Michael had trampled Hexthalion into the ground, and it looked very much as if Michael would like to do that again right now.

'Let me tell you a story,' Hexthalion said. 'Once upon a time a poor woman fell pregnant in this very city. This was back in the time when this city was still great, when more than a million people lived here, and the roads flowed in and the roads flowed out. Back when there were houses and factories and shops. Galleries and offices and schools. Hospitals for the sick, parks to wander in, places to worship in. There was no labyrinth in those days. Do you remember, Michael?'

Michael nodded.

Maya settled down in the sagging chair by the stove. She loved stories and she loved hearing about the old days, the happy long-ago days, though she had a feeling that the story Hexthalion told would be a different one from those she knew.

'But this was a time of war,' Hexthalion said. 'Do you remember? Men fought men for gold and oil and power and God, although their gods bore no resemblance to the ones we knew. And angels fought fallen angels. Everything was awash in blood and suffering. And then a troupe of young men – freedom fighters, terrorists, soldiers, it doesn't matter anymore – they went into Oil City Two with explosives strapped to their backs and – kaboom – everything was finished.

'It was not a good time to be pregnant. This poor woman – I don't even remember her name – was one of very few to survive. Just a motley collection of angels and fallen angels and the few city people fortunate enough to make it to their shelters in time. The sky was black, the dust blocked out the sun. All the water was poisoned. Fires burned and burned, and sickness was rife. No, it was not a good time to be alive, let alone alive and carrying twins. But then, slowly, the dust cloud began to clear. The first few flowers began to open up their petals again. It rained pure clear water and the birds started singing. And this poor woman gave birth to twins

– a boy and a girl and there was hope and new life in the wreckage of the old. There was singing and celebration. You were there, Michael, you and your chums, and you proclaimed that the babies were gifts from God. You claimed them as yours, promised that angels would always watch over them. You said these births showed that you had won, that God's precious angels had prevailed. Gifts were bestowed upon them – health, wealth and happiness, long life and eternal beauty. All that twaddle. And all night there was dancing and music and celebration. And in the midst of it all, you must have forgotten to invite me to the party. I was not pleased.'

Hexthalion cast his eyes round his audience and smiled. One of the Cherub twins crawled into his lap and he patted the thing like a lap cat. Maya watched him and felt something stirring inside her. Not fear exactly, something more like longing. For some reason, she thought of her mother, lost and crazed in the labyrinth.

'But you know how it is: the wicked fairies always come to the ball. I brought gifts of my own.'

'Not gifts,' Michael said. 'Curses.'

Hexthalion nodded. 'Gifts, curses. What does it matter in these godless times? It was petty of me, I admit. I cursed those darling babies right there in what was left of the cathedral, in God's house. The sun came slanting through the stained glass and colours danced on the floor and I stood there, in the reflected glory of the saints and angels and I cursed the boy to die on his sixteenth birthday, and the girl to live but wish she died.'

'I deflected the curse,' Michael said, 'I did what I could, but it couldn't be broken, not completely. The best I could do – the boy would not die, but would sleep eternally, would live only in the dreams of others, the girl would have happiness, but not here, not in this city. We protected them, we did everything we could. I tasked stray dogs and cats, the birds in the trees to watch over them. I gifted some of them with sentience and speech. Those children were our hope, our future, they must be protected. Of course, other children were born, but the twins were the first. They symbolised the new world and that it could be better. We tried to protect them, we told them to be careful, to be mindful of strangers, not to touch anything unless they knew what it was but—'

Hexthalion smiled. 'The bad things always happen in the end. It was such a small simple thing to happen. A careless seamstress, it seemed, left a needle in the boy's shirt and it pricked his finger and the wound festered, became infected, and the boy fell asleep, and sleeps still. He lives in our dreams, he chases away the nightmares. He became our Dream Lord.'

There was a silence in the kitchen. Even Cracker resisted the urge to make proclamations of evil and bad tidings.

Maya stared from the angel to the demon and saw that although there were many answers in their story, there were just as many questions.

'What about the girl twin?' she asked.

'She saw her brother fall sick. She saw the prophecy fulfilled and she vowed to find a cure for him,' Michael said. 'She turned the city upside down looking for— I don't know what she was looking for. And when she couldn't find what she was looking for, she vowed to search the wilderness outside until she found the way to awaken her brother. She left, taking nothing with her but a cat, a dog and a crow. They went out into the wilderness never to be seen again.'

'And we became crazy and insular,' Hexthalion grinned. 'We were scared of the Ash Plains and the ruins of the Oil Cities. We were frightened of the people who crossed the plains to the city. We killed them, but still they kept coming. We dreamt of monsters. The Dream Lord chased them away, but we knew they were real. We built a labyrinth around this city to protect it. We swathed its walls with barbed wire and spikes and broken glass, we built terrible traps into it. And we let the nettles grow up, the nettles and brambles, the briars that bloomed poisonous blooms. People couldn't get through the thorns, the monsters stopped trying. Centuries passed, and we stopped believing there was anyone else left out there. We forgot about her. We made people of clockwork and metal to fill our empty buildings. We take census every month, not just because we are afraid of strangers but because we hope, without hope, that one day we will count and there will be someone extra. Someone new. And there never is.'

'And she's here?' Maya asked. 'The Dream Lord's sister is here? Did she find what will wake him?' She looked from Michael to Hexthalion to all the familiar faces around her. 'What will happen when the Dream Lord awakens?'

'Doom,' Cracker said, 'Bad news, evil.'

'Shut up, bird,' Hexthalion said and this time he threw the teapot at the crow, showering those unfortunate enough to be underneath with tea and broken china.

Maya stood up. 'I'm going to see,' she said. 'I'm going to see the Dream Lord.'

'Maya, it's not safe,' her father said.

Maya didn't listen She pushed through the crowd to the door and out into the city. She started to run, and the others ran after her. Fenella caught up with her and Oleander and Azriel were a few steps behind her. The others followed in a mob of clanking and barking, grinding gears and flapping wings. At the Dream Lord's house, Maya tore up the pathway and into the house and then stopped dead in the dining room doorway.

The Dream Lord was gone. The table where he had lain for all of Maya's life and all the centuries before was empty, but there was a woman leaning against the dresser. She was dressed like a man in a long black coat and a wide-brimmed hat. Flags of long black hair hung around a face that was weathered and scarred but still looked like the Dream Lord's. She looked at Maya and then beyond her to the others.

'I once had a cat that was insufferable and bossy, a dog that was faithful and loved me no matter what I did, a noisy bird that wouldn't shut up,' she said. 'They were the best companions I ever had.'

'Where's the Dream Lord?' Maya's father asked. 'What have you done to him?'

'I kissed him, and he awoke. He's gone,' the woman said. 'He awoke, and he went. Out into the labyrinth and the Ash Plains. To freedom.'

'But there's nowhere to go,' Maya said. 'This is the world: the city and the labyrinth and the Ash Plains. There is nowhere else. And we're all the people that there are.'

The woman raised one eyebrow and didn't speak.

'Aren't we?' Maya asked, her voice very small.

The woman straightened up and crossed the room to stand before Maya. She smiled, and her smile was full of light and laughter and promises. 'Maybe,' she said, 'and maybe not. You can find out, little one. Follow the Dream Lord out into the darkness and hope that something wonderful jumps out to get you. Or stay here and stay safe. It doesn't really matter anyway.'

Later, many years later, Maya realised it had never been about the Dream Lord. It made no difference whether he slept or woke. What made the difference was his sister arriving from outside, from somewhere else, and watering seeds that had already begun to germinate in Maya's mind.

The Dream Lord's sister left the next day. She said she'd catch up with her brother in the labyrinth and show him the way through. She said that anyone who wanted to could go with her, but no one did. Not then.

Maya waited until after the next census, dutifully standing with her father ticking off the names in her notebook:

- o Human beings – 15
  - o men – 3
  - o women – 5
  - o children (male) – 3
  - o children (female) – 3
  - o children (indeterminate) – 1
- o Angels - 22
  - o fallen – 6
  - o not fallen – 12
  - o in process of falling – 1
  - o half-angels – 3 (2 x male, 1 x female)
- o Talking animals – 4
  - o dogs – 1
  - o cats – 2 (plus six possible talking kittens, too early to tell)
  - o crows – 1
- o Clockwork people – 6 (plus one in need of repair)
- o Dream Lords (asleep) – none

That night, she packed a few things in a bag. In truth, she didn't know what to take so settled for just a sharp knife, a change of clothes, a book of fairy tales and a miniature picture of her mother and father on their wedding day.

She amended the number of children (female) in her notebook and left it on the kitchen table with a note for her father, promising to come back when she had found whatever there was to find out there beyond the Ash Plains.

'Really?' a voice said from the hearth. 'You're really going without saying goodbye?'

Maya turned and saw Fenella sitting on the mat.

'And that's all you're taking?' Fenella stood up and walked over to Maya. 'Not even a gun? Just some piddly little kitchen knife? Have you even got a map?'

'Fenn, I'm sorry. I was going to write you a note too, but I didn't know what to say.'

'No, need to be sorry,' Fenella said, 'I'm coming too.'

Maya hid a smile. 'But what about Lucy?'

Fenella made a hissing noise. 'She's up the duff again,' she said in disgust. 'I despair of that cat, I really do. And besides, she has nine kittens to look after, six of whom might be talkers. I've no wish to hear what any of her offspring might have to say. All gossip about alley cats, I expect.'

They stepped out into the street. The moon lit up the broken buildings and climbing vegetation, all the strange beauty of the city. Near where the Dream Lord used to live, two figures slid out of the darkness and fell into step beside Maya and Fenn. Maya grinned at Oleander and punched Azriel gently on the arm.

'Doom,' Cracker shouted from the branches above them, 'disaster, calamity. Bad news. Bad news.'

Maya laughed. Cracker swept down from his branch and settled heavily on Azriel's shoulder.

'Adventure,' he said and cackled. 'Doom, death, bad news.'

'Let's just settle for adventure,' Maya said.

They walked to the edge of the city, where the city ended, and the high walls of the labyrinth began. Maya looked back at the city and saw there was a light burning in her father's tower and wondered if he could see her. She blinked back tears. She thought of her mother and of the Dream Lord's sister who had set off on her own adventure long ago with a talking cat and dog and bird for companions. Maya's own companions were no less strange: a talking cat, an angel in the process of falling, a boy who was half human and half angel, and a doom-singing bird that wouldn't shut up. And herself, the census-taker's daughter, just an ordinary girl living in a very strange time on the edge of a story of her own.

She took a deep breath and together they stepped into the labyrinth.

Behind the Glass...
Author's Afterword

The Lord of the Looking Glass

Fairy tales have been written and re-written to death, so I was looking to do something different with this. I had thought to tell the story from the point of view of the wicked queen, but at the same time I was writing about magical mirrors and the things that might live inside them for a longer piece of writing, so the idea of retelling the story from the point of view of whatever lives inside the magic mirror grew.

The Post-Garden Centre Blues

I, too, have become the kind of person who enjoys spending an afternoon at the garden centre. Although this isn't a fairy-tale retelling, it does have a fairy in it. I'd heard of fairy seductresses, but they didn't interest me. It was only when I got a copy of Brian Froud's *Good Fairies, Bad Fairies* that I realised there was a male version and that was much more interesting. It's about getting older and the realisation and acceptance that your life hasn't gone the way your younger self would have wanted it to. I think it's a very upbeat story – as long as you're happy and do no harm, you can live your life however you want.

The Piper

I started this story without any real idea of where I was going with it. I'd been thinking about a retelling of the 'Pied Piper of Hamelin' from the point of view of the Piper, but I couldn't get going with it. It was only when I threw in some spider-worshipping villagers that the idea took form.

Fiona McGavin

The Frog Prince

I think my writing career must be more shaped by *Shrek* than I realised. I had great fun writing this story. My writing often has a tendency towards gloom, doom and amoral characters, but this is just a piece of light-hearted silliness to counteract all that.

The Contraption

In the summer of 2017, I went on holiday with my mum, sister and two-year-old nephew and we watched a lot of *In the Night Garden*. If you Google the Night Garden, you'll find a lot of theories that it's all about death, that the Night Garden is the afterlife and the characters are versions of the people you knew in life. This story grew from that idea. I also always feel vaguely uncomfortable when I walk through an area where all the houses are displaying the Neighbourhood Watch signs in their windows, as if I don't have any right to be there. I'm not a fan of zombies, but I had a lot of fun writing the crazy conversations between Annie and the dead man – I hope the silliness balances the sadness of this story.

Grey

Herons are probably my favourite bird. There's something otherworldly and elegant in their stillness. I always get excited when I see one. I grew up in the Scottish Highlands and people I knew at school and university had families who were involved in managing the wildlife on shooting estates. I've never been quite sure what I feel about that.

Roses

This was the second piece of writing I had published, and I was reading a lot of Gothic literature and Anne Rice at the time. I was working for a small company when I wrote this and I didn't have enough to do, so I think I wrote and edited the whole thing at my desk.

Wintertide's Eve

I wrote this when I was trying to shape the world of my *Dream and A Lie* trilogy. The trilogy, and the vampires in it, ended up quite different, but there are elements here that I used – the witch burnings, the bleak industrial city and the beautiful but deadly priest. The idea of hearing someone's footsteps on the other side of the world comes from a poem called 'Tonight' by Iain Crichton Smith. When I read this poem, I thought it was incredibly sad and romantic, and I knew I wanted to use the idea in my own writing.

Dr Franks and Mrs Stein

It's a long time since I read *Frankenstein,* so I'm not sure where this story came from. I was out on a walk when the idea popped into my head and by the time I'd finished the walk, I'd pretty much plotted the whole thing in my head. I went home and wrote it down in one sitting. It's about monsters, but it's also about human kindness and decency.

Bridge 52

Bridge 52 is real place where the M1 passes over an old railway line on the outskirts of Milton Keynes. It's also supposed to be haunted by an Irish labourer, who is reputed to have been murdered and his remains hidden in the concrete pillars that support the bridge. There are a few lines about him in a book of local ghosts I have, but if you Google him, you come up with nothing. I've been intrigued by this for a while and had several false starts trying to write this story. It was only when I fell off my bike under a different bridge that I found the hook I needed to move the story forwards.

Magpie

I first heard about battlefield looters in a history lesson at school and the idea stuck with me – who were they, what kind of person would make a living from something like that? The crow wife who features in this story is a kind of female version of the Walking Man who also appears in a couple of my stories.

Driving Home for Christmas

I wrote this specially for Immanion Press's *Darkest Midnight in December* anthology of Christmas ghost stories. Whenever I drive past a roadside memorial, I wonder about the people they commemorate and the people who keep them. I'd planned this just to be a simple revenge story, but when I came to the end of the first draft, the twist just came to me and I think it gives this story an even darker turn.

Cosmic Ordering for Vampires

I often write short stories when I'm trying to get my thoughts together for a longer piece of writing and this is one such story. I love the idea of a bored, amoral vampire steadily working his way up the hierarchy in an office just because it's something to do. Woe betide anyone who borrowed his stapler and didn't give it back… Matthew Askew is one of my favourite characters in this collection and I've written the first draft of a novel about his life but it needs a lot of work. It also features Solomon Hollowman.

The Lottery Lady

This story is unusual for me because it has no supernatural element in it, although it does have the kind of morally askew characters I enjoy writing about. For most of my adult life, I've worked in offices and I'm fascinated by the different personalities and interactions and power games that take place. I like the idea that you can spend five days a week with your colleagues and hardly know them at all. For a long time, I was part of an office syndicate and we rarely won anything. There's no question that anything dishonest was going on, but I never knew what the numbers were. I was just handing over my money and putting my trust in someone else. At that time, I was working for a bank and quite bored, so my imagination started running wild and I thought I'd figured out how to rob the bank from the inside. I hadn't, as it happened, but the idea for this story started to take form.

The Last Days of the Jesus Star Mission

So, strictly speaking, this isn't an office story, but I imagine being part of the crew of a spaceship might be a bit like working in an office – the same hierarchies and cliques could form and if you're bored of your life on earth, you're going to be just as bored and jaded up in space. I started writing this during a workshop for a creative writing course I was taking. I never read it out to the class, because everyone else seemed to be writing very worthy and gritty stories that were firmly embedded in the real world (alcoholism and homelessness featured very strongly). The first draft of this story also included a time-travelling space alien and I was aware that I was on a completely different page from everyone else. I hid it under the desk and smiled and told everyone how much I liked their work – pretty much as the main character in this story would have done.

We Are Not Who We Think We Are

I've had the idea of writing a horror novel set in an office for years. It's an office that somehow slips into another dimension and where everyone has a backstory and gets picked off one by one – sort of like *Lost* but set in an office block instead of an island. This story was an attempt to try and clarify some of the ideas and the characters. I was getting nowhere with it – too many distractions at home, so I checked myself into a local hotel so I could write without any interruptions. As I was writing about the Walking Man, I started seeing things moving in the reflections on the widescreen TV and noises in the room next door to me, which reception had told me was empty. I finished the story and went to bed and then woke up a few hours later freezing cold and convinced that there was someone walking backwards and forwards down the corridor outside. Sleep paralysis, I guess, but for a brief moment I was convinced that the Walking Man was coming for me.

A Tale from the End of the World

This was originally published in *Visionary Tongue* magazine, more than twenty years ago, and it was the first thing I ever had published. It's one of the first pieces of writing that I dared to show to anyone else. It's not quite what I'd write if I was writing it now, so I've tweaked it a bit, but the spirit of the story is the same. I'm a fan of post-apocalyptic fiction and love the idea of the world re-wilding itself into a huge Wilderness full of madmen and monsters and desperate people trying to survive. It's a place I'm planning to return to.

He May Grow Roots

This is a companion piece to 'A Tale from the End of the World'. At the time I was playing with the idea of some sort of intelligent plant life that wasn't a triffid sort of thing, and I was also interested in the Blood twins and their world. Before I started writing this, I had a very clear picture in my mind of a man walking through a ruined city with a rifle and two big dogs on a leash.

Ginevra Flowerdew

I think of this as being the third story in a set along with 'A Tale from the End of the World' and 'He May Grow Roots'. It's set in a very similar world and although the twins don't feature, their servant does (maybe he got fed up of them and changed jobs). It's about twenty years since I wrote this, and I think I originally intended to write a mermaid story. I seem to remember telling a friend I was going to write a story about a girl who gives birth to a fish and getting a very strange look.

The Plague Doctor

This another story I wrote as part of the creative writing course. My tutor assumed that this was set during the Black Death, but I'd always intended it to have a post-apocalyptic setting, mostly because I'm lazy about carrying out research, but also because when I was picturing the houses the doctor and his men were looting, they were modern. The character of the Plague Doctor came to me first. I could see him very clearly – his patchwork coat and silver hair, footfalls ringing out through empty streets, a good man gone bad. I have some plans in the back of my mind to write more about him.

The Walking Man

I wrote a story called 'Twilight' for *Visionary Tongue* several years ago. I was never happy with that story, so when I was putting together the stories for this collection, I decided to give it a few little tweaks. Those tweaks turned into a complete rewrite and the version here doesn't bear much resemblance to the original. The Walking Man appears in various forms in a lot of my writing both here and in various drafts and unfinished bits and pieces. There are elements of him in 'The Plague Doctor' and 'The Piper', and the wife in 'Magpie' is a female version. And, of course, he has a starring role in 'We Are Not Who We Think We Are'. Sometimes he has a dog and sometimes he's alone. Sometimes he's utterly malevolent and sometimes, as in this story, he's less so. I see him very clearly in my imagination, and there's something about the idea of a figure who just walks relentlessly across the landscape and the mythologies that might spring up around him, that appeals to me.

The Census-Taker's Daughter

I really enjoyed writing this story. It's based around one of my favourite fairy tales and it's got pretty much everything I like in a piece of fiction in it: a post-apocalyptic setting; fallen angels; dreams; ghosts; shadows; scary heads in jars; mysterious strangers; the word 'kaboom' and talking animals. Talking animals! I'd always avoided including talking animals in my writing because I thought they were twee and juvenile, but I couldn't resist throwing them into the mix and I'm so pleased that I did. I have plans to try and expand this story into a novel using this setting and characters. If anyone's interested, the real Fenella was a grey cat called Laurel who never hesitated to tell me how dissatisfied she was with things.

Fiona McGavin
February 2019

About the Author

Fiona McGavin was born and brought up in the Scottish Highlands but now lives just outside Milton Keynes. She has a degree in history from Stirling University and is currently studying (very slowly) for an MA in Creative writing with the Open University.

As a child her parents surrounded her with books and encouraged her to read and write voraciously. Early influences include Tolkien, Richard Adams and Mary Stewart as well as medieval Scottish history. When she discovered Tad Williams, Stephen King, Storm Constantine and Elizabeth Hand in her early twenties, the nature of her writing took a darker turn.

She has always been interested in folklore, magic and anything spooky or odd and is particularly interested in how folklore and mythologies reinvent themselves to remain relevant in through the ages.

She works in an office, enjoys trips to the garden centre and lives with an elderly black and white rescue cat called Sophie-Bananas.

IMMANION PRESS
Purveyors of Speculative Fiction

Strindberg's Ghost Sonata & Other Uncollected Tales
by Tanith Lee

This book is the first of three anthologies to be published by Immanion Press that will showcase some of Tanith Lee's most sought-after tales. Spanning the genres of horror and fantasy, upon vivid and mysterious worlds, the book includes a story that has never been published before – 'Iron City' – as well as two tales set in the Flat Earth mythos; 'The Pain of Glass' and 'The Origin of Snow', the latter of which only ever appeared briefly on the author's web site. This collection presents a jewel casket of twenty stories, and even to the most avid fan of Tanith Lee will contain gems they've not read before. ISBN 978-1-912815-00-5, £12.99, $18.99 pbk

A Raven Bound with Lilies by Storm Constantine

The Wraeththu have captivated readers for three decades. This anthology of 15 tales collects all the published Wraeththu short stories into one volume, and also includes extra material, including the author's first explorations of the androgynous race. The tales range from the 'creation story' *Paragenesis*, through the bloody, brutal rise of the earliest tribes, and on into a future, where strange mutations are starting to emerge from hidden corners of the earth.
ISBN: 978-1-907737-80-0 £11.99, $15.50 pbk

Voices of the Silicon Beyond by E. S. Wynn

Vaetta is not human, but far more than a mere robot. Her world is overcrowded, its resources at breaking point. The humans who govern this parallel Earth need a solution to these problems. Then a strange, androgynous visitor appears from an inexplicable portal to another world, also seeking help. His world is sparsely populated, following the demise of humankind and the rise of a civilization known as Wraeththu. Vaetta is chosen to scout this new world and begin preparations for invasion, but what waits for her on the other side of the portal doesn't make sense to her, until a fatal meeting through which she discovers a history with far-reaching implications covering all realities. (A novel set in Storm Constantine's Wraeththu Mythos.)
ISBN: 978-1-907737-97-8, £9.99, $14.99 pbk

Songs to Earth and Sky edited by Storm Constantine

6 writers explore the 8 seasonal festivals of the year, dreaming up new beliefs and customs, new myths, new dehara – the gods of Wraeththu. As different communities develop among Wraeththu, the androgynous race who have inherited a ravaged earth, so fresh legends spring up – or else ghosts from the inception of their kind come back to haunt them. From the silent, snow-heavy forests of Megalithican mountains, through the lush summer fields of Alba Sulh, into the hot, shimmering continent of Olathe, this book explores the Wheel of the Year, bringing its powerful spirits and landscapes to vivid life. Nine brand new tales, including a novella, a novelette and a short story from Storm herself, and stories from *Wendy Darling, Nerine Dorman, Suzanne Gabriel, Fiona Lane* and *E. S. Wynn*. ISBN 978-1-907737-84-8 £11.99 $15.50 pbk

Madame Two Swords by Tanith Lee

An unnamed narrator, in the French city of Troy, finds an old book of the writings of the revolutionary, Lucien de Ceppays, who lived and died in the city two centuries before. She feels a strange bond to the life and thoughts of this long-dead man – what is the mysterious truth behind her obsession? Perhaps she did not find the book at all – perhaps it found her. Some years later, impoverished after the death of her mother, the narrator – in a state of desperation – find herself inexorably guided to meet the peculiar and unnerving Madame Two Swords, an old woman with a history, and her own enduring bonds to Lucien – as well as the book. For the narrator, reality seems to unravel, as she begins to penetrate just how intimately she is connected with Madame Two Swords and Lucien. Previously only available as a limited-edition hardback in 1988, the long-awaited new edition of this vintage-Tanith novella includes illustrations by Jarod Mills. ISBN 978-1-907737-81-7 £11.99, $15.50 pbk

The Lightbearer by Alan Richardson

Michael Horsett parachutes into Occupied France before the D-Day Invasion. Dropped in the wrong place, badly injured, he falls prey to two Thelemist women who have awaited the Hawk God's coming, attracts a group of First World War veterans who rally to what they imagine is his cause, is hunted by a troop of German Field Police, and has a climactic encounter with a mutilated priest who believes that Lucifer Incarnate has arrived... *The Lightbearer* is a unique gnostic thriller, dealing with the themes of Light and Darkness, Good and Evil, Matter and Spirit. ISBN 9781907737763 £11.99 $18.99

http://www.immanion-press.com
info@immanion-press.com

NEWCON PRESS

newconpress.co.uk

The very best in fantasy, science fiction, and horror

David Gullen – Shopocalypse

A Bonnie and Clyde for the Trump era, Josie and Novik embark on the ultimate roadtrip. In a near-future re-sculpted politically and geographically by climate change, they blaze a trail across the shopping malls of America in a printed intelligent car (stolen by accident), with a hundred and ninety million LSD-contaminated dollars in the trunk, buying shoes and cameras to change the world.

Kim Lakin-Smith – Rise

Charged with crimes against the state, Kali Titian (pilot, soldier, and engineer), is sentenced to Erbärmlich prison camp, where few survive for long. Here she encounters Mohab, the Speaker's son, and uncovers two ancient energy sources, which may just bring redemption to an oppressed people. The author of *Cyber Circus* returns with a dazzling tale of courage against the odds and the power of hope.

Best of British Fantasy 2018 – edited by Jared Shurin

Jared spread his net wide to catch the very best work published by British authors in 2018, whittling down nearly 200 stories under consideration to just 21 (22 in the hardback edition) and two poems. They range from traditional sword and sorcery to contemporary fantasy, by a mix of established authors, new voices, and writers not usually associated with genre fiction. The result is a wonderfully diverse anthology of high-quality tales.

www.newconpress.co.uk

CPSIA information can be obtained
at www.ICGtesting.com
Printed in the USA
BVHW030903230519
549121BV00001B/131/P